FATED TO MONSTERS

Book Cover Design by Night Witch
Editing by Cruel Ink Editing
Proofing by Tiffany Hernandez
First Edition 2023
ASIN B09WJFT9PS (ebook)
ISBN 978-1-957238-07-4 (Paperback)

FATED TO MONSTERS

FALLING FOR THE ENEMY (BOOK THREE)

LUNA PIERCE

Don't give up.

I

WREN

My head throbs with a force that makes my vision blur more than it already was.

I scrape my fingers along the ground, desperate for any indication of my location. The air is cool and fresh as I suck in each gasping lungful, and despite it making no sense at all, gravity itself seems to have changed, too.

I blink once, twice, three times. My chest heaves, matching the same frantic energy as every other ounce of myself.

"Wes!" I call out into the abyss. "Bo!" I pause. "Dash!"

Slowly, I rise to my feet with my hands out.

"Where the fuck am I?" I whisper into the nothingness around me.

So, help me Angels, I will murder Tremont if he betrayed us.

The last thing I remember is holding on for dear life while being shoved into a vacuum of darkness. I'm not certain how much time has passed, or if we all made it out alive, let alone to the same place.

I close my eyes and steady my breath before opening them again. This time, my surroundings come into focus, and the ringing in my ears fades to a dull murmur.

A writhing body draws my attention from a few feet away, and I rush over to it without another thought.

"Wr-Wren, is that you?" Jade squints at me and sits upright. "Where's—" She glances around and I watch as her eyes widen. If I had to guess the same panic I'm feeling is now coursing through her. "Everest?" She scrambles to her feet. "Where are we?"

Clenching my jaw, I scan the vicinity and try to make an educated guess. But it's too dark. Too different. Too unfamiliar to state a conclusion.

"I don't know." I swallow harshly and beg the Angels help me locate any of the men we came here with.

"There." Jade points ahead and takes off toward another lump of a person littered in this desolate forest.

I run past her and skid to a halt beside the body. Gripping the collars of his shirt, I shake him harder than I probably should. "What the fuck have you done?"

Tremont snaps his gaze up at me. "It worked."

Within a split second, I slide a small knife out of my

waistband and press it to his throat. "Where are they? Tell me what you did to them or I'll gut you right here and now."

He wiggles under my grasp but it's no use, not when I've already made up my mind.

"You have five fucking seconds...four..." I push the blade deeper into his skin without fully penetrating the soft flesh.

Jade reaches for my shoulder, but I shrug her off.

"Where are they?" I yell at him. "Where are *we*?"

A sly grin eases its way across his face.

"Arthlia." But it isn't Tremont's voice, instead, it's that of my fated mate.

My sights dart from the man I was poised to kill and up at the man who appears from the shadows ahead.

"Wes." His name is barely a whisper lingering on my lips. I drop Tremont with a thud, and rise to my feet once again, rushing over to throw my arms around Wes.

His strong grip catches and drags me toward him. "My girl." Wes inhales deeply and hugs me tighter. "We did it."

It's then that Dash and Bo come into my line of sight behind Wes, and Everest follows up the rear.

"Did I hear you threaten to kill someone, Birdie?" Bo says as he approaches. "Not going to wait for me?"

Wes sets me on the ground, and I pull Bo and Dash in for a group embrace.

"Aw." Bo pats my head. "You missed us."

I release him and punch him in the shoulder. "I thought you guys were goners."

Dash kisses the top of my head. "Going to have to try harder than that."

I exhale and bask in knowing that all three of these men are safe, but the overwhelming realization that we did the impossible punches me in the gut.

"Wait a minute." I point toward Wes. "You said we're in Arthlia. How?" I train my focus on the man responsible for our escape. "Is that true?"

Tremont rubs at the spot on his neck where the blade nicked him and pushes up onto his feet, dusting his legs off and glancing around. "Well, like I said, there was a weak spot in the fold."

"No." I shake my head. "You..." I desperately try to recall our last moments in Prania. "You said you didn't need it because..." I shift my gaze to the ground but struggle to recall the memory of the time not too long ago.

"We're here now," Jade tells us. "We're safe. And that's a win in my book." She clings to Everest's arm, and he seems to gravitate toward her with equal force.

"It's darker than I thought it would be." Wes cranes his head toward the sky.

"It must be a new moon," Tremont announces. "See that bright star right there? That's Polaris, the North Star. We can follow that and head north until we find somewhere to stay."

"Together?" I ask him.

The older man nods. "I didn't anticipate stranding you in unfamiliar territory."

"Why?" I narrow my gaze at him.

"Because that's not who I am. Not anymore. You're the reason I'm free of that place. The least I could do is give you some advice before parting ways."

"Advice?" I cross my arms over my chest.

"Yes, Wren, advice. For starters, humans don't take kindly to being threatened within an inch of their life."

"How else am I supposed to get information out of them?"

"Like this. With your words." He motions between us. "You communicate."

I sigh and roll my eyes. "Seems ineffective."

The throbbing in my skull picks up its tempo, my body tilting off balance as I struggle to regain composure.

"Wren." Dash steadies me with his soft but strong hands.

Wes appears in front of me. "What's wrong?"

"I'm fine, really." I swallow down the aching in my head and take a few steps toward Tremont. "This North Star, where is it leading us?"

"Hopefully someplace where we can find food and shelter."

"Are we in danger here?"

He glances over at me like he's about to spill a secret but decides to keep it to himself. "No. You have nothing to fear from the humans, so long as you don't give them a reason to cause trouble. They're rather ignorant and oblivious."

"But." I flit my gaze behind me at Wes temporarily. "Humans aren't the only creatures in this realm, correct?"

Tremont continues his trek forward. "That's right. Many supernatural beings reside on Earth."

Supernaturals can't even get along amongst themselves, how are they able to with a whole other species?

"The supernaturals keep their existence a secret. Ensuring the humans stay in the dark is what allows peace between them."

"But how? That doesn't make sense. How is it possible for them to fly so far under the radar that they are undetected? No one sees the horns or claws or fangs or the magic?"

"The supernatural living on earth make it a part of their life's mission to keep the truth a secret. Because if the humans were ever to learn that truth, there's no telling what they would do. It's safer this way, for everyone involved."

I walk next to him without any real idea of where we are going. A million questions fill my head faster than they can be answered. Supernaturals are just allowed to exist in this realm without consequence? Safely and peacefully? While we've been fighting for our lives in a neighboring realm and knowing no sense of freedom.

Guilt flows its way up my back and sends a chill

down my spine. My stomach tightens at the thought of all the monsters I left behind to rot and never escape the hell hole I once called home.

"And it's not like they go around with their claws and fangs and horns out in the open. Those with non-human-like traits avoid those things ever being seen. Most of the supernaturals here blend in with the rest of humanity. The witches don't use their magic out in the open. The vampires feast discreetly. The werewolves go deep into the forest during a full moon. The others find homes in sleepy towns or long-forgotten cities where they can go undetected and live their lives without concern for being found out. Not everyone is as cautious but the majority of them are. Because they know what's at stake if their secret comes out into the open."

I let his words simmer before asking another question. Surely things can't be this simple in this realm. There must be a catch. Something he isn't telling me.

Tremont looks back at the hodgepodge group following closely behind him. "You can all pass as humans if you don't let your magic rise to the surface and give you away." His gaze lingers on me. "Although you may want to find some different clothing. Something that fits this realm and doesn't make you look like you came out of a fantasy movie."

"Movie?" I pinch my brows together.

"Mmhm. A motion picture." He sighs and continues on his way. "You have much to learn about Earth."

But Tremont stops after a few steps and holds out his arms to stop us, too.

Instinctually, I press the hilt of a blade into each of my hands and ready myself for the threat. "What is it?" I whisper to the man and attempt to locate the source of his concern.

"It...It can't be."

My sights settle on a large building in the distance. Its shape is massive, and it's barely visible with the minimal illumination from the night sky. "What is this place?" I ask the man leading us through this uncharted territory. "Have you been here before?"

I study the way his shoulders tense, and he harshly swallows the lump in his throat.

"Yes," he mutters. "A lifetime ago."

"Is it safe?" Jade says softly from behind us.

"I'm fucking starving," Bo tells us as he shoves his way forward. "This place better have some fucking food. I could eat twelve loaves of bread."

"What an oddly specific number." I follow behind him and hope there's no danger ahead. We've already been through hell and back; we could use a little break from the chaos.

I want to believe things will be better but a voice in my head reminds me that the worst is yet to come.

2

BO

I'd be lying if I said Arthlia wasn't way fucking better than Prania.

Fuck Prania. That place sucks in every single regard.

The food sucks. The water sucks. The people suck. The fucking atmosphere sucks.

I don't know what they put in the air here, but my lungs are grateful to not have to breathe in that garbage from back home.

And whoever it was that decided to invent something called a Hot Pocket, I'd love to give them a big wet kiss on the lips. It is quite literally a hot pocket of bread filled with gooey cheese and various ingredients. I am on my fifth, and I don't see myself stopping anytime soon. There's nothing like it in Prania. Sure, we have bread and we have cheese, and something could maybe be fashioned over an open fire but they have these things called microwaves here that blast frozen food with electricity until it's hot and ready to eat.

Who needs hunters and gatherers when you have access to places like Costco?

"And this Costco," I say to Tremont. "They have cases upon cases of these frozen treats?"

"Yes," he responds. "But that's not all. They have a whole bread aisle. All the types of cheeses you could imagine. Frozen and fresh meat. Vegetables. Fruit. Cakes. Ice cream. You name it, they probably have it."

"I..." I get lost in thought as I imagine an endless supply of food at my fingertips. "I must go there."

Tremont holds out his hand when I stand. "Perhaps another time. Not tonight."

Despite wanting to snap his neck I comply and sit back down. We've only just got here; Costco can wait for another day. There's so much to learn of this world before I foolishly step out into it. I've never been one to shy away from danger but it's not just me who is affected now.

I shift my stare across the room at my long-lost sister who is no longer the little girl that was taken from me all those years ago. Now she is grown. She has seen things, and the world has treated her with such cruelty. And if it weren't for the fact that this Everest fellow brings a smile to her face, I would rip the skin from his flesh and gouge out his eye sockets.

"Here, try this." Dash hands me a plate with a strange-looking goo on it.

"What is this?" I ask him while shoveling a forkful of it into my mouth. "Mmm," I mumble.

"Peanut butter pie. I had trouble getting it out of the pan, that's why it looks like that."

I scrape every last bit of it off the plate and lick the fork clean. "Is there more?"

Dash grins and nods. "Yeah." He walks through the large, but dimly lit kitchen to retrieve said pie from the counter. "Does anyone want any more?"

When no one takes him up on his offering, he comes back over and sets the thing in front of me.

I blink at it, and then at him. "Did you want some?"

He shakes his head and nudges it toward me. "It's all you."

"This building," Wren says while looking right at Tremont. "Who does it belong to?"

Tremont pats the corners of his lips with his napkin. "An old friend." But when his gaze doesn't meet hers until after the words are spoken, I grow suspicious.

"And where is this friend?" She takes a cautious look around the big, open space. "Is he human? Or supernatural?"

"He is long from this world." Tremont pushes his plate forward and puts his elbows on the table. "As is his wife. Although, I would assume the house was inherited by their son. They had a rather difficult relationship, so I'm not at all surprised to see the house unoccupied."

"Who would abandon such a place?" Jade trails her finger along the stone countertop and walks from one end of the kitchen to the other.

"Given the provisions stocked in the freezer and refrigerator, I would assume it hasn't been abandoned completely. It just isn't his main residence. Which means our time here is limited. I advise we keep a low profile. Recover from the cross-realm travel and depart at sunup. Now that I know where we are, I can navigate us from here."

Damn, just when I was thinking we could finally stop for more than a few hours, we'll soon be on the run again.

"Feel free to find a room to sleep in and a bathroom to freshen up but do so by candlelight, and try to stay away from the windows. We don't need to bring any unwanted attention to us."

"I thought you said they were friends." Wren stares across at him through her lashes.

"*Were.* Past tense. Things were different then, and I've been gone for years. There's no telling how a home-coming will go, especially with having many guests."

"You didn't say what they were," I add. "Human or supernatural?"

Tremont breathes through his nose sharply before exhaling. "They were witches."

"And their son? Is he a witch, too?"

Tremont nods.

One measly witch is nothing I haven't handled in

the past. Sure, they have some tricks up their sleeves, but they aren't a major threat.

My focus moves to Wren as she presses her fingers gently along her neck where I had marked her. I'm not entirely sure if she knows she's doing it, or if it's simply an unconscious reaction. Either way, it completely entrances me.

"If anyone needs me, I'll be in the first room on the right at the top of the stairs." Tremont latches onto one of the candles lighting up the space and takes it with him. "And this should go without saying, but please don't break anything." His gaze lingers on me far longer than it does on anyone else.

Once the door to his room creaks shut, I'm the first to break the silence. "Should we make a run for it?"

Wren runs her hand through her hair and sighs. "If we knew anything of this world, I would say yes, but we don't, Bo. We don't know what's out there."

"I'm with Wren," Wes chimes in.

Of course, he and his stupid mutt are with her.

Dash scoots in closer. "He's lying about something, isn't he?"

"Definitely," Everest adds. "But I agree about staying until morning. We're in no shape to go wandering around a new realm right now."

Jade reaches across the table and places her hand on top of mine. "Promise me we'll stick together this time?"

I clench my jaw. "Fine."

"We'll figure this out tomorrow, okay?" Wren stands from the table. "In the meantime, I think we could all use some rest." She extends her arm toward me. "Come on, grumpy."

I roll my eyes but rise to my feet, too. "I'm picking the room." Plucking a candle from the table, I go in the direction Tremont went, turn, and go up the winding staircase to the upper level of this large house.

The floorboards creak under my steps despite doing what I can to be quiet.

The landing opens up to a long corridor that seems to go on and on. Six doors are easily visible, and given that Tremont has chosen the first one on the right, I select the first one on the left. That way, we can be near if he tries to pull anything while we're waiting out the night.

I grip the cold metal door handle and open the door, shoving the candle through to illuminate the space.

It's large, like one would expect considering the size of the rest of the house.

Dust particles float around the flickering flame, and a chill drifts out to greet me.

"Don't go too far," I tell Jade as she and Everest pass us in search of another room.

"I missed this overprotective brother thing." She stops at the door just past the bedroom I chose and disappears inside without another word.

I step fully into the bedroom and peruse the

contents, noting the squeak of a faucet being shut off in the near distance. Tremont must have finished washing up.

"This is nice," Wren says as she plops onto the bed with four giant wooden things coming out of each end.

"What are these for?" I grip one of them and shake it.

"Decoration, I think." She pokes the intricate design and reclines onto her back. "I wonder what it's like to be this wealthy."

I raise a brow at her. "You weren't exactly living in squalor, Birdie."

Wren props herself up onto her elbows. "This is different and you know it."

"Yeah."

"There's a bathroom through this door." Dash clears his throat. "It's equally extravagant."

Wes opens another door. "There's a closet here." He goes in, his entire body vanishing into the space. "Looks like it's men's clothing," he calls out from inside.

I spot a lounge chair near the front of the room when I do a full circle. That will do for keeping post while the others rest their little heads. No fucking way I'm getting a second of sleep when Mr. Secrets is just across the hall, scheming Angels know what.

Wren hops off the bed and fumbles with the fasteners on her top. She pulls and yanks and tugs until she breaks free of its confines and discards it onto the floor.

Wes walks over like an obedient puppy and picks her shirt off the floor, folds it neatly, and sets it on top of the nearby dresser.

I lean against the bedpost and watch her performance.

"What?" She looks up at me as she leans down to drag her bottoms over her bare body.

I shrug and grin. "Just watching."

"That's your thing, isn't it?" Wren stands there, completely naked, waiting for my response.

I swallow and do everything I can not to gawk at every inch of her.

Would I rather march over there, throw her onto the bed, and spend the rest of the night learning where every freckle and scar marks her porcelain skin? *Absolutely.*

But this whole situation is more complicated than that, and I cannot be that reckless. Not when it comes to her. Not when everything is already more complicated than it should be.

She is a hunter. She is my enemy. She is fated mates with Wes, a hellhound with more power than me. And she's clearly in love with Dash, too, a creature we thought was only real in fairytales—a phoenix.

"Well, are you going to just stand there or do I have to drag you over here?" Wren snaps her fingers in front of my face.

"What?" I focus on the angelic features of her face.

"Come on." She latches onto my hand and pulls, but

when I don't budge, she turns around and glares at me. "I will not ask again. *Come on.*"

And because there isn't anything I wouldn't do for her, I move in her direction.

I would follow her to the ends of the world and back, and given that we're quite literally in another realm, it's safe to say I'm a man of my word.

For now, I will submit to her requests, but there will be a point in time I have to resist her if I stand any chance of keeping her in my life.

3
WREN

"This shower is nicer than the one at Everest's safe house." I adjust the knobs on the wall and watch the stream of water as it changes. "Does the one over there do that?"

"Yeah, Birdie. But you're going to break it if you keep fucking with it." Bo stands under the other showerhead with his face fully submerged. He runs his fingers through his long black hair and then wipes the droplets off his eyes before settling his sights on me. "Look who's staring now."

I roll my eyes but turn to hide my blushing cheeks. Scanning the labels of the bottles tucked into the shelf in the wall, I locate the one labeled *shampoo* and squirt some into my hand. I work the substance into my hair and bask in how damn good it smells. Upon rinsing the suds from my locks I note how clean they feel. I'm going to have to get a bottle or twelve of that shampoo whenever we settle into a place of our own.

My stomach knots. *A place of our own.* What if none of these men intend on sticking together once we learn the ways of this world? They always have in the past but that was when they were running for their lives and trying to survive. Without that threat here what if they choose to go their separate ways? What if they choose to start their lives over, and I am not a part of that? I can't assume that they would want me to be in their new normal just because of our short time together. But I also can't imagine any future without them. I never meant for the feelings to start but now that they have there's no turning back. Not for me.

Being with them is the only certainty that I actually have in my life. Everything up until this point has been a fucking lie. I devoted my entire existence to fighting on the side of a war that was unjust. And now that I know the truth, what else do I have? I used to wake up every day with one single thing on my mind—killing as many demons as possible. Without that my life has no meaning, no purpose, no drive. The only silver lining was that I found them. Or well, they found me. They saved me. Not only from death but from a worthless existence.

But things haven't really changed for them. Hunters still want them dead. Parla is still out there plotting her revenge, and it's no doubt because of my interference. They may be safe temporarily but until

Parla is gone and the soldiers that still wish to carry out her mission, the clock will continue ticking like a time bomb.

We were able to escape Prania but what will happen once she figures it out too? Her desire to kill all demons will no longer be confined to one realm but to potentially all of them. At what point will it be enough for her? She will stop at nothing until she has killed every last one of them.

Wes and Dash and Bo included.

How can I sit back and let that happen? I've already done too much to enable her and her sadistic plan to take over the world, I refuse to not use every resource I have to take her the fuck down.

I can't expect any of these men to want a future with me if they can't even expect to have a future for themselves. What kind of person would I be to even ask that of them without ensuring their safety?

"You okay in there?" Dash's gentle hands cup my cheeks and pull me out from under the water. "I thought you were trying to drown yourself for a second."

I blink through the droplets still trickling down my face. "Yeah."

"You okay?" Concern hides in the soft corners around his eyes.

"I will be once you kiss me." Because if this world has taught me anything it's that we must take advantage of the little downtime we get. It never fails to be gone before we least expect it, and there's no telling when we will ever get it back again.

"Are you sure?" Dash glances behind him at Bo who has both hands resting against the shower wall and his face down as the stream pelts his back.

Bo might be one grumpy son of a devil but damn is he a fucking masterpiece. Every sinewy piece of muscle is highlighted by the shimmer of the water.

"I'm sure," I tell him while grabbing his hand and placing it around my waist. "Don't worry about him."

Dash steps forward, his naked body meeting mine underneath the stream of water, reminding me of our very first time together. It seems like a lifetime ago when all of us were enemies, and I was held captive by the men I was supposed to execute. There was no telling how much longer I had until they killed me, so I did the unthinkable; I slept with one of them.

I hadn't admitted to myself at that point that I already had feelings for Wes. I knew *something* had blossomed between us, I just assumed it was a new form of hatred. Is it possible to hate someone so much that you end up falling for them? I guess there is a very thin line between love and hate.

But with Dash, things were completely different.

I didn't instinctually hate him the way I had Bo and Wes. Dash showed me kindness. And there was always this innocent part of him—a wholesome harmlessness that I had never experienced. I knew Dash wouldn't hurt me, not in the traditional sense. And my attraction to him was without question. Maybe that was because he didn't remind me of all the other men I had interacted with in the past. Whatever it was, I felt confident enough to act on it and satiate that hunger I felt toward him.

The same hunger I still feel, that has yet to dissipate in any capacity.

With Wes, I assumed it was the fated mate bond making my feelings for him so fucking strong. And with Bo, I chalked it up to the alpha marking he left on my neck.

Dash has none of those supernatural ties to my soul, and still, I feel for him the way I do with Wes and Bo.

Is it possible that what we share is as simple as an honest connection?

How could I have gone my entire existence and felt nothing resembling what I do for them, and now all of a sudden, I'm drawn to three drastically different men?

A hellhound. An alpha of alphas. And a phoenix.

The fiercest demon assassin of all falling for the three most enigmatic monsters.

Maybe it's not a coincidence—maybe it's something else entirely. There's so much I have yet to uncover about my past, and maybe once I do, it will uncover our future.

I'm brought back to reality by Dash's tongue dancing with mine. He runs his hand up into my hair and digs his fingers in, pulling me toward him. I melt into his embrace and savor every fucking second of this, afraid it will be gone too soon.

His erection grows between us and presses to my stomach. He moans into my mouth when I wrap my hand around his girth.

I want nothing more than for him to take me here, right this instant. But Dash doesn't give in as easily to the frenzied passion. Instead, he creates distance between us and breaks away from my kiss.

"Let me take you to bed," Dash says while staring into my eyes. "I want to take my time."

Without needing any convincing, I reach for the lever of the shower.

"Leave it on," Wes tells me when he enters the large bathroom. "I'm right behind you." He grabs two towels from the counter and holds them out for me and Dash.

"Thanks." Dash takes one and gives it to me before taking the other and blotting his face with it.

Wes tugs his shirt over his head and puts it neatly onto the counter. He reaches for the buttons of his pants.

I swallow and dry myself off, the memory of Bo watching me bringing a grin to my face as I do the same thing to Wes. I look over my shoulder to Bo, who's still in the same position he was in minutes ago. "You coming, big boy?"

Out of all these men, I never expected Bo to be the one who needs to be persuaded into following a naked woman. I've practically spread myself open and begged for it, and he still won't have sex with me. Sure, he's let me tease and stroke him, but he doesn't take things all the way.

Is it something I've done? Is it because he really doesn't want to?

He jokes around like he does, but when it comes down to it, he's the most reserved in that department. Maybe he's not attracted to me the way I am to him. Maybe the feelings are only one-sided, and the alpha mark is the only thing keeping him from finishing what he started.

My chest aches at the idea of my feelings not being reciprocated, but I cannot force myself on him if that isn't what he wants.

"We'll meet you in there." Wes brings my hand to his mouth and kisses my knuckles. He releases me and steps into the steamy shower with the man who still hasn't responded to me.

I sigh and follow Dash into the bedroom.

"He's always in a bad mood, don't take offense to it." Dash guides me over to the bed and nudges me onto the mattress.

"You don't think I did something to piss him off, do you?" I scoot onto the newly changed blanket—one that doesn't produce dust particles with each movement.

"There's no telling what's going through his thick skull." He trails his lips up my leg, starting from my ankle and ending near my center. Dash glances up at me. "Is this okay?"

I swallow and nod, the anticipation of where he's going to touch me next killing me.

Dash dips his tongue along my slit and grips both of my thighs with his hands.

"He didn't say anything?" I ask him.

"Wren." Dash doesn't look up as he continues teasing me. "You have nothing to worry"—he twirls his tongue again—"about. Nothing to be insecure about." He slows his pace. "Not now, not ever."

Insecure. Worry. Those are two things that I have never experienced, so why am I feeling them now? Not too long ago I was a strong, independent woman who gave zero fucks about men. And here I am concerned about three of them.

Wes, I don't worry about. Fate has already made that decision for us, and I find a strange comfort in that. In knowing that no matter what the thread connecting us is permanent and binding. Is it terrible of me that I revel in no longer having a choice in the matter? I've always been a fan of free will, but I also love certainty. And what's more certain than a fated mate bond?

When have I ever been in my head this much over something that isn't life or death?

A sexy, red-headed man is going down on me, and I'm questioning whether another man is into me or not. What the fuck is wrong with me?

I sit up on my elbows. "I'm sorry."

Dash kisses my inner thigh and up my stomach,

stopping at my chest to give attention to each of my nipples.

I drop my head back and become lost in him. In his warm mouth on my eager body. On his patience despite my lack thereof.

He drags his lips over my neck, nibbling but not biting the soft flesh. Just on the other side are marks from Bo and Wes. They are reminders of the commanding and dominant nature of both men. The contrast between Dash's delicate and gentle personality is a beautiful contradiction. Together, we are four people who shouldn't make sense.

"You have nothing to apologize for." Dash brings his face to rest just against mine. His skin on my skin. His breath mingling with my breath. "You've been through hell and back," he whispers into me. "I can't expect to understand that, but your feelings are valid either way."

"How are you so perfect?" I stare into his baby blue eyes.

"I'm not." He softly presses his lips on mine. "But I know what it's like to have more questions than answers. To wonder and worry and not be able to make sense of things."

"You're perfect to me," I tell him without really comprehending it myself. There isn't much I'm certain of, but there's one thing I know for sure: Dash is too good for all of us.

Dash positions himself between my legs and climbs

on top of me. He reaches for my hands and tracks them over my head, pinning them down. He glides his cock over my entrance and draws in a breath before positioning himself into place.

"You're already hard." I blink up at him.

"I've been hard since the moment I laid eyes on you, Wren." He grins bashfully. "I'm a little obsessed with you, if you haven't already noticed."

With his sights still set on me, he slowly pushes inside of me, his eyes flickering shut momentarily.

"Fuck," he whispers. "You feel so fucking good."

I stifle a giggle at hearing this sweet as sugar man curse twice in a row. "Yeah?"

He moves deeper. "Oh, yeah."

I bask in the fullness and tighten around him.

The weight of his body presses down onto mine, and he picks up his pace.

"I dreamed of this, being this near to you, over and over again when you were taken away." Dash kisses me and thrusts himself harder.

I rock myself with him and pump against his movements. Freeing one of my hands, I wrap it around the base of his neck and weave it into his hair to pull him closer and intensify the kiss. I break away for only a second to say, "Show me how badly you missed me."

Dash takes his free hand to wrap it around my waist and lift me toward him, the new angle sends pleasure through me in a whole other way. He fucks me harsher, our bodies crashing into each other in pure bliss. He's never been this rough, and I love every fucking second of it.

My core tightens, my breath catching as my climax rises to the surface.

Like he's fully aware, Dash moans into my mouth and grips the hand above my head tighter, his cock hardening inside of me with each thrust.

I dig my nails into his back and inch him farther, deeper, harder until I cry out into him and pleasure ripples through my entire body.

He pumps into me and slows his pace, his ragged breath matching mine. "Fuck, that was intense." Dash rests his forehead on mine as he comes down from the high. He softly kisses me while pulling out and collapses onto the bed next to me, his arm flopping over his sweat-lined forehead.

I smile triumphantly at seeing this side of him—his take charge side. Somehow he's still very Dash-like, but at the same time...he's more possessive.

My gaze shoots across the room to the man standing in the doorway, his body pressed into the frame, his arms crossed over his broad chest.

"Always such a lurker."

Bo remains firmly in place without saying anything.

"Afraid I might bite?" It's a phrase humans throw out as a joke but the possibility of that happening in a room full of supernatural creatures is pretty high.

Bo finally breaks from his stone-cold stare. "I wish you would."

"Come here and I will."

"You don't know what you're asking for, Birdie." Bo drags his hand over his solid jaw.

"That's not the first time you've said that, Bo."

"And it won't be the last." He shoves off the wall and stalks over slowly. "What is it you want from me?"

"Isn't it obvious?" I inch my legs apart without overly exposing myself any more than I already am.

The towel around his waist barely covers his wide frame, and with each step, the corner where it's bunched together loosens little by little.

But Bo reaches down in time and secures it back into place. His sights return to me. "Did you kill him?" He darts his attention briefly to Dash.

I side-eye the beautiful man who's quietly snoring next to me. "That could be you."

Bo latches onto my ankle, the heat of his skin sending a wave of pleasure up my entire body. He slides me to the edge of the bed, and my ass nearly hangs off the end. He holds one of my legs in the air and the other cups his body. "Is this what you want, Birdie?"

He leaves my leg leaning against his shoulder and skims his rough palm down.

I shiver at his touch.

"You want this..." Bo keeps his dark gaze on me as he swirls his fingers over my center and teases my clit. "You're throbbing, Birdie."

I rock my hips toward him in a desperate attempt to feel any friction against my aching desire.

"What about this…" Bo circles my entrance, and just when I'm certain he's playing one sadistic game, he shoves two fingers into me.

I bring my hand up to cover the gasp that escapes my mouth and clench my pussy around his long fingers.

"Or what about…" He drops to his knees at the foot of the bed and hooks his hand over my thigh to drag me closer while keeping my leg still propped on his shoulder. Bo leans in and takes in a deep breath. "Angels, you smell…" Finally, after what can only seem like an eternity, he presses his lips to mine, his tongue darting out and joining the party. "And taste"—he whispers into my pussy—"like heaven."

My chest heaves and I grip the bed sheets to ground me in this magical experience. This is the first time Bo has truly touched me, and damn if it isn't everything and more than I thought it would be.

I want him inside of me, on top of me, all over me, but fuck if this isn't glorious, too.

He thrusts his fingers in deeper, the force moving my body back and forth as he glides his tongue and lips over my most sensitive areas. Bo grips my thigh tighter and the pain from his touch only intensifies this whole experience.

I reach down and rake my hand through his hair and grab a fistful.

He moans against me, the vibration sending me further into paradise.

Bo surprises me by filling me with another finger,

the width of all of them spreading me wider. He heaves them deep and pinches my clit between his lips.

"Fuck," I whimper and tug his hair tighter.

It only takes one more thrust of his hand and I come undone around him, my whole body quivering with pleasure.

Bo slows his torment but continues to lick and suck me. He glides his fingers out, spreading me open for him to get a better access point with his mouth. His tongue slips inside of me, going further than I imagined it could. He softens his hold on my leg.

I spasm on his tongue and release my hand from his head, dropping it to the side and melting into the bed.

After another minute of exploration, he concludes his tour by leaving the gentlest kiss on my pussy lips. He runs his fingers down my thigh as he stands. Still licking my desire off his lips, he says, "Is that what you wanted, Birdie?"

I stare up at him through my lashes. "That...and more."

He shakes his head. "You can't handle more."

"You don't know that." I push down the anger that instinctually rises to the surface.

Bo tips his head toward the bathroom. "Hound boy is finishing up. He can have you next."

"Excuse me?" I rise up onto my elbows. "What do you think I am, some whore you can all have your way with?"

"That's not what I said." Bo takes a step back as I push onto my feet in front of him.

"Sounded like that's what you meant."

"It isn't what I meant and you know it."

"That's the thing, Bo." I glare up at him. "I don't know. Because you won't fucking tell me. You're full of arrogance and banter but refuse to say anything real."

Bo remains standing there, his mouth pinched in a hard line.

"See." I shove his chest. "Nobody is forcing you to be here, Bo. Leave if that's what you want." But before he can see the tears welling in my eyes, I turn away from him and march to the bathroom, and shut the door.

"What's wrong?" Wes asks the second I'm in the closed-off space. He comes over from his spot at the counter.

"Nothing," I lie. "What were you doing over there?"

Wes glances back and then focuses on me. "Just being nosey and looking at all the stuff in the cabinet. This human world fascinates me." He sighs and pulls me to his chest. "Tell me what happened."

I close my eyes and savor the comfort of his body, his truth, his unfaltering loyalty to me.

"Bo being Bo," I finally mutter into him.

Wes pats my back gently. "Want me to kill him?"

I peel myself off him. "Kind of." I force a laugh. "Just kidding. Don't actually." My fingers trace the outline of the alpha mark on my neck. "Especially while I'm still connected to him."

Maybe that's why Bo sticks around; he feels bad about the alpha mark. If he leaves, it will ignite the beacon and alert demons to my whereabouts. But, if that's the case, why doesn't he just remove it and be done if being around us is so fucking terrible?

"Did he tell you how to remove it?" I ask Wes.

"No, just that my hound wouldn't like whatever it is."

"And I asked if any of you had to die, and he said no. What else could it be?"

Wes shrugs. "I have no idea."

Whatever it is, it's bad enough that he's keeping it from us.

4

WES

I wait in the bathroom for Wren while she rinses off in the shower.

When she's finished, I stand there, my arms outstretched with another clean and soft towel to wrap her up in it.

"You sure are a gentleman, you know that?" She grins up at me from her spot tucked close to my chest.

"I've been waiting my whole life for this. There isn't anything I wouldn't do for you."

And that doesn't just apply to me, it goes for my hound, too.

He's constantly foaming at the mouth to break free and murder anyone who dares to look at her cross. Her happiness is his main priority, and I couldn't be any more relieved that we're at least on the same page about that.

"You know it's the same for me, too, right?" Wren stares into my eyes, her gaze intense.

I swallow and tuck her damp hair behind her ear. "Is it?"

"Yes."

I told you, my hound declares.

"Let's get you to bed." I kiss her forehead and with my arm still wrapped around her shoulder, I lead her toward the door.

Only once we're in the bedroom, her body goes rigid upon the absence of Bo.

"Bo's a night owl, he's probably just exploring the property."

"I thought you couldn't lie."

"I'm not lying. Bo is weird. Nothing he does makes sense."

Wren hugs her body tightly.

"How about some clean clothes?" I guide her over to the side of the bed. "Give me a second."

Helplessness cascades through me at not being able to mend what is happening between her and Bo. I never thought that I would accept my mate being with another but I also never thought I would fall for a hunter. My hound doesn't prefer it, but her happiness supersedes his. Nor could I have anticipated being here, having escaped Prania. I've always dreamt of Arthlia and what it might be like to flee the confines of our homeland. Freedom, autonomy, safety. It was a pipe dream, and now it's real.

In the past, when I thought about my future, there was always this void. This emptiness I thought I would never be able to fill. I imagined a life outside of Prania, but I was alone—or alone with Bo and Dash.

No matter the scenario...I was alone.

It wasn't until she came to kill me that I realized she was what I was missing all along. My soul had locked onto her with a force unlike anything I had ever known. I suppressed it. I tried to hide it. I attempted to resist every bit of the pull she had on me. But there was no denying what was already there. Fate had decided it long ago. And I have never been more grateful for anything in my entire life.

I wasn't lying when I said I would do anything for her. I would kill for her. I would die for her. And when Parla tried to tear us apart, I chose to live for her.

I fumble through the clothes in the closet and locate the smallest T-shirt I can find. I settle on a pair of sweatpants in one of the drawers and grab something for myself, too. Luckily, whoever lived here in the past left their belongings behind. Only the pit in my gut tells me they haven't abandoned this place completely. And with Tremont being as cryptic as he is, there's no telling what's in store for us. Tomorrow we will get answers and figure out how to move on in this world. How to start over.

I exit the large closet to find Wren lying along the edge of the bed with the towel still clung around her delicate body, and her eyes closed. My chest flutters at the sight of her, and a smile creeps its way across my face. It's amazing how such an angelic creature can be so fucking deadly. But maybe that's what makes me love her even more, that she is not what she seems. She is fierce and strong and intelligent, but she is also kind, compassionate, and sensitive. She tries to act tough but she cares more than she lets on. I see it come through in the way she treats others. How she refused to leave people behind at Rockbridge. For a woman who was born in blood and violence, she still has a way of radiating such light.

With great caution, I slide the legs of the pants over her dainty feet and up her legs, tying the string around her waist tight enough so they won't fall completely off.

She stirs, her eyes fluttering open to meet mine. "I fell asleep."

"Here," I tell her while she's awake. "Put this on." I help her up, tug the shirt over her head, and pop her arms through each hole. "There. That's better."

Wren grins with her eyes closed and yawns. "I'm tired."

I untuck her hair from inside her shirt and scoop her into my arms, carefully gliding her under the covers and closer to Dash, who remains completely zonked out with his arm resting over his head and his mouth agape.

Once I've dressed, I walk across the room to shut off the lights and climb in next to her.

I settle into the plush mattress and wonder where this level of support has been all my life. No hard lumps. No lack of pillow. No thin blanket. And to top it off, a beautiful girl nestled into the crook of my neck and intertwining her body with mine.

Is it possible I've died and gone to heaven? Because I can't imagine anything fucking else that could be better.

I sleep better than I ever have in my entire life, only, it's cut short by about fifty-seven hours when we're woken by the sound of an argument.

I shoot out of bed and rush to the door.

"Where are my knives?" Wren shows the same level of concern that I do.

I blindly point to where I put her armored clothing and slowly turn the door handle. I peek through the thin gap and see Tremont standing at the end of the hall and another man, easily half his age, a few feet in front of him.

This newcomer has his hands in his dark, curly hair, and he seems distraught but has no visible weapons and he hasn't done any harm to Tremont. Maybe this threat is not as severe as it appears.

I hold out my hand to Wren to hopefully stop her from going into full defense mode.

"We can talk about this," Tremont says to this other man.

"What is there to talk about?" The man draws in a breath and shakes his head. "You shouldn't be here. This ended years ago."

Tremont nods. "I can assure you, I am a changed man, Sydney."

Sydney—the man has a name.

"If she finds out you're here, she'll kill you herself. Tell me why I shouldn't do it right here and now." Sydney remains in place a few feet from Tremont, and Tremont makes no effort to evade him.

"What's happening?" Wren whispers as she tries to see through into the hallway.

Dash stretches and yawns.

Wren and I turn and shush him at the same time.

He offers a quiet, "Sorry."

"I have..." Tremont pauses to find the right words. "Information."

"About what?" Sydney rubs his chin. "What information could you possibly have that she doesn't already? You have no idea the power she wields now. You're a nobody."

"I know." Tremont doesn't dare argue with this other man, yet he tries to plead his case. "I mean no harm, Sydney. I am ashamed of what happened and the role I played in it. I wouldn't have come here so foolishly if I didn't mean that."

"Why did you come here? Huh? This is the worst possible place you could have chosen."

"Because I'm telling you the truth. I was going to find you, or Silas, or anyone. I needed to give my travel companions time to rest. They are not from this world."

Sydney's eyes go wider. "What kind of evil did you bring here, Tremont?"

My hound overpowers my arm and forces the door open, exposing myself and Wren to this random man assuming the worst of us. And if my hound continues to call the shots, he's going to be proven right.

Sydney doesn't jump, he doesn't falter, he simply turns his attention on me. "Who are you?"

Tremont steps between us. "This is Wes, he's from another realm. He and his family have sought refuge here on Earth."

"From where?" Sydney eyes me and then Tremont.

"Prania."

"Prania?"

"Yes. There is a terrible war and a great injustice to his kind."

"His kind?" Sydney steps to the left to avoid Tremont's obstruction. "What are you?"

I clear my throat. "I'm a hellhound."

Sydney's brow rises. "You're a man."

Summoning my powers, I let them rise to the surface, only showing a fraction of my true form. The flames flicker along my skin and comfort me in a way that the luxurious bed of his never could.

"And who's behind you?" Sydney points past me.

Wren shoves her way through the door. "I'm Wren. Wren Oliver."

Sydney's mouth falls open slightly and his gaze trains itself onto Tremont. "What are you trying to pull here?"

"Nothing, I promise you. Get a truth stone, do whatever you need to do, but trust this, she is who she says she is." Tremont moves out of the way to give Sydney a better view down the hallway.

I shift to put myself in front of Wren. "She's not on show here."

"What is she?" Sydney tilts his head around to look at Wren.

Wren does her best attempt to shove me out of the way. "I'm right here, you don't have to talk about me like I'm not in the room."

Sydney runs his hand through his hair again, a nervous habit. "You're right. Sorry. I don't mean to be rude, this is just all very...unexpected." He focuses on Tremont. "Have you not told them about our past?"

Tremont shakes his head. "Not entirely."

"Perhaps they would no longer put their lives in your hands if they knew the truth."

"My life is in my hands, and no one else's," Wren says to Sydney. "We only met him briefly before fleeing our realm. Whatever past you two have together has nothing to do with us."

"And yet you're traveling with him."

"Out of necessity." Wren steps closer and I clench my hand into a fist to shield my desire to force myself in front of her again.

"You come here bearing the name Oliver, so very conveniently." Sydney crosses his arms over his chest. "I don't buy it."

"Why would I lie about that?" Wren matches his movement and folds her arms, too. "Does that name mean something?"

Sydney laughs abruptly. "Really?" He points to Tremont. "This must be hilarious to you, isn't it?"

"Care to explain the punchline?" Wren asks him.

"You show up, after all these years, out of the fucking blue, claiming you want peace, using *this house* to find refuge, and with a girl bearing Willow's last name."

"Who's Willow?" Wren speaks the question that was on my mind, too.

"Really? You're telling me you have never heard the name Willow Oliver, that Tremont doesn't have you going along with whatever game he's playing? I find this way too convenient to have a shred of truth in it."

I shove around Wren and put myself back into his line of sight. "I've had enough of you accusing her of being a liar. Get your little truth rock and do what you must, but if you so much as hint at one more bad thing toward her..."

"Ah." Sydney grins. "The violent welcome party I

expected." He looks me up and down. "Why don't you try?"

He saw the flames licking my skin, and yet he's standing there completely unfazed by what I could possibly do to him. He wields no weapons and hasn't even hinted at having magic of his own. He's unmatched and unbothered, meaning only one thing, I'm underestimating him entirely.

And when I take another step forward and am met with the sturdy wall of an invisible forcefield, I realize he had the upper hand all along. I was just too stupid to see it.

5

WREN

"Are you okay?" I grip Wes's shoulders as he stumbles back.

"Yeah." He regains his footing. "What is this?" Wes places his palm against seemingly nothing.

I fight the desire to lose my entire mind at being held captive *once again*. First, it was by Wes, then Rockbridge, and now, this.

Will I ever be truly free?

Even before Wes found me bleeding out in that building where I was supposed to kill him, I spent my existence in a chokehold by Parla and her merciless cause. I've never been of my own free will, why did I expect things to have ever changed? If only I had just died that day with my mother, none of this would have happened. Wes and Dash and Bo would be living much better lives without me, and so many wouldn't be dead by my hands.

"It's a barrier spell," Sydney tells him. "To keep all of you contained while I figure out what to do with you." He nods down the hallway. "How many more are there?" He raises his voice. "Show yourselves."

Dash comes out of our bedroom with his hands in the air. "Uh, hey, I'm Dash. I don't have any special skills or anything, I'm just really good at dying. I mean, not dying, but like, coming back to life. I don't know, that doesn't make sense. I'm not making sense."

I take one of his hands and lower it, weaving my fingers into his and pulling him toward me. "Everything is going to be okay, don't worry." It might be a lie, but it's what he needs to hear. The truth is, I won't let anyone hurt him, not if I have any say in it.

Sydney's brows bunch together. "Your specialty is dying?"

"Yeah, I'm a—"

Tremont cuts Dash off. "He's harmless is what he is. And until you start negotiating our release, I don't think they should have to give you any more information."

"Do you not realize how sketchy that sounds, especially coming out of your mouth?"

"It's fine, I don't mind," Dash speaks up. "I'm, I guess I'm a phoenix, whatever that means."

Sydney leans against the railing to the stairs. He trains his focus on Wes. "You're telling me that you're a hellhound." Then on Dash. "You're a phoenix." And then on me. "And you're a witch."

I shake my head and interject. "No. I'm not a witch. I'm a hunter."

"A hunter? But..."

"She's been in Prania her whole life," Tremont adds. "She was raised as a hunter. Her magic has lied dormant. Ring any bells?"

I step toward Tremont. "When are you going to realize that I don't have any magic? None of my own at least."

"What's that supposed to mean?" Sydney grows defensive.

"It's complicated." How am I supposed to explain something that doesn't make sense to me either?

"Right."

"Is this where we introduce ourselves?" Jade pokes her head out of the bedroom she and Everest share.

Sydney throws his hands up. "By all means, just keep them coming. Anyone else hiding in there?"

"Just me and Everest." She walks out with her hand tucked into his, the two of them side by side, declaring for the whole world to know that they're *together*.

If Bo saw this, he'd be foaming at the mouth.

Bo. My heart stutters from the realization that he's not here, and that he never came back last night.

My fingers trace the scar he left behind on my neck, the constant reminder of his presence in my life. It doesn't burn, doesn't run hot, but it's how it normally is when he's nearby. Which means he hasn't abandoned us completely. No, he must be lying in wait for his time to strike. Or, he's gorging on the rest of the hot pockets in the freezer downstairs. One option is just as possible as the other.

"And what might you two be?" Sydney narrows his gaze at them like he's trying to decide for himself before they answer.

"I'm..." Jade holds her hand to her chest.

"No," Wes cuts her off and turns toward Sydney. "I need to know that no harm comes to any of us." He flits an apologetic look toward Tremont. "I understand you two have history, but the rest of us have done no wrong other than eating some of your food and sleeping in your beds. I will do whatever you wish to repay you for that, but I beg of you to show mercy to the rest of us."

Sydney takes in Wes's request and chews at his bottom lip. "You two, the hellhound and the phoenix. You're with her, the *hunter*?"

"They have names," I blurt out. "Wes and Dash."

Sydney smiles. "You're more and more like an Oliver with each passing second."

"See," Tremont says. "I told you so."

"Silence." Sydney stares right at Tremont. "I've heard enough from you." He steadies his gaze on Wes. "No harm will come to you so long as the same is recip-rocated. The second I find out you're lying to me, I will have no choice but to take back my word."

Wes and Sydney exchange a swift nod.

"So then you'll free us from these confines?" I ask the question that's no doubt on all our minds.

"I still don't know what those two are." Sydney motions down the hall.

Jade steps closer. "I'm a banshee, and Everest is…"

"I was born a hunter, as was Wren, but I do not associate myself as one."

"Let me get this straight." Sydney rubs his hands together and pauses momentarily. "You three are some of the rarest, if not completely obsolete supernatural beings in existence. And you." He focuses right on me. "You're a distant relative to my wife."

"I…" But no other words come out of my mouth. I have family? Living relatives? In another realm outside of Prania? Is this possible? I thought I was the last of my bloodline. That's what Parla told me when she helped me trace back my lineage. Although, when has anything that bitch has ever said or done been without some hidden fucking agenda behind it? Maybe Parla realized how powerful and significant I would be when she was pretending to be my friend, and instead of telling me the truth, she fed me more lies to keep me under her authority.

Because had she told me then that there were more of my kind, I would have done everything in my power to find them. And that alone would have ruined her carefully laid out plan.

She didn't just take my life from me, she tried to take away my future and my past, too.

Is this why Tremont was shocked when Dash had called me by my last name? Because he knows the woman who is married to Sydney? Tremont mentioned he had history with Sydney's parents, but how does that affect Sydney or his wife? It clearly does, because Sydney is labeling us all the enemy just for being in Tremont's company. What could Tremont have done that was so bad to make Sydney hate him so much?

Unless...

"Sydney." I grow worried about the question I'm about to ask. "Is your wife, this other Oliver, is she dead?"

"What?" He shakes his head. "No. She's very much alive."

"Oh." I let out a sigh of relief. "Sorry, I thought you were mad at him because he hurt her."

At least I don't have to add *dead relative* to my list today.

"You really don't know, do you?" Sydney stares at me.

But before either of us can say anything else, a dark flash darts up the stairs.

"This party is over." Bo grabs Sydney by the neck and lifts him off the ground. "This fucking spell, you take it down, *now*."

I choke on a gasp. "Bo, stop!" I rush forward, not sure where the boundary of the barrier spell is in place. But when I bolt past where I'm certain it was without being stopped, I continue pushing my feet forward until I'm latching onto Bo's arm. "Please, Bo, don't hurt him."

Bo's dark gaze meets mine and he blinks, like he's wondering how it's possible Sydney complied with his demand so quickly.

"See, I'm right here, the barrier spell is gone. You can let him go."

"Uh, Wren," Wes says from somewhere behind me.

I turn, expecting him to be closer than he is, but he's still in the hallway, where everybody else remains.

"What are you waiting for?" I ask him. "Come on."

He shakes his head and places his hand along the rippling magical edge of the boundary which is very much still intact.

"Bo, I command you this instant, release him."

Bo drops Sydney onto the hardwood floor, where he wheezes and clutches at his throat.

"Fucking psycho," Sydney spits out.

Bo squares his shoulders. "If you don't release them, I'll show you a true psycho." A growl rumbles in his chest.

Sydney scoots back and up onto his feet. "I'm not letting Tremont out."

"I don't care about him. But the rest of them, let them out, *now*."

I step in front of Bo and inch carefully toward Sydney. "What he's *trying* to say is, would you please let our people free? We have spent a lifetime in captivity." I glare over my shoulder at Bo. "He lacks the proper manners to ask politely."

Sydney rubs at his throat and flits his gaze between us. "Don't make me regret this." He snaps his fingers and a moment later, everyone except Tremont is free of the barrier.

"You can't just lock me up in here." Tremont pounds his fist on the invisible forcefield.

"I can, and I will." Sydney swallows harshly. "Could I have a word with the rest of you downstairs?"

"Yeah, of course." I shove Bo from his spot firmly in place. "Knock it off, grump ass." I wave my hands at the rest of my group. "Go ahead, I'm right behind you." I hang back to make sure they go without causing an issue and then walk down with Sydney.

Something in my gut tells me he wouldn't hurt me, not if he doesn't have a reason to. If my distant relative trusts him enough to marry him, that means I should be safe to be near him.

"Is he"—Sydney nods ahead—"one of your mates, too?"

I bite at my lip. If he had asked me yesterday, I would have said yes without hesitation, but now I'm not so sure what Bo is to me. Is he simply the alpha who left a mark on my neck? Or is he more? To me, he is one of the men I care deeply for, but I cannot force someone to want to be with me if they don't want to. And I surely won't be reduced to a piece of meat they take turns sharing. Perhaps Bo and I were always destined to remain enemies and nothing more.

I settle on responding, "It's complicated." Because that's the truth and I'm sick of lies.

"I'm familiar with complicated." Sydney matches my stride down the winding staircase. "My wife has four mates."

My eyes widen and I turn to take him in, to assess whether this is another deceit. But when he offers me a soft smile, I conclude that he's being honest, too.

I want to ask him more, to let the million questions rattling around inside my head spill, but upon reaching the bottom of the stairs, the rest of the group stands there in wait for their next command.

"Through here." Sydney motions ahead and walks past them, leading us down another long hallway and into a grand living room with a large fireplace and lavish furniture. "Have a seat while I tend to the fire."

Wes follows him over, mumbling something along the lines of, "I can help with that." I don't catch everything that's exchanged, but it seems civil to say the least.

Sydney throws a few logs onto the fire and steps back, waiting for Wes to do his magic.

Wes balls his hand into a fist, the fire of his other half rising to the surface and creating a blazing orb that he tosses onto the wood in the brick hearth. The thing ignites instantly and settles down once the wood has been engulfed.

The two of them say a few more words and make their way over to the rest of us who have chosen a seat among the many in this room.

"For the sake of clarity, could we agree to be honest with each other?" Sydney glances around the room at the faces he's only met moments prior in an equally hostile situation. "We didn't exactly get off on the right foot, and I have to admit, you being anywhere near that man upstairs makes me immediately suspicious."

"And you locking them into a wing of your house isn't doing you any favors either," Bo mouths off.

"I don't know how it works back where you're from, but there's this thing called breaking and entering here, and it's illegal." Sydney leans against the arm of the couch Jade and Everest have taken up residency on. "Human law, not even supernatural. So the fact that you're supernatural makes it that much more complicated when I show up to my childhood home to find a misfit bunch of creatures sleeping in my beds. Plus, the fact that they're shacking up with my literal enemy. Anyone else may have killed you on the spot, but you caught me on a good day."

Dash raises his hand. "I would have come back. And you'd have had to clean up all the ash and soot, and I'm not going to lie, it's pretty messy."

"Noted." Sydney crosses his arms. "Someone want to tell me what you're doing here. The truth this time."

And that's what I do. I tell him the truth. That our homeland was in a forever-long war, that demons and hunters would stop at nothing to rid each other from the realm. That up until I met these men, I was considered the most feared demon assassin of them all. That I was brainwashed into thinking they were the enemy when in reality, we were the evil plaguing our land, and I didn't learn that until it was too late. But that we found a way out, that we rallied together to escape an inescapable prison, and we banded together to outrun those that wished us dead. Our enemies turned into allies, and we chose to blindly put faith in those around us because it was the only thing to do to stay alive.

"So you didn't know Tremont long?" Sydney asks.

"He was my cellmate," Wes tells him. "He told me he knew of a way out, not of the prison, but of our realm. I had no other choice than to believe him." He draws in a breath and continues. "We've all made our fair share of mistakes, and the man I met in that prison cell showed genuine remorse."

"Did he tell you what he did?"

"No, not really. He mentioned a past he was regretful of. That he lied, and stole, and let people down. I recall him saying he was a bully, and that he went through painful withdrawals in Prania but that when it was all said and done, he was glad because he realized that he was wrong for what he had done. He said he wanted to make amends but thought it was too late. I didn't pry any of the details out, not when the most important thing on my mind was getting her out of here." Wes grips my hand tighter and rubs his thumb along mine. "I would have formed an alliance with the devil himself if it meant saving her."

"Are you going to keep tiptoeing around it or are you going to tell us what he did?" Bo folds his fingers into his palm and looks at his nails. He's never really been one for patience.

But when Sydney opens his mouth to speak, he's distracted by something else.

Dash, who was sitting on the edge of the chair being his sweet and opposite of Bo self, falls face first into the table, banging his head on the side and collapsing onto the floor.

"Angels." I rush over to him and turn him over onto his back.

Blood pools from the open wound on his forehead, and his eyes remain shut. His body starts trembling uncontrollably.

"What's wrong with him?" I say to anyone listening.

"Here." Sydney gets to my side, a small pillow from the couch in his grasp. "Put this under his head." He meets my gaze. "Has this ever happened before?"

"I..." But I haven't been with Dash long enough to know if it has or not.

"No," Wes chimes in. "Never."

"What did you do?" Bo accuses. "Did you poison him?"

Sydney lets out a gruff breath. "I'm not as cruel as you think I am." He presses his hand to Dash's chest.

"What are you doing?" I grab at his wrist a bit too hard.

"I'm trying to see if I can figure out what's wrong with him." Sydney's eyes flutter closed.

I hold my breath, hoping and waiting and praying to the Angels that Dash will be okay.

Because if he isn't, I might just become the villain that Sydney suspects is in this room.

6

DASH

Darkness. Pain. Isolation.

A blast of light. A crack of a whip.

A woman yelling.

My hands dig into the dirt, and it consumes my fingers, shielding the smallest piece of me from harm.

I wish to sink deeper, go farther, until I am buried in the ground and surrounded by nothing but dirt to protect me.

Another slice across my back. Agony courses through me. Numbness. The scent of fresh blood pooling.

I tremble and will it to stop. Please stop.

Please stop.

Please stop.

Please.

Stop.

Please.

I pinch my eyes shut, convinced that if I pretend I'm not here, I'll disappear.

Maybe I can just disappear.

Disappear.

"Come back to me," a whisper floats to me.

It is kind, gentle, safe.

I focus on it, even if it is only a figment of my imagination.

Anything is better than this.

Another torrent of the whip. I am ripped open.

I shake.

Hands, warm hands, grip my shoulders.

"Dash," the voice calls out again, this time with more urgency.

Is this person in danger more than I am? Do they need me? How can I break away from my hell to save this other person? No one should be helpless, scared, afraid. I must find a way.

"Please," they say. "I need you."

I fight. I scrape. I push with every ounce of strength.

And when I open my eyes, I am no longer in hell, but in the arms of the woman who I care most about in this entire world.

"Dash," she pulls me to her. "Angels, are you okay?"

I hug her back, grateful to be gone from whatever nightmare I was just living through. It felt too...real. No dream has ever made me experience such torment.

"I'm fine. I'm sorry I worried you."

She releases me but keeps me at an arm's length. "Are you really apologizing right now?"

"Sorry."

Her cheeks turn up into a smile. "Dash."

I pinch my lips together to keep myself from saying sorry again.

Wren blots at my forehead with a towel.

Bo rises from his chair in the corner of the room and moseys over. "Thought you were a goner, bud." He pats my shoulder. "Where did you go?"

I scoot up and rest my back against the headframe of the bed we slept in last night. Someone must have brought me here when I...

"The last thing I remember was we were in a big room." I avert my gaze to attempt to recall the memory. "There was a fireplace. And I was listening to everyone talk." I glance at Wren. "Is this right?"

She nods.

"I can't really remember what they were saying. But I got hot, real hot, real fast. And woozy. I thought I was going to throw up. And then I fell." I place my hand on my forehead where a bandage covers the spot that must have made impact.

A breeze from the open window licks at my cheeks.

"Damn, that feels good." I kick my legs over the edge of the bed and stand.

Wren grips one arm while Bo holds the other.

"I'm not going to fall. I'm fine."

"Better safe than sorry." Wren doesn't let me go until I'm leaning on the windowsill.

"What happened after that?" Bo presses his shoulder into the wall and crosses his arms over his chest.

"I had this terrible nightmare. I was being tortured." I reach toward my back and replay the anguish. But when I touch a spot, it actually *feels* tender. "Uh, will one of you do me a favor?"

"What is it?" Wren comes back over with a glass of water in her grasp.

I drag my shirt up my back and turn toward them. "Do you see anything out of the ordinary?"

Wren sucks in a breath. "Angels." She extends her hand but doesn't touch me.

An indicator that my hunch was correct.

"How is that possible?" Bo asks us.

"What does it look like?" I ask them.

"Like someone just got done beating you senseless." Bo steps forward.

Wren adds, "Your scars. They're not open wounds, but they're red and swollen. Not all of them. But quite a few. Like they're fresh. Do they hurt?"

"No," I lie. "They're sore." I let my shirt fall over them and turn around to sit near the window again.

That nightmare didn't feel like a nightmare. It was more like a memory. But a memory that I don't have. And a memory that could somehow hurt me. None of that makes sense.

"Anyway," I say. "What did I miss?" Because I would do anything to change the subject and escape from the sad and pitiful stares they're giving me right now.

"Dash..." Wren places her hand on my shoulder.

I bring it to my face and kiss the soft flesh before putting my hand over it. "We have more important things to deal with than my mystery scars. We're in a different realm. In someone else's house. And traveling with a potential asshole."

Wren sighs. "Bo isn't just a *potential* asshole."

"Hey, now, that's the nicest thing you've said about me all day." Bo continues to lean against the wall.

Wren rolls her eyes. "Sydney was about to tell us what Tremont had done when you face-planted into the table. Bo carried you up here, and we've been at your side ever since. Sydney left. He said he was going to get some rock to see if you had a *glitch*, whatever that means. But we have no way of contacting him to let him know you're awake. Tremont is confined to his room, and the rest of our group is downstairs giving us some space. That pretty much catches you up to where we are now."

"How long was I out?"

"A half hour or so." Wren glances at Bo, who nods stiffly.

I lower my voice. "And we still don't know what he did?"

She shakes her head. "Something bad enough that Sydney hates him for it."

"I don't trust him," Bo chimes in.

"You don't trust anyone." Wren faces Bo. "What is it? His enormous manor. The fact that he didn't kill us for breaking into his home? His giant freezer full of delicious food? That he was willing to go find something to help Dash?"

Bo stares right at her, expressionless. "Tremont, not Sydney."

"Oh."

Bo huffs. "I'm going to tell the others you didn't die."

"Actually," I reach out toward him. "You. Stay. Wren will inform them."

"Yeah, of course." She kisses my cheek before leaving the room.

When I'm sure her footsteps have hit the stairs, I glare at Bo. "Spill."

"I don't know what you're talking about." Bo presses his hands on the windowsill and shoves his head out the window. "The air is different here, have you noticed that?"

"Yeah, it's fresher, and it doesn't smell like soot and rotting flesh. But don't try to change the subject."

Bo sighs dramatically. "I can't change the subject if I don't know what the subject is."

"Don't play dumb with me. You're too smart to be that stupid."

"Aw, you think I'm smart." Bo brings himself back inside and returns his arms to the crossed position over his chest, shutting me out like he does everyone else.

"What's going on between you two? And before you ask me who, I'm talking about you and Wren. What happened?"

"Nothing happened."

"Something happened."

"Why are you so worried about it?"

I pinch the bridge of my nose between my fingers. "Because she's important to me, and you're important to me. I'm not an idiot. Something is clearly going on. This is a different kind of banter. I can literally *feel* the fucking tension when you're both near each other."

Bo's dark eyes widen. "Did you just say *fucking*?"

"Why does everyone get so alarmed when I cuss?"

"You're the sweet and innocent one of the bunch." Bo shrugs. "It's uncharacteristic of you."

"Maybe I'm sick of being the odd man out. And for the twenty-seventh time, stop deflecting the conversation. I'm not going to leave you alone until you tell me what it is."

"And then what, Dash, what does it matter?"

"It matters. To you, to her, to me, to all of us. You're going to tell me, and then we're going to fix it."

"What if it can't be fixed?"

"Then, you better start groveling. Sooner rather than later." I stick my arm out the window to let the breeze wash over my skin. "What did you do?"

"It's more like what *didn't* I do?"

"So you admit that you did something wrong?"

Bo runs his hand through his long hair, tugging it and letting out a breath. "I don't know. Yes. No. Kind of. Everything has been wrong from the start. And I'm..."

But he doesn't finish his sentence, not even after a full minute of silence.

"You're what, Bo? You're sorry? You're worried? You're angry? What are you feeling?"

"I'm afraid."

Two words I never expected the man in front of me to ever say. He's never been fearful of anything. He takes danger head-on with a sly grin on his face. But this...this is something different. It's not something he can beat or fight or outmaneuver. No, caring about someone is a new kind of fear that he's only known in small blips. Romantic feelings are entirely different than that of family—because family is forever, love is chosen, it's all or nothing, and quite literally the fiercest competitor he's ever had.

"Hey," I say softly and place my hand on his shoulder. "You're going to get through this." I bob my head up and down. "You will."

Wren comes back into the room, her warm presence a welcome comfort. "They made some food if you guys are hungry."

Bo shrugs me off and leaves me behind at the window, marching past Wren and disappearing in the direction she just came.

"Good talk," she mutters on her way over to me.

"Don't worry about him."

"Oh, I'm not." Wren sits across from me in the window and stares outside. "Not one bit."

I hide the way my lips turn up. "Uh-huh. Okay."

"What?" She glances over at me. "I'm not!"

"What did he do?" I ask, despite knowing both of them are equally hot and cold on whether they're willing to talk about things.

"What didn't he do?"

Her response, so similar to his, makes me laugh.

"Sorry," I tell her while covering my mouth and regaining my composure. "Is there something specific this time?"

She inhales and looks outside prior to exhaling and focusing back on me. "Promise you won't say anything?"

"I promise."

"Last night, he basically implied I was some piece of meat you guys pass around."

My jaw clenches and without realizing it, I'm standing, both of my fists balled tightly. "I'll kill him."

Wren stands, too, to block me from going any further. "You said you wouldn't say anything."

"I did, didn't I?" I force myself to sit back down.

It's no wonder Bo is worried about things, he fucked up. Never should anyone feel the way that Wren most likely does since he said that. Regardless of the context or the tone or whatever was going through his thick skull, he should have kept his mouth shut. Wren is so much more than that to us—to me, at least—and if I have to be celibate with her to prove that, I'll do it in a heartbeat.

"On behalf of men," I say to her. "I apologize." I take her hand in mine. "And I'm sorry if us being together last night brought this on."

"You didn't do anything wrong, Dash. You're perfect, really." She returns to her spot next to me. "I just don't understand Bo. He's into me one minute, and not the next. He shows he cares, or is worried, but then he's so distant and reserved. I never know what he's actually feeling or thinking. And if the only thing connecting us is this stupid mark, I'd rather it be gone so he could go his separate ways."

Tears well in her eyes but she blinks them away and stares out the window.

"I'm sorry," she tells me, her focus returning. "You just went through hell and here I am blabbing about boy trouble."

"Shh." I hold her hand tighter. "You brought me back, okay? I'd do anything to make you feel better."

"Don't worry about me, I'm fine, really. That stuff isn't important."

"You're important," I remind her.

"Well, so are you, Dash. And you're probably hungry, aren't you?" She stands and tugs me up with her. "Come on, you should eat before Bo wipes the entire house of all its food."

"Now that, that wouldn't surprise me." I weave my fingers through hers and walk the length of the room by her side.

Oh what I would do to make this our every day. The problems we face are that of arrogant men who don't know how to share their feelings and nothing of wars and revenge and running for our lives.

I want that with her. A human life. Or at the very least, a human-adjacent life here, where the air is fresh and we can stop looking over our shoulders in fear of what's coming next. That's what I will fight for because it's what we all deserve.

And although I don't want to break my promise to her, it's going to be difficult to not confront Bo and make him pay for the hurt he's caused her.

7

WREN

"Glad to see you're back on your feet," Sydney tells Dash when we file into the large kitchen. "I was worried we'd have a mess to clean up for a minute there."

Dash forces a smile. "Just keeping everyone on their toes."

We settle into two empty chairs at the end of the table where everyone else is sitting. Well, everyone aside from Bo. No, Bo chooses to scarf down his food while standing in the farthest corner of the room like the rest of us might give him the plague if he comes too close.

Whatever.

"Here, give me your plate." Wes takes the shiny white dish in front of me and scoops some food onto it, along with a hunk of bread. "Pass that over to Dash." He hands it to me, and I'm wafted by the heavenly aroma as it crosses in front of me and over to Dash.

"Damn, that smells amazing." My stomach growls and reminds me that eating more should move up on the list of priorities.

During our stint in Rockbridge, there was no telling when our next meal would be. Not to mention, whether it would be edible. Usually, it was some sort of greyish sludge that could have been borderline toxic waste. Sometimes there would be a cup with a small amount of water, and rarely, a moldy piece of what resembled bread. We were only there for a short period, and yet the experience isn't something I wish to ever go through again.

My gaze darts across the table to land on Jade, who spent, from my understanding, years in that horrid place. How is it possible she survived that long on scraps of nearly nothing? But when I see Everest push his plate toward her, I realize the answer to that question.

He was the light in the darkness that kept her going. Her lifeline when all hope was lost.

And he was more than likely a huge catalyst in not just her survival, but ours, too.

I thought I was the only hunter who fought against our kind, but maybe Everest and I aren't the only ones who see the errors of our ways.

"There's cheese on this." Wes picks up the piece of

bread on my plate and points to a gooey substance on top. "And this." He latches onto a peculiar tube and pops the top. "You can sprinkle on the pasta."

"It's called parmesan cheese," Sydney says from down the table. "Try it."

I reluctantly take the thing from Wes and sprinkle some on top of the pile of food on my plate. Taking the fork from beside my plate, I swirl some of the pasta and shove it into my mouth. My eyes instinctually close and a moan escapes me. "This is," I say with a mouthful. "So fucking good."

Wes grins and sets the bread back onto my plate, but I snatch it up and bite off a chunk, chewing it with the pasta.

I practically drown the noodles with more cheese and mumble through each bite.

"I didn't have any breakfast foods stocked in the house." Sydney walks over to the large refrigerator, which is apparently powered by electricity, not magic.

To me, they're one and the same.

An entire home with running water and lights and heating, that sounds magical.

"Is this not *breakfast*?" I pat my mouth with my napkin and reach for the glass of water in front of me. "Because I could eat this for every meal."

Sydney chuckles. "Usually humans eat eggs or meat, pastries, pancakes, fruit, things like that, for breakfast. With coffee or juice."

"I could go for some ale." I point to the tray of bread

in the middle of the table and whisper to Wes, "Can I have another?"

"Ale? Hmm." Sydney continues browsing the contents of his fridge. "I have this spiked cider." He pulls out a bottle and brings it over to me. "Deghan got a six-pack the last time he visited."

"Deghan?" I take the thing from him. "Will they mind if I have this?"

He shakes his head. "He probably forgot all about them."

What a luxury to have so much that you forget about things. I may lose track of an apple here or there, but I would know if someone took something like this from one of my safe houses.

"And who is this Deghan? A friend?" I fumble with the thing covering the end of the bottle.

"Here, let me help you." Sydney twists the cap off and tosses it onto the table.

I sniff the end. "It's kind of fruity."

"Yeah, it's fermented apples."

Everyone except Bo and Sydney stares at me in what I can only assume is anticipation of my response to the drink.

I bring the bottle to my lips, the cool fizzy liquid pooling into my mouth. I swallow it down and shrug. "It's not bad." I hold it out to Wes. "Want to try it?"

"Sure." He takes it from me, then passes it to Dash. "Not bad at all."

"I can get more, if you'd like." Sydney opens a

drawer and pulls out a notepad. "And to answer your question, Deghan is one of my wife's husbands."

"Wife plural or husband plural?" I ask him to clarify.

"Husband, sorry, I should have been clearer. I have one wife, she has four husbands. And each of us are married to only her."

"Is that common here on Earth?" Because it's not something I'm super familiar with.

"Um, yes and no." Sydney makes a note on the pad of paper. "Relationships with multiple partners are becoming more widely normalized and accepted. Legally speaking, no, you can't technically marry multiple partners. Our ceremony wasn't traditional in the sense, and more so to connect us on a spiritual level. It meant more to us than having a legally binding arrangement."

It's comforting to know that I'm not the only one who finds being with more than one person appealing. It isn't that I want to collect men until the end of time, but there's no denying that I have a connection to each of my guys, and if forced to choose between them, I don't think I could. Each of them makes me feel a different way and imagining a life without any single one of them seems dull and void. Even Bo, who drives me completely fucking insane.

I'm not open, available, or interested in any other suitors—I just want my three demons.

"It's more common in the supernatural world," Sydney adds.

Jade speaks up from her spot at the end of the table with Everest. "What are you going to do about Tremont?"

A question no doubt on all our minds. I don't particularly care either way what happens to him, but I am curious.

Sydney draws in a long breath and leans against the countertop. "I haven't made a decision." He runs his hand through his shaggy hair. "If I'm being honest, this entire situation has thrown me. Between him, you, being back here—I'm unsure what to do about any of it."

I sip more of the cider. "Are you going to tell us what he did?"

"It's...complicated." Sydney glances down at the floor and back up. "And kind of a long, twisted story." He shakes his head. "One that I thought was behind us."

"Maybe just give us the highlights, or well, the low lights. His worst offenses." I understand where he's coming from, because if someone asked me to explain things with Parla, I'd be lost at where to begin, too.

"The worst?" Sydney drinks from his cup, the condensation trickling down the side and dripping onto his shirt. "He hurt my wife." He nods. "That's something I'll never forgive him for, no matter what amends he tries to make."

"Is she okay?" I ask.

"Yeah, she's better than ever, growing in strength every day, no thanks to him."

He must care a great deal for his wife if he's *this* mad at someone for harming her.

"What does she say about him, and us, being here?" I can't help but wonder what she must be like—this distant relative of mine. I wonder what features we share, what things we have in common.

"I haven't told her, not yet, not until I know more. I don't want to burden her, she already has too much going on as it is."

A part of me grows worried that he never will, and we will remain locked away in this house, in this other realm, without any hope of a real future.

But I push that intrusive thought away. It's only been a day; I need to not jump to conclusions. I've spent a lifetime in captivity, what's a little longer?

"Here's the deal. Tremont hurt her in more ways than one. He hurt you, too." He looks directly at me when he says this. "He's the reason your magic was suppressed for all those years. He conspired with my parents to steal magic from an entire bloodline in some sadistic power-hungry rampage. Up until not too long ago, the Oliver name was cursed, and he played a huge role in making that happen."

Rage boils within me at each word he speaks. It's no wonder he was shocked when he found Tremont shacking up in his house and threw together that barrier spell. Hell, I would have killed him on the spot if I were him. Sydney has more willpower than me, or maybe he's not accustomed to that kind of violence. Or is it that things aren't handled that way here on Earth?

"I say we kill him." Bo finally breaks his silence.

Leave it to Bo to say the thing on my very mind.

I flit my attention at him briefly before settling my gaze back on Sydney. "You really believe I have hidden magic somewhere within me?"

"Without a doubt."

I thought Parla took everything from me, but it seems Tremont was a key component in trying to ruin my life, too. What if I came into my powers sooner? Could I have stopped the war in Prania earlier? Could I have saved myself a lifetime of serving that heartless bitch? Would I have been strong enough to prevent my mother from being murdered when I was a child? I'll never know, and it's his fault I'll never find out.

"I think he knew." I recall the memory of him taking my *magic* to break the barrier spell at Rockbridge, the one that was keeping us confined inside the building.

He acted shocked, like my power was somehow alarming. I passed it off as him getting a jolt of all the demon essence I harnessed, but in reality, he was getting a taste of what he already knew. *Oliver magic.* He gave himself away again when he questioned my last name, and insisted I would be capable of cross-realm travel without a weakness in the fold. He knew the whole time, and never once thought to tell me who I was, who I am. And because I was blind to the truth, I never truly picked up on any of it. My biggest concern was getting my people to safety, and in that, I over-looked the enemy right at my side.

But if he truly meant ill, would he have brought us to the very place where those secrets would no doubt come to light? He had to have known how dangerous it would be here, and that it would only be a matter of time before I learned what he had done.

The entire situation makes no sense from his perspective if he had some nefarious plan.

Regardless of whether his intentions were good or evil, it still makes me want to kill him no less.

He may not have known he was hurting me when he suppressed the Oliver magic, but the impact of what he did runs deep. His actions very well could be the catalyst that set my entire life on the path that it took.

Would my path have crossed with Wes's if he hadn't, though?

Or what if we had met sooner, under different circumstances?

"Oh, he did, for sure," Sydney confirms. "I'm guessing he brought you here as a bargaining chip, for his freedom."

How dare someone use me for anything, especially for forgiveness of such heinous acts.

"Wait." I play the details of what he said back in my mind. "Your parents, what became of them?"

Sydney's jaw tenses. "They got what they deserved. And now they're serving out the rest of their days in Balial's hell dimension." He puts his arms up. "This was their home, the one I grew up in. I can't bring myself to part with it but being here is a constant reminder of a childhood I don't wish on anyone else."

That makes two of us with a screwed-up adolescence.

Wes grips my hand under the table.

None of us have had it easy, that's for sure. But if I have any say in our future, it's one that isn't plagued with memories we beg to forget.

"I'm guessing you didn't share your parent's ambition?" Dash stands from the table, taking his empty plate and the one in front of me.

"No, my parents and I had nothing in common. They hated me and what I stood for—what I was."

"How could a parent hate their child?" The question leaves my mouth without me really meaning to say it out loud.

"I was a reminder of what they would never have. True angel given power." Sydney glances around. "I don't know how much you know of your ancestry, but we all have some level of light and dark magic coursing through our veins. Every supernatural being does. The lighter, the more powerful. That isn't to say darker can't be potent, too, but lighter is purer, a more direct link to the Angels. My parents, with the help of Tremont and many others, going back centuries, had been suppressing and harnessing the Oliver line, because it was stronger than anything they could have naturally."

The comparison of what Parla had me doing to the demons of Prania is so eerily similar to what Sydney's parents were doing to my bloodline.

At the end of the day, what makes me any different than him?

What if he was manipulated and convinced that what he was doing was the right thing?

How can I hate him for doing exactly what I had been doing?

I didn't just steal their source of power, I killed them in order to take it.

If anything, what I did was fucking worse.

I swallow down a lump that forms in my throat and grow ill from the damage that I had caused.

I knew I was taking their essence, and I had no reservations about ending their lives. I thought I was doing my realm a service to free us from the creatures that plagued our lands. But all they were trying to do was survive. Sure, they fought back and caused their fair share of mayhem, but they were doing what they had to do to stay alive—and with me out there, fueled by nothing but vengeance, they stood no chance. None of them did. The only thing stopping me from making sure Wes had met that same fate, was fate itself. If the curse hadn't been lifted, would I have even known who

Wes was when I locked eyes with him? Would I have killed him without knowing he was my fated mate? When would it have ever registered in my mind, in my soul, that I was responsible for his death?

Suddenly, I find myself grateful for whoever, or whatever freed the Oliver bloodline of their curse.

"How? How were we set free?" I hold Wes's hand tighter and silently thank the Angels that he's here with me today.

"It wasn't easy," Sydney tells me. "There was a series of obstacles, but ultimately, it came down to Willow, my wife. She went through hell and back, quite literally, multiple times even. There were a few times I didn't think she'd make it, that any of us would, but somehow, she overcame the impossible." Sydney smiles softly. "I'm not sure there isn't anything she can't do once she sets her mind to it."

The love he has for her radiates through each word he speaks of her. He's protective, proud, supportive. It's a beautiful thing to see despite all the ugly I'm familiar with.

"I'd love to meet her." I would settle for anything to help me wrap my head around the information that's been thrown at me.

Nothing about my life is what I thought it was. And every day, something else seems to change. What else do I not know about who I am, who I was, or who I could be?

"I need to process things before bringing her into

this." He lets out a breath. "I hope you understand. This is rather unexpected, and my primary concern is her well-being. I don't know how she'll react to any of this. I want to tread lightly, be cautious."

And given I'm the worst monster of them all, I don't blame him for wanting to shield her from me.

8

WREN

Tremont stays tucked away inside his room.

I don't bother knocking, or paying much attention to him aside from imagining him bursting into flames and experiencing a painful demise.

I shower again, doing what I can to rid myself of the lingering remains of his touch. He didn't hurt me, but I can't help being repulsed by the idea of him having access to my power.

Let me in, he had said.

I gave him entry to my magic without realizing the severity of the situation. But if he was going to abuse that gateway, wouldn't he have taken more? Taken so much that it rendered me completely powerless.

Nothing of this makes sense, and the more I try to rationalize what has happened, the more confused I become.

So instead, I sit in the large expanse of the shower

and let the water wash over me, the heat reddening my pale flesh.

How much longer will we remain in this house? What will happen to us once Sydney makes up his mind? We're at a standstill on how to move forward, especially considering Tremont was going to be the go-between for teaching us the ways of this world.

Without that, we pose too many risks to be set loose on Earth. One hour of Bo being free and he'd probably eat an entire town for lunch and out the supernatural world by the end of the day.

These beings have spent their entire lives maintaining the secret of their existence, what kind of people would we be if we fucked that up our first week?

They have peace here, or at least, some form of it. They get to exist and live without fear of someone like me or Parla coming after them to take what is theirs. Granted, that's my understanding of how it is here with the minimal information I've gathered from talking with Sydney.

There's always the possibility of him lying and feeding us a line of bullshit to keep us from leaving this house but what would he gain from that? I'm sure he wants us out of here just as much as we do.

"Hey." Dash pokes his head into the steamy shower. "You okay in there?"

I blink through the water covering my face and wipe at my eyes. "I'm good."

"Those clothes Sydney brought for you are clean.

You wouldn't believe the machines they use. It makes doing laundry so simple once you figure out which buttons to push. Although, I do warn you to use caution when filling the cup with soap. There's a line on there for a reason."

I stand and turn the faucet off, not yet growing tired of the endless hot water supply this house has. What a plethora of wonders this world has and we've only just visited one place.

"And Bo," Dash adds. "He found something called *Netflix* on this large thing on the wall. I thought it was a black piece of artwork but he found this other little black thing with buttons and started pushing them. The artwork lit up so he kept clicking and found this thing that apparently has motion pictures inside of it that you can watch."

"Tremont said something about a fantasy movie." I towel dry my hair and wrap the soft fabric around my body, focusing on the man in front of me. "How are you feeling?"

Dash shrugs. "Totally fine. How are *you* feeling?"

I tilt my head at him. "Dash."

"Wren." He mimics my movement.

I roll my eyes. "Would you tell me if something was wrong?"

He sighs dramatically. "If I thought it was a big enough deal."

"What if what we think is a big deal are two different things?" I slip into the shirt sitting on the dresser, noting how it fits tighter than the other clothes I've been borrowing since being here.

Sydney was kind enough to locate some women's clothing since most of what's in this house is either men's, or weird fancy clothing left behind by his mothers.

It's like the woman never wore sweatpants or T-shirts.

Don't get me wrong, I appreciate her commitment to the look she was going for, but it's too stiff and swanky for me. And I'd be lying if I said it didn't remind me of the way Parla dressed.

My gaze falls on the armored clothing I was wearing when I got to this realm. My fingers itch to reach out to touch it, but I restrain myself. I'm safe here; I don't need to hide behind the thick layers. Running for my life and constantly fighting battles is a thing of the past.

But I'd also be lying if I said I didn't miss it.

And maybe because it's all I've ever known, or maybe because it's a part of who I am.

Either way, I must come to terms with the fact that it is not my future.

Dash settles his hands on my shoulders. "You don't need to worry about me, okay?"

"I could say the same to you." I raise a brow knowing that he's aware that what he's asking is easier said than done.

"Not fair."

"I'm a skilled assassin, Dash."

"And I'm an immortal phoenix. That has to count for something."

I reach up and cup his face in my hand. "You might not be able to die, but you can still get hurt."

And the fact that it can happen in his nightmares is even more alarming.

How can I protect him when I can't even see the threat until it's already sunken its claws into him?

"This is proof." I skim the bandage on his forehead where he split his head open on the table in the living room.

"I'll heal." Dash's bright blue eyes look back and forth between mine. "So, what do you think, want to watch a Netflix?"

I breathe in, separating myself from this beautiful man and finish putting my borrowed clothes on. "I don't know."

"Because of Bo?"

I shrug and sit on the edge of the bed. "Kind of. He pisses me off."

Dash smiles. "He pisses us all off."

"That's the truth."

"You have enough going on, don't let him ruin your day. You should get to enjoy your time in this new place, too."

"And how are you liking it here? Well, with the limited exposure to this realm."

Dash leans against the bedpost. "I love it. It's nice

not to be constantly running for your life. And the food, well, that speaks for itself."

"It really does, doesn't it?" I imagine that warm, cheesy bread melting in my mouth.

"The bed." Dash pushes his hand down onto the mattress. "I don't think I've ever rested that soundly in my life."

It sure beats the measly thing they had shoved in a corner of their tiny house.

I thought things were bad for me in Prania, but everyone I came here with was struggling in ways I'll never imagine. It's no wonder they're settling in with ease.

Still, I can't ignore the itch in my core telling me not to get too comfortable.

"Can I ask you a question?" I chew the inside of my lip.

"You just did." Dash chuckles. "Sorry." He brushes my shoulder playfully. "What's up?"

"Does it bother you, you know, that I'm *with* other people?"

"Honestly..." He pauses for what feels like an eternity. "Not at all. Maybe if it was anyone else than who it is, but I'm still not sure I would be *bothered*. I trust your judgment. My only concern is that you're happy and cared for. Other than that, I'm thrilled to be involved."

How did I get lucky enough to find someone so kind and understanding?

"I don't plan on adding anyone else," I tell him, just to make sure he knows.

"And that's a bridge we can cross if it comes up. I would never hold you back from living the life you desired." He stands from his post. "But, for the record, you're the only woman for me."

Dash holds out his hand toward me. "Now come on, let's see what this Netflix thing is all about."

Apparently, this giant home has more than one living room. The one we talked to Sydney in is technically considered a *sitting* room, while this one has a *television* and is somehow different than the other. Elaborate furniture fills both, along with dark paint and large windows, covered by decadent drapery. Someone took great concern while decorating this house, and it shows in the finest of details.

What a different world to find myself in after having spent my life ignoring and being completely oblivious to those types of things. It's not that I didn't appreciate it, it just wasn't on my radar in any capacity.

With Dash and Wes at my sides, Dash leans his head on my shoulder while Wes drapes his arm around me, resting his hand on Dash. The comfort of their presence almost drowns out the magnetic and negative energy Bo radiates.

"So, you're telling me," Bo says loudly. "This guy

can stalk and murder people and it's considered romance, but when I do it, it's bad?"

Jade presses a button on the remote, pausing the show. "Bo. I love you like a brother, you know this, but if you don't keep it down, I'm going to be the one murdering you. I want to know if he's going to kill her boyfriend or not and I can't hear over your outbursts."

Sydney comes in from behind us. "Ah, you're watching *You*, that's a good one. But hey, let me see that." He points toward the button clicker thing in Jade's hand. "If you push this." He does as he says and pokes the thing a few more times. "You can get subtitles on the screen, so you can read what's being said, too." He hesitates before handing it back to Jade. "That is, if you can read English. I only assumed since you speak it."

"We don't call it that back home, but yes, it's the same." Jade takes it from him and turns the show back on.

"Wren," Sydney says. "Can I have a word with you? Privately."

I nod and scoot myself up from the depths of the comfortable couch and the warm bodies I'm pressed between. "Of course, yeah."

He tips his head, a signal for me to follow him.

"I'll be back, guys." I glance over at Jade. "And gal."

Bo does a poor job hiding his stare when I get up and leave the room, but I don't bother giving him a blip of satisfaction by acknowledging him.

I follow Sydney down the long hallway with dusty artwork and doors that lead to unknown places. We end up in the kitchen, where Sydney goes straight to the counter and points to a seat for me to take.

"Would you like some coffee?"

"Sure." I've grown to like the bitter hot liquid and besides, it would give me something to do with my nervous hands. Usually, they're filled with knives or chains or whatever weapon of choice for the day.

It's going to take me a hell of a lot longer than a couple days before I grow used to not knowing what to do with all this idle time. Even when I had breaks between cases, I would spend the time training or preparing for my next battle. Here I have nothing to worry about other than what type of snack I'd like between meals.

Is this all humans do? Or Earth folk in general? Is life this mundane that it revolves around eating, shitting, and watching television shows?

It could be worse, that's for sure, but it's nothing at all like what I'm familiar with.

But that could simply be because we're confined to Sydney's parent's estate, and we haven't ventured out into the *real* world.

"I never properly asked, but you're a witch, right?" The hunter radar within me that typically alerts me to these things hasn't really worked properly since I was taken captive by Wes. None of my skills ever really came back fully.

"Yes, that's correct." Sydney fills two mugs with coffee and nudges one across the counter to me. "There are many like us here, and with the curse finally being lifted, more and more come into their powers each day." Sydney blows on the steaming drink. "Although with time it has slowed a bit, the first initial wave was intense. A multitude of new witches that had no idea they had magic suddenly started presenting signs of magical use. It took the majority of our resources to get it under control and get everyone the assistance they needed."

"What do you mean? What do you do for people like that?"

"Well, aside from explaining what was happening to them, we had to open new schools across the world to accommodate the teachings of magic. We couldn't run the risk of being exposed so we had to act quickly to get everything in order. It was so overwhelming that Willow had to temporarily step down from her position on the supernatural council to make sure everyone was taken care of. She still advises, and has recently regained some of the responsibilities, but her main concern is of the people, not the power. She's less about politics but the two go hand in hand, unfortunately."

I put my palms around the mug to warm them. "She sounds...incredible."

The kind of woman I aspire to be.

But I'm aware the things I have done will make that nearly impossible. My mistakes won't be so easily forgotten and it will take many lifetimes to offset the damage I have done. I must atone for my sins if I wish to seek redemption.

"She is." Sydney stares off blankly. "From the moment I laid my eyes on her, I knew she was special, and every day, she continues to amaze me." He blinks to center himself. "Anyway, I wanted to talk to you. We have much to discuss, and so much to learn of this world, but I was curious, what are your intentions here?"

I tilt my head and take a cautious sip of my drink. "What do you mean?"

"You came here, to Earth, or Arthlia as some refer to it, to seek refuge. Are you planning on staying long-term, short-term?"

"I..." I find myself unsure what to say considering we've only just arrived.

"I only ask because it will impact how I handle our approach. Obviously, the choice is up to you, and those you've traveled with, but if it's meant to be a short visit, I'm not convinced we should spend our time focused on the insignificant details."

"We, uh, we don't really have anywhere else to go." When we fled Prania, I had no idea we would land here, in Arthlia. This place was always considered a fever dream, something talked about in drunken conversations at the bar. A paradise of sorts that none of us had ever been to, but hoped to visit someday. We all knew it was impossible, that's why we talked about it the way we did.

But now, now that I'm quite literally standing on the other side, I can't help but feel like someone should pinch me and wake me up from this dream.

"Did you intend on coming here when you traveled between the realms?" Sydney leans his butt against the counter and crosses one arm over his torso while he keeps his mug out in front of him.

"No." I shake my head and try to recall the moment everything changed. "We were there. A wendigo army was closing in on us, we had nowhere to go. We were pressed between the border and countless demons that wanted us dead. Tremont latched onto me, told us all to hold on tight, and the next thing I knew, there was a bright flash of light and we were waking up in the darkness."

"Why hadn't you ever left before if things were that bad?"

"We couldn't. Prania had been closed off for realm travel long ago. Centuries maybe. I'm not keen on the actual origin date."

"If my research is accurate, and that's the case, the power Tremont harnessed from you was what granted you access, and that was because of your bloodline. And if I take it one step further, the realm that you ended up in is the one that the angels decided you should be in."

"You're telling me the angels transported me here?"

Sydney nods. "In theory. But that goes both ways.

Tremont was no doubt sent to Prania because it was inescapable. His ultimate punishment."

"Then why would they let him out?"

"That is the million-dollar question." Sydney exhales. "This is all speculation based on what I've gathered. We have a past with cross-realm travel because of our experience with hell dimensions but never with a realm that doesn't exist on paper. I scoured textbooks and couldn't find anything on Prania. It's almost like it doesn't exist."

"But it does," I tell him. "I spent my entire life there."

"I know. I believe you. But it does beg the question, why was it completely erased from history?"

9

BO

I stand just outside the kitchen, leaning against the wall, and eavesdrop on Wren and Sydney's *private* conversation.

How dare he think that he can whisk her away to chat without involving the rest of us?

It's nothing that juicy either, only some minor details about our entire homeland pretty much being completely unknown to the world outside of Prania.

But I'm no stranger to my past being erased completely.

Us demons did what we could to preserve the buildings that housed the literature and recordings of our existence, but hunters did everything they could to make sure not even an ounce of us remained.

They killed us, and then removed any trace of what we may have left behind.

Our legacy disappeared out of sight like dust in the wind.

So the information leaving Sydney's mouth is no surprise at all.

The hunters want us gone in every way possible.

And they have stopped at nothing to make that happen. Only, Wren threw a big fucking wrench in their scheduled programming when she turned on them and got herself a fated mate that was one of the most powerful demons of all.

It's kind of funny, really, if you think about it.

The one major component in their plan for world domination ended up being the very person that brought it to a staggering halt.

Sure, Wren may have evaded Parla's grasp, but Parla is still in Prania, slaughtering innocent demons and following through with whatever eradication she can.

Wren being gone isn't going to stop Parla from being a conniving bitch.

Maybe *innocent* was a bit of a stretch but still, they're unjustly killing people that don't deserve to die. I don't know what could be more innocent than that.

Wren has taken her fair share of demon lives, but so have I. Not only demons, but hunters, too. Anyone who threatened me—or Dash and Wes—met the fate that I decided was best fit for them.

It's a shame I didn't get a chance to end that wendigo before we were thrown into another realm. It's no surprise that we desperately needed out, but it would have been nice to have a bit less unfinished business in a realm that I have no clue how to get back to.

Parla and that wendigo need to die, and it won't sit right with me until they do.

Although, they would be doing me a solid if they went ahead and offed each other since they're enemies anyway.

But then that would deprive me of the gratification of doing it myself, and I don't think I'm ready to give that up.

Wren shoves her head around the corner and into the hallway. "You're not being subtle, Bo. I can hear you all the way in here. Either stop breathing or get in here."

"Birdie, I was just…" I run my hand through my hair and pretend she didn't give me a slight start.

"Chop chop, big boy." She snaps her fingers, and it's like every fucking fiber in my stupid body responds to her command.

I hate the control she has over me.

She could say *sit, Bo* and I'd sit.

Roll over, Bo, and I'd roll over.

I'd do anything for her, other than what's right, because all I seem to know how to do is the wrong thing.

Every word that leaves my mouth is interpreted an entirely different way than intended, and despite my best attempts, I fuck up left and right.

She'd be better off if I disappeared and never came back.

But I can't. Not when she bears the mark of my bite on her neck, and my distance means the flesh-hungry demons of Earth would be able to track her down and kill her.

I made a mistake marking her. I just didn't realize the severity of it until after my feelings developed. Hatred was replaced by something I didn't and still don't recognize. I do, however, get glimpses of what it should be when I see her with Wes and Dash.

We could have that, but I won't allow it. Not when I'm no good for her and her main attraction toward me is a result of the stupid fucking mark I gave her without her consent.

And ridding her of the beacon my mark exudes would be a worse fate than she's already met, and I can't bring myself to do that to her either.

Instead, I have to be around her with this ache in my chest and the knowledge that she will never be mine—not truly.

"I'm coming," I tell her, my trail hot on hers. I breathe her in, her scent lingering in the air with each step she takes.

The soaps in this world do nothing to mask her true, delectable scent.

I can even catch whiffs of the blood pulsing through her veins and causing my throat to burn with a lust unlike anything I've ever felt.

I want so badly to sink my fangs into her neck and

taste her once again, but if I do, there's no telling if I'll have the self-control to stop this time.

She tastes better than I ever could have imagined, and just the thought of my mouth pooling with her blood makes my cock throb in my pants.

Her desire rivals the decadence of her blood, and if I had my choice, I would drown in both and die a happy fucking man.

My dick pulses at the thought of pleasing her while she's on her moon cycle, my two favorite things paired with the idea of bringing her to climax.

"Actually, on second thought. I have to go." I throw my thumb up and point behind me.

"What?" She turns on her heels. "Where?"

"I, uh, I have somewhere to be." I glance at my wrist despite not wearing a watch. "Yeah, the time." I take a few steps back, and once I'm out of the room, I dart down the hall and disappear out of sight.

"Bo," she calls out but it's too late, I'm already gone.

I rush up the stairs, ignoring the usual appeal I have to tear down Tremont's door and rip his limbs from his body, and go into the bedroom Wren has claimed as hers. I drag my shirt over my head, toss it onto the floor, and step out of my pants on the way to the bathroom. I close the door and lock it behind me. With a deep breath, I step into the shower and yank the faucet on, turning it to its coldest setting.

I stand under it for a full minute, my hand pressed into the wall and my head down, the water rolling over my face. It does nothing to rid my mind of the image of her soaking wet and spread in front of me. I lick my lips, the taste of her so fresh in my memory that I can still smell her delicious lust.

With my free hand, I grip my cock and stroke its full length, hoping that will be enough to stave off my hunger. But when my eyes close, and the thought of her pussy clenching around my fingers fills my head, I grow even harder in my grasp.

"Angels," I whisper.

I want her so badly it hurts.

I change the water from freezing cold to scalding hot and return my palm to my dick. I rock it up and down, squeezing tighter and deciding that the only thing I can do now is find a release. Maybe if I come, I won't be so fucking tense and ready to kill anyone. Who am I kidding though? That's how I always am regardless of whether I'm horny or not.

Imagining her hand in place of mine, I stroke myself faster, wanting this whole experience to be behind me. It's not that I don't enjoy a good self-pleasuring moment, but when it's to stop yourself from making bad decisions, the fun kind of goes out the window.

"Did you really come in here to jerk off?" Her voice fills the entire bathroom and rattles through my entire core.

"Maybe," I tell her. "But if you don't mind, I'd like to finish, so either stay and watch or get out."

"How about I do you one better?"

I glance over my shoulder to find her undressing.

Fuck. I can't be *this* horny and near her naked body at the same time. It's one thing to be around her when I have a bit more self-control, but now I worry I won't have the same level of restraint.

Wren strolls over, the water sprinkling her as she approaches, the droplets beading on her breasts and running down her perfect fucking body. Taut, petite, subtle round edges. Her dark eyes meet mine, her lust-filled gaze fueling my erection that much more.

"What are you doing?" I ask her, my jaw tense.

"Whatever I want." She reaches for my cock, sliding her hand beside mine.

"Wren," I breathe.

"Do you want me?"

I swallow and fight every carnal desire I have to throw her against the wall and fuck her with a force that might kill us both.

"You know I do," I tell her the truth.

"Then if a climax is what you so desperately need, allow me to give it to you." She drops down onto her knees, her doe eyes staring up at me through her thick lashes.

Fuck, I'm a goner.

She licks her lips, her gaze leaving mine and settling on my cock that's only inches from her pretty little mouth. Wren strokes my length and positions it at the edge of her lips, the heat from her breath alone sends a wave of pleasure through me.

"Angels, Birdie." I grip the base of my shaft and shove into her, the warmth consuming me instantly.

Wren widens herself for me, cupping her tongue and allowing me to go deeper. Water pelts her face but she doesn't seem bothered as she focuses solely on my cock in her mouth. She grabs the backs of my legs, pulling me toward her, a silent permission to give her more.

I try to hold back, to control myself, but it becomes more difficult with every second I'm inside of her.

My hand weaves its way through her hair, gripping her skull and holding her in place. I rock my hips, fucking her harder.

Wren digs her hands in and pushes back to free herself, and I fear that I may have taken things too far. My erection softens at the immediate and unfamiliar concern.

She looks up at me. "Plug my nose."

"What?" I blink at her.

"Plug my fucking nose. Water keeps splashing me and it's distracting." She strokes my cock.

"You won't be able to breathe."

"I'd rather die from asphyxiation than drown." She latches onto me tighter and pulls me toward her. "Do it, Bo."

I comply, pinching her nose between my fingers as she takes me into her hungry mouth.

"Fuck," I moan and slide myself deeper until I hit the back of her throat.

She keeps me there, in the depths of what she's able to take of me, and meets my gaze. Wren bobs her head in her attempt to consume more, not daring to come up for a breath, yet her lifeforce becomes swallowing every inch of me she can muster.

I grow harder and my inhibitions lower as a side of me that I beg to keep hidden rises to the surface. Releasing her nose for a second, I return my hold and use my other hand to grab the back of her head and fuck her gorgeous face.

Her moans vibrate against my shaft, and my climax builds.

I blow deep inside of her throat, refusing to pull out and allow her the breath I'm sure she desperately needs. I grunt through the pleasure and accidentally shift, my demon side taking over my more human-like nature—my cock included. Small barbs poke out, sinking their way into her mouth like a bunch of tiny bee stings, only the stingers stay in place and keep her there, her blood rolling down her throat with my orgasm. I thrust one last time and force my demon side to return to its hidden capacity and pull out of her.

She gasps and wipes at her bottom lip, not at all fazed by what just happened.

"Are you okay?" I ask her, tilting her head up toward me.

Wren nods. "Yeah, what the hell was that?"

"I...I didn't mean to." Because showing her that side of me, truly exposing who I am, was never what I wanted to happen and part of the reason why I can't *be* with her.

"Bo," Wren rises to her feet but still has to look up at me. "I'm not afraid of you." She stands taller and presses her body closer to mine. "You're not going to hurt me."

But haven't I already? Both physically and emotionally?

She slides her finger down my arm and latches onto my hand, slowly moving it between us and tracing it over her clit and down her vulva. "I want you, Bo. All of you." She continues moving me as she spreads her legs slightly. Wren lifts her leg and holds it against my side, and without thinking and simply letting myself do what it wants, I thrust two fingers into her.

Her head tilts back. "That's it."

And in a sheer millisecond, I shove her into the wall, lower myself in front of her, and with her leg over my shoulder, I taste her once more. I'm more aggressive this time than last, my tongue morphing into my demonic tongue, the end splitting and touching both sides of her clit before diving down and lapping up her juices. I fuck her harder, giving her another finger to fill her fuller while dragging my other hand up her body and pinching her nipple between my fingers. I cup her breast in my hand and return to her nipple, squeezing harder when she moans louder.

Her pussy tightens around my fingers, and I thrust them in deeper and harder, my knuckles hitting her pelvic bone. I suck on her clit and bare my teeth, my fangs slicing her ever so softly. Considering how ravenous I am, I remain in control, only allowing myself the smallest indulgences.

But when the taste of her blood tempts me, I nearly lose it all.

I breathe in, desperate to not tear her apart right here and now, and center myself on the subtle movements of her body. I focus on her heartbeat, her ragged breaths, and the pulsing of her pussy on me.

Wren whimpers and comes undone, her pleasure satisfying me in an entirely different way than I was only moments ago.

She finishes and I stand, gently lowering her leg onto the damp tile floor.

Together, we step fully back under the steaming hot water and rinse off in silence.

I grow worried with each quiet moment until finally, she speaks.

"I'm still mad at you."

I tuck her hair behind her ear and study the shape of her jaw and trail my gaze up to meet hers. "I wouldn't have it any other way."

"Why are you so difficult?" she asks me.

"Why do you expect me to be anything else?"

Wren sighs. "Touché."

I don't say anything else. Instead, I listen in a manner that only someone who's paying great attention could. Her chest rises, her heart stutters, and she swallows harshly. She's thinking about something that makes her unsteady.

"If you don't want to be with me, why don't you just tell me?" Wren avoids making direct eye contact with me.

I don't mean to, but I smirk at her shy vulnerableness. She's the most badass woman I've ever known and here she is, showing insecurity.

But who am I to judge—I'm in the same exact boat. All this boils down to my fear that once the mark is gone, she will no longer want me, and with its removal, I'll never actually know.

"That's what you think this is?" I lean against the wall of the shower and avoid gawking at her naked and wet body.

"What else would it be?"

That I'm scared, terrified really, and for the first time in my life, I have someone I want to keep but have no idea how to make that happen because from the very moment I laid my eyes on her, I've been making mistake after mistake and setting us up for nothing but failure.

I don't say that though.

Nor do I mention that I have no idea how I'll fit in, in this world. It's unfamiliar and new and different and a demon like me can never exist with humans. I get angry and kill people and take what I want when I want it. That doesn't work here, at least not in reality, only in fiction. Being a murderous psychopath is frowned upon, and I don't know how to be anything else.

If she wants to stay here, there's nothing I can do to stop her, nor would I. I might be a blatant asshole, but I do actually care about what's best for her. And if living out her days in this realm with Dash and Wes is what she wants, I will suffer from a distance without putting her in danger.

"Bo," she says, snapping her fingers in front of my face. "What else would it be?"

I shake my head and run my hand through my wet hair, the tangles catching on my fingers. "It's complicated, Birdie." Kicking away from the wall, I take a step toward leaving.

She catches my arm. "You're the one making it complicated, Bo."

Each time my name leaves her lips, my heart constricts tighter.

"This is the way it has to be." I yank free of her and leave the shower, latching onto the first semi-clean-looking towel I can find.

The faucet creaks as she turns it off and her foot-steps pound on the floor behind me. "Fine, if that's the way you want it, we're done."

Her last two words cut like the sharpest blade through my heart.

I want to protest, to scream and fight and beg and plead but I can't bring myself to say a fucking word.

10

WREN

"Hey," Dash says upon entering the bedroom. "Sydney's ready."

Fuck. In the chaos of things with Bo, I completely lost track of time and the plan that was already set in place.

Dash catches my shoulders and steadies me, his blue gaze meeting mine. He keeps his voice low. "You okay? What's wrong?"

I force a smile. "Nothing. I'm good." Because I refuse to let Bo hear a single word that I'm anything other than completely fucking okay about what just happened.

If he wants to keep his emotions at bay, then two can play this fucking game.

I rush over to the pile of women's clothes and rummage through until I find something to throw on. I shove my feet into my boots and go over to the mirror, smoothing down my hair and pinching my cheeks to bring some color to my otherwise pale face.

"You look beautiful," Dash tells me without even having to ask.

Always the gentleman, that one.

Bo, on the other hand, he's everything but.

I meet Dash's gaze in the mirror, ignoring Bo dressing off in the corner. "Do you want to come with us? Be good to get out of the house."

Bo perks his head up immediately. "You're leaving? Like leaving, leaving?"

"Are you sure?" Dash steps closer.

"Of course. You're the only one I don't have to worry about unleashing your powers. I can't imagine Sydney would have any issue with it either."

"Is someone going to tell me what's going on?" Bo marches over to where Dash and I are standing.

"No. It's none of your business." I cross my arms over my chest and turn toward him. "Now if you'll excuse me, we have somewhere to be."

Bo catches me in the same way I had caught him when he tried to leave the shower. "What about the mark, Wren?"

The usage of my name only means that he's doing what he can to get under my skin more than he already has.

I shrug him off. "I've been informed it isn't but more than a few miles, nothing we haven't dealt with before. The *mark* you put on me shouldn't fully engage so long as you stay here."

The mark is a burden tying us together despite the very fact that he wants to get far, far away.

Maybe if he hadn't acted like an irrational idiot, we wouldn't be stuck in this mess and he could be free of me like he desires.

"Come on," I tell Dash while sliding my hand into his.

The sun shines through the window and casts light across the room, one that I imagine will feel warm and comforting on my skin once I'm outside. I've spent all my time inside this house, only venturing out in the darker hours when I'm most comfortable.

But with Sydney as our escort, I'll get to go out during the daytime.

The sun hasn't shone in Prania in centuries, at least, that's what I'm told. There were moments the sky would be clearer than others, but the ruins of that world taint the atmosphere with a relentless cloud of smoke. It's thick and heavy and completely different than here in Arthlia.

"You can't be serious," Bo calls out after us.

I don't bother turning around, instead, I tug Dash along with me into the hallway and down the stairs of this massive house.

Sydney waits at the bottom, his attention turning from the small device in his grasp to the two of us. He clicks a button on the thing and shoves it into his pocket.

I'll have to ask him what that is later.

"You don't mind if Dash comes, do you? He's harmless, I promise." I wait for his reply, watching the way he rubs at his neck and hesitates to answer.

"Uh, I mean…" Sydney glances between us.

Wes approaches from another one of the hallways and plants one hand on my shoulder and one on Dash's. "He's practically human aside from coming back from the dead."

"Yeah, I suppose that will be okay." Sydney shrugs. "Things are already weird enough, why not bring a phoenix along for the ride?"

Wes kisses the top of my head and whispers, "Be safe, and come back to me, okay?"

My cheeks blush even more than when I pinched them.

"Thanks for not throwing a fit about me leaving." I turn to tell him, my gaze flitting to Bo, who stands at the top of the stairs like a fucking statue as he glares at me.

Maybe he could learn a thing or two from Dash and Wes about how to engage with a woman. Bo might be expertly skilled in the bedroom but he's an idiot otherwise. An infuriating and sexy idiot.

"You can explore the grounds if you'd like. It's a rather nice day today, but please don't venture beyond the tree line. I'd rather people not ask questions we can't give them answers to just yet. The less you draw attention to yourselves, the better." Sydney looks at Wes the whole time, almost like he's putting him in charge while he's gone.

He's typically the most reserved and rational of us all, so it makes total sense Sydney would gravitate toward thinking along the same lines.

I don't imagine Jade and Everest will need much convincing to keep themselves concealed, but I wouldn't put it past Bo to defy the orders just because he can. Sydney may have been better off encouraging Bo to roam as far as he pleases, and Bo would probably stay in and be a lazy bum.

Tremont is supposedly still confined to his room, so it's unlikely he'll cause any issues.

Dash and I follow Sydney down another hallway that leads to a part of the house I have yet to venture into. A strange unease rises through me at being led away by a stranger, but in these few short days, Sydney has shown me a different side of what being supernatural means.

Where I come from, everyone is filled with hatred and darkness—but Sydney has this pure aura about him that I can't help but put trust in. Like my gut knew before I did that he would be on my side.

Perhaps it's that there are no sides. Instead, a common good that the people of Earth, or at the very least, Sydney, and from the sound of it, Willow, want for everyone.

The Angels sent me here for a reason, I should put a little faith in that.

Air hits my cheeks, warming them and spreading throughout my body. I blink a few times to adjust to the light and take in a deep breath. "Angels, this is…"

"Welcome to spring," Sydney says. "We've been having unseasonably higher temperatures lately but none of us are complaining. Winter was rough and aside from Deghan, none of us are really a fan of the snow."

"Is Deghan a witch, too?" I ask him since he's mentioned him enough that it seems an appropriate question to have.

"Deghan is a werewolf." Sydney points toward a shiny-looking thing with wheels. "My car."

"Car," I say, getting a feel for the word on my tongue. "Does it operate on magic?"

Sydney chuckles "No, it uses fuel to function. Gasoline."

Fuel. Gasoline. Car. Not magic. Got it.

"Interesting."

"You don't have cars where you come from?" Sydney opens a door on the side of the car and motions for me to enter. "You can sit in here. Dash, you okay sitting in the back?" He points across from my seat. "I have to drive otherwise you could sit up there with her."

"Yeah, no problem at all. I'm just happy to be here."

Dash reaches for the handle the same way that Sydney had and slides into the seat behind mine.

I climb in, unsure what I'm supposed to do with my hands, and sit there, waiting for my next instruction.

Sydney shuts my door, closing me into this metal contraption, and walks around the front to get in the other side. He shoves a key into a slot and turns it, the death trap roaring to life and rumbling my entire body gently.

"What is that?" I fight the urge to panic. I am safe here, with Dash, with Sydney, in this foreign place.

"The motor." Sydney pats the *car* and reaches toward the door to retrieve a belt-like thing. "This is a seat belt. It keeps you from flying out of the car."

"I'm going to fly out of the car if I don't put it on?" My heart picks up its pace. I thought my old world was threatening, but this is an entirely new kind of concern.

"Only in emergencies, like if we were to crash. It's unlikely, but a precaution that I suggest taking." Sydney latches his into a hook that seems to keep it in place.

I glance in the back. "Does Dash have one to keep him inside the car, too?"

Dash has his in his hand and secures it in the holder, leaving me the only one not belted in. "Got it." His smile warms my heart more than the sun did my skin.

"So yeah, seat belt for the car that is fueled by gasoline. It's not magic but it might as well be. I never really understood mechanics at all." Sydney grips a stick with a ball on the end of it and moves it, causing a clunking of sorts to take place before the entire thing we're in moves.

"We have wagons," I say to distract myself. "They're powered by magic, but usually only the wealthiest hunters can afford them. I've ridden in a few in the past. It was nothing like this. This is…" I run my hand over the door and the fabric of the seat. "More sophisticated."

I push a button on the door, and the glass of the door lowers. I gasp. "Angels, I didn't mean to do that. Did I break it?"

Sydney laughs again, his humor at my expense somehow making me feel less concerned. If I broke something, he probably wouldn't find it funny.

"No, that's the window. They go up and down. You can keep it down if you'd like."

Dash pushes the button on his, too, lowering it and shoving his arm out of it, his fingers spreading and waving about delicately.

"Is he allowed to do that?" I turn toward Sydney.

"Absolutely. You can, too. Here, look." Sydney follows suit and once his window is down, he puts his arm out, and weaves it about. "It won't hurt you."

Is that what I'm afraid of? Something hurting me? Haven't I already been through enough in the past to not be fearful? Maybe it's not fear of being hurt, but more-so fear of the unknown. I've always been in control of every aspect of my life. Down to the way I handled killing demons. I had a protocol and a specific method, and that all changed when I was tasked with the assassination of Wes.

I lost control, and since then, I've fought to regain my footing in life.

Nothing makes sense, and the more I try to figure it out, the more that unravels.

I've always been more of a loner, going through the motions of life on my own and dealing with problems myself when they arose. It worked that way. There wasn't anything I couldn't handle. No demon too strong, no task too big. There was no teamwork, no concern for anyone else's safety. I researched things, I paid attention, the risk was mine and mine alone.

Now, I worry about other people constantly and grow terrified that if I make the wrong decision or don't do things correctly, they will suffer—or worse.

What if it's my fault they get hurt or die? What if I don't know all the variables, and I'm the reason for our demise? Things were different when it was just me, and that terrifies me worse than any monster ever could.

"Try it," Sydney tells me with one hand out the window.

Carefully, I lift my arm, inching it toward the opening, the air whipping by my fingers. I push it through, somewhat expecting there to be pain or discomfort, but instead, a rush of adrenaline courses through me. I move my wrist, spread my fingers, and become one with the air cascading by.

"One of the simple pleasures of life." Sydney glances over and looks back at the road.

"What do you mean?" I ask him with my hand still waving about like I'm attempting to catch the wind in my grasp.

"This, for instance." Sydney holds his hand up higher and then swoops it down. "The sun on your face after a long winter. The first sip of your morning coffee. Canceled plans when you really wanted to stay in. Finishing a good book. Freshly baked cookies. Making someone you love smile."

Hearing him rattle off examples makes me wonder what it would be like to live somewhere those things could actually happen. He doesn't appear much older than me, but he speaks as though he's lived such a grand life. I want that for myself one day, only, I'm not certain it's possible, not after everything I've done. Do I really deserve any of it considering what I've put so many through?

Still, I can't help but imagine the endless possibilities.

Would any of the guys want that? How do people like us transition to a life unlike anything we've ever known?

Even Dash, the sweetest and most innocent of us, has grown familiar with the violence and turmoil of our homeland.

Yet, it hasn't broken him, not entirely. He remains optimistic and ready to try new things. This new world doesn't have the same impact on him as it does on the rest of us.

And with my constant paranoia, can I get used to not constantly assuming anything I don't know is a danger to me and those around me?

How will I differentiate between a threat and something harmless when everything seems so foreign?

"That sounds nice," I tell Sydney.

"There's much to enjoy in this world, if you'll give it a chance." Sydney pushes a button on the console of this car, and noise quietly fills the space. "Music is another simple pleasure. You won't like all of it, but you'll end up preferring some styles over others."

"This one is nice." I lean back in the seat and allow myself to relax with my arm resting on the windowsill. Trees whip by, blurring into one indistinguishable shade of dark green.

"I like it, too," Dash says from behind me. He reaches through and gives my shoulder a gentle squeeze. "I think we'll be happy here."

I have zero doubts that Dash will fit in nicely in Arthlia. Calm and peaceful is kind of his thing. But will I be able to abandon my violent tendencies and resort to a life of domesticity?

How can I come to terms with my past and accept that I abandoned Prania and left it in the hands of Parla?

"What are you going to do about Tremont?" I tilt my head toward Sydney.

His hair wafts in the wind like slow-moving clouds, and his gaze darts down and then onto the road again. "What do you think I should do?"

I chuckle. "I don't think I'm the right person to be asking. In my homeland, things like this usually ended in violence."

Sydney nods his head. "That's what I'm trying to avoid, but I can't ignore the fact that he nearly ruined everything for me—and for so many others, too."

"But he didn't. You were able to stop him."

"That doesn't change what he did."

I chew at the inside of my lip, his words stinging worse than he intended. "What are your options?"

"That's the thing, I'm not sure. I guess I could kill him, that's the obvious one. But that doesn't sit right with me, not with who I am now. Not to mention, it's super illegal."

Does that mean that's who he was in the past? Maybe we aren't that different after all.

"Releasing him is another option," he continues. "But what if he's lying and he has wicked reasons for being here? What if he causes more chaos and hurts people? I'd be responsible for any harm he inflicts if I let him go."

"So you can't kill him, and you can't free him." I scratch at my chin.

"You could imprison him," Dash suggests.

My stomach clenches at the sudden recollection of my time spent in Rockbridge with Wes. Surely their prisons are nothing like Prania, but still, wouldn't that be a worse fate than ending his life?

"In theory, holding him hostage and imprisoning him is also illegal." Sydney flips a lever and a faint clicking sound appears. He turns us onto another road, and then the sound goes away.

"What does that mean though? What are the consequences?" I scan the new road in total amazement over how lavish this land is.

"Well, the humans, the people living on Earth, have these groups of higher-level officials called the government. They have them at all levels. Cities. Counties. States. Countries. We live in Harper County which is located in the United States." Sydney runs his hand through his hair. "I'll have to teach you about geography sometime. Or maybe there's a crash course I could have the academy put together for you. We school new supernatural creatures; I don't know why they couldn't make an exception for your situation."

My mind struggles to catch up with the fresh information.

"The government is in charge of making laws and there are law enforcement officers who, well, enforce them. There's a justice system, so when someone breaks a law, they go through a set process and they're either proven guilty or not, and then depending on the crime, there are different punishments. Something simple like a parking ticket is not punishable by jail time, but simply a fee that has to be paid. More severe crimes, like murder, that's going to get you locked up for a very long time. There are instances of accidental murder, or self-defense, which are taken into account when the decisions are made. Basically, bad things are off-limits here. No killing." He takes a second to look over at me. "No drugs. Most violence is a no-no. Weapons are pretty much off the table, too, unless you have a license for them. And one of the most sure-fire ways to get in trouble with the government is tax evasion."

I blink and come to terms with the fact that Arthlia is sounding less and less fun by the minute. But with these strict rules, the burden of being constantly in a state of worry reduces. If Prania had these types of laws, maybe things wouldn't have been in total anarchy.

"What's tax evasion?" Dash asks.

"Citizens of the United States have a duty to pay taxes on the income they make. Some people try to avoid doing so, for various reasons. But if the government finds out, you can be charged with tax evasion."

"What do they do with the taxes? The government?" Dash leans forward a bit in his seat.

"It depends on which level. There are taxes at the city level, all the way up to the federal. A lot of it goes to funding public services for things like health care, education, and transportation. They spend it on our military, um, what else, I don't know, there's probably a website I could find with more information if you're really invested in the topic."

"No, I was just curious. It's fascinating." Dash smiles softly.

Sydney turns the car again, but this time, we pull onto a one-lane road with no yellow or white lines like the rest. He drives slower, barely moving us down the long lane. "This is where we live, Willow and the rest of us."

My mouth goes dry, and my hands sweat within seconds of hearing the words leave his mouth.

A house that rivals the size of Sydney's comes into view. The lane circles around the front, making a perfect loop in front of the massive structure. Greenery weaves its way up the sides of the building, and perfectly sculpted shrubs line the entryway.

"You guys are *rich* rich." Dash says the thing that was on my mind, too.

Sydney laughs. "We inherited this home shortly after Willow became head of the supernatural council. We're fortunate for the resources that were provided for us. Not everyone is so lucky."

I had safe houses back in Prania, but none of them were *mine*. They were property of Parla and the hunter's organization. I only got them when I advanced through the ranks and proved what I could do for them. Other hunters weren't living the way I did because they weren't as skilled as me. I got preferential treatment because I worked my ass off for it. I vetted the witches that spelled the houses, but I only had access to them through my position working for Parla.

Witches. That reminds me of what Parla had been angry about at Rockbridge. She claimed I was working with a witch to stop her from harvesting the demonic power I had been harnessing from those that I killed and consumed. What if that had something to do with what Sydney had told me—of my bloodline being connected to Willows? Was it *my* powers that stopped her from taking what was mine? How strange that Willow fought a war to regain the magic that was stolen from her, and here I was, doing the same fucking thing to demons? The similarities are chilling.

I'd love to know the truth that Parla was asking for, but I'd have to confess to my crimes, and I don't think I'm ready to face the ghosts of those demons just yet.

The punishment of losing the people I care for is far worse than anything a *government* could do to me.

II

WREN

I hold my breath upon crossing the threshold into Willow's home.

Dash slides his fingers through mine, and it's like I can breathe again, the comfort of his touch holding me together. He always has a way of settling my soul in times of disarray.

He smiles and my heart warms to his presence.

"This way," Sydney says, guiding us through the entry.

Two staircases hug the walls on both sides, curving and leading up to a second story with an open walkway. The floor is made up of something hard and shiny, like a polished rock that had been cut into perfectly sized squares and laid with such ease that not a piece is out of place. A mirror hangs on a wall we pass, the gold frame of it beautiful in a peculiar kind of manner.

Our footsteps patter on a hard surface, then on a long rug, winding us through the labyrinth of this home before Sydney brings us to a halt.

"Wait here." Sydney points toward a sitting area. "I'll be right back for you."

He disappears through a door, the thing almost closing but not quite latching all the way shut.

Dash settles into one of the seats without question, his palms rubbing the arms of the chair. "This is nice."

I appreciate the carelessness in his demeanor and how he's not bothered by the unknowns of this world. He goes with the flow and despite having a nightmare that quite literally hurt him, he doesn't seem impacted by it.

Or, he's just really good at masking what's wrong.

I hate to think something could upset him and I wouldn't know about it. Out of the three men in my life, he's the one I want to shield the most from harm. Bo and Wes are supernaturally strong and capable of fighting their own battles, and it's not that Dash isn't, but he isn't as equipped as the rest of us; naturally, my concern falls mostly to him.

Dash is pure, and he deserves more than this world has to offer.

And I'm convinced that anyone who ever meets him would think the same thing.

I pace the space Sydney left us in but pause when I hear faint conversation from inside.

"Can you send them through processing, Syd? I don't really have time today." Her sweet voice floats out toward me.

I swallow down the unease at her not wanting to see us.

"This one's different Wills."

The nickname he has for her brings the corners of my lips up faintly.

Papers shuffle and she sighs. "How so?"

"Just let me introduce you to her, and then we can go from there. Five minutes, that's all I'm asking."

"This is very unlike you, Syd." She pauses for a brief second. "Come here, I want a kiss first, then I'll meet this mystery girl of yours."

I wait patiently outside the room for them to do what they need to do, my stomach growing wild with the realization that I'm seconds away from seeing her face-to-face.

My relative. My kin. My blood.

The door swings open, and I take a hurried step back.

Sydney's face greets me. "Come on in." He motions for me to enter. "Dash, you can come, too."

Willow, at least who I assume is Willow, stands from behind a large desk, her smile soft and her features delicate but somehow also sharp and etched like the angels themselves took extra caution bringing her to life. Her nearly white hair, with a long strip of black down one side, billows in subtle curls over her shoulders and falls the length of her elbow.

Automatically, I'm drawn to her, my chest pulling and tugging me toward this woman I've only just laid eyes on.

She raises her brow and shifts her focus on Sydney before focusing back on me. "Willow Oliver," she steps around her desk, walks toward me like she's gliding across the floor, and extends her hand. "And you are?"

I blink and blink again, my heart stuttering but my arm inching up and sliding my hand into hers. "Wren... Wren Oliver."

The second our skin touches, a sort of current zaps me, but not painfully. I suck in a breath and meet her gaze. "Is that normal?"

Willow releases me and reaches toward Dash. "Only sometimes."

"I'm Dash," he says. "Just Dash."

She shakes hands with him, too. Willow holds on a bit longer and narrows her gaze. "It's kind of my job to know what type of supernatural creature people are but I'm drawing a blank with you. You're not human."

"No, ma'am." Dash plasters on his typical Dash politeness. "I'm a phoenix."

"A phoenix," she repeats. "Interesting." Willow shifts her attention between us.

"I told you," Sydney says from his spot off to the side.

Willow grins at him. "Such the know it all." She

nods toward the far corner of the room. "Perhaps our guests would like something to drink."

Sydney goes over without question. "Coffee, tea, water?" He pauses before adding. "I could run to the main kitchen if you'd like juice or something else."

"Coffee is fine," I mutter and look at Dash.

"Same."

Willow motions toward a sitting area in her large office. A long couch lines the wall with two plush chairs opposite of it. A table with a few books rests on top, along with a pot filled with flowers with tiny petals.

I settle onto the couch with Dash at my side.

He rests his hand on my knee, and I thank the Angels that I asked him to come along today. Does Dash know how much support he's providing by simply being near me?

Willow takes the chair closest to me and props her elbow on the armrest. "Where are you from?"

Such an innocent question that harbors more than she's bargaining for.

"Prania," I tell her.

Willow tilts her head, another display of her beauty shining through with each movement she makes. "I'm not familiar with Prania. What state is that in?"

A lump forms in my throat and multiplies in my stomach. Why am I so fucking nervous about speaking to her and telling her my truth? Maybe it's because if I talk too freely I will ruin this for all of us.

Sydney comes over with a tray in his grasp. He carefully sets it on the table and distributes the steaming mugs. "Prania is another realm, dear." Sydney lowers himself onto the other seat and joins our conversation fully. "They traveled across the fold."

"I've never heard of Prania, though, in our time researching other realms." Willow presses her palms around the mug like she's warming her hands, the same thing I do; it's one of the reasons I love coffee.

"I hadn't either until they told me about it." Sydney sips his drink. "Could ask the headmaster about it. You have a meeting with him later today."

"Who's that?" I ask her while suddenly realizing there are probably a lot more people in this realm that I'm unaware of and will come across. When we were confined to Sydney's house, our interactions were limited, but now we're out in the world, there's no telling how many I'll encounter. How will I know if they're supernatural or human? What if I say the wrong thing to the wrong person? How is she able to determine someone's species just by shaking their hand? Is that something she could teach me?

Too many questions and not enough breath to speak them all.

Willow interrupts my rampant thoughts. "He's in charge of the local shadow academy Sydney and I both attended. Headmaster Walker. He's highly knowledgeable of the supernatural world and the academy itself houses an expansive library full of supernatural literature. Surely there's something between him and the books that would shine some light on Prania." Willow speaks with such confidence and elegance that it makes me sit up a little straighter in my seat.

"I'm sorry, did you say *shadow* academy?"

"Mmhm." She sips her coffee. "Much like a regular undergraduate college, except half the students are supernatural and attend their magical classes without the human faction having any idea of their powers."

"That seems...dangerous."

Willow shrugs. "Existing in their world has its risks, but this way, students learn how to balance the two and navigate keeping their abilities concealed. Of course, there are times when that is tested, but for the most part, it works well without issues."

Humans and supernaturals living in tandem, going to college together, peacefully. What a strange place Arthlia is. And how incredibly fascinating.

"And what of your parents?" she asks me.

"My mother," I chew my lip. "She died when I was young, and my father left before that."

Willow nods like she somehow understands what I'm saying. "That makes sense." She reaches out her hand and her tone shifts. "Not about your mother dying, for that I am so terribly sorry, but your father, that is a common Oliver situation. It was part of the curse." She turns to Sydney. "How much of this did you already tell them?"

Sydney shrugs. "Some of it. It's a lot of information."

"It really is." She glances down at her watch. "Listen, I don't mean to cut this short, but I have another pressing matter to attend to." Her mesmerizing gaze meets mine. "Would you walk with me for a moment?"

"Yeah." I rise to my feet without question because what other option do I have? I'd do anything she asked if it meant taking one step closer to finding out the truth of my continuously mysterious life.

"Syd, keep Dash company while I steal her for a few minutes?" Willow gives Sydney's shoulder a gentle squeeze and offers Dash a kind smile.

"You okay?" Dash mouths to me.

With a nod, I confirm that I am, despite the aversion to leaving him behind. It's not me that I worry about, but Sydney has been considerate enough to allow us to get away with breaking into his home and using his amenities. It wouldn't be farfetched to assume he wouldn't keep Dash alive for a few more minutes.

My footsteps patter quietly along the floor behind Willow's. Once we're outside her office, she slows her pace to fall beside me, walking in unison like equals.

"I apologize for my shortness," she tells me. "It's not at all uncommon that we have new witches, but one actually bearing the Oliver name...that's a surprise."

"You don't have any direct relatives?" I match her

strides but give her the lead since I'm not exactly sure where she's taking me.

"Mother and father, yes. My uncle isn't a blood relative." She leads us through a swinging door, the aroma of berries and warm bread greets us with a warm embrace.

A man with honey-colored hair looks up from his spot at the counter, his eyes beaming once they settle on her. His cheeks turn up and he exposes his teeth. "You're just in time." He dusts his hands off over a doughy mixture and wipes them on the towel tucked into his apron.

Willow continues toward him. "Cam, I have someone I want you to meet."

A buzzer goes off. "Hold that thought." Cam presses one finger up into the air and turns on his heel. He slides a mitten onto his hand and reaches into the oven to pull out a batch of whatever he must be baking.

My mouth waters at the sheer scent of it but I restrain myself from latching onto the hot pan and running out of here like my life depends on it. Food is not a scarcity here, not like it is back home. I may not have lived like a demon on the run, but even as a hunter, things like substance and shelter weren't always easily accessible. And considering only the elite had the best of what our world had to offer, the provisions we got weren't anything compared to what Cam just placed on the counter between us.

"You didn't have to." Willow walks around and

throws her arms around his torso and presses her lips to his.

He returns her kiss and hugs her tightly before releasing her. "I knew you had a busy day ahead of you." Cam brings her hand to his face and kisses that, too. "Anything for you."

Willow blushes and gives her attention back to me. "Wren, this is Cameron, my husband. Cam, this is Wren Oliver."

Cam's brows perk up. "An Oliver, ey?" He extends his arm. "Always nice to meet family."

Family. Is that what this is? I shake his hand, noting how nothing sparks at our touch the way it had with Willow. Does that mean he's not supernatural? Or is it possible that the reaction I had with her was only because we share the same blood? Either way, I'm grateful for the connection even if it doesn't have the same *spark*.

A week ago, I had no one, and now I have Willow and her husbands.

"Can I offer you a blueberry muffin?" Cameron plucks napkins out of a square wooden holder before taking two warm muffins out of the tray and setting them on the counter.

"Thank you," I tell him. "That's mighty nice of you."

What did I do to deserve the kindness that these folks have had to offer? Sydney has been gracious in introducing me to Willow and giving us a place to stay.

And Cameron is willing to part with one of his delicious concoctions.

"Cam is the best baker in the state." She elbows him gently. "Angels, maybe the whole world. Can't say I've had a blueberry muffin that tastes better than this." She takes one from the counter and hands it to me, then keeps the other for herself.

"I think *world* might be an overstatement, babe," he tells her.

"Doubtful." Willow kisses Cam's reddened cheek. "I'll try to be back for dinner, but don't wait around on me. You know how Deghan gets if he misses a meal."

"Speaking of, have you seen him? He was gone before I got up." Cam scratches at his scruffy chin and leaves behind some of the white debris that was still on his hand.

Willow pats him with her napkin. "He's out with the wolves doing wolf stuff."

"Oh, right, that new pack is in town. I forgot he's training them." Cam nods as if he's just had a realization. "That explains why two pans of brownies were missing this morning."

"Are you surprised?" Willow chuckles.

"Not even a little bit." Cam steadies his baby blue gaze on me. There's something so soft and innocent about him—wholesome, really. He reminds me of Dash with his genuine and caring nature. He lacks the overbearing masculinity that I've grown familiar with in my lifetime. Most men make it a mission to assert their dominance and be seen as the top alpha in the room. Cam and Dash are both okay with their position in the ranks and seem to thrive in the truth of who they are. It's calm, endearing, and a welcome breath of fresh air in a sea of men and their pissing matches.

I don't need a man to protect me—I need respect.

Dash has given me that from the start. He's been on my side even when I wasn't and continues to stand by and support my desires. Bo could learn a thing or two from Dash. My relationship with Wes hasn't always been easy, but given our complicated attachment to each other, it makes sense that it wouldn't be smooth sailing. What relationship ever really is? Maybe I'm being too demanding for thinking that the situation with Bo should be anything less than difficult? He and I are exact opposites. We were brought up to hate each other. And not too long ago, we were enemies.

I shouldn't compare Bo to Dash, nor should I compare any of the guys. Every one of them is different, along with my connection to them. I should accept that some may come easier than others, and some might take a lot more work. But what if I'm the only one willing to put in the work, and Bo doesn't even feel the same way at all? I guess my biggest issue with the entire situation is not knowing whether he actually wants me. I could handle his bad attitude, temper, and short-fused nature if I was certain of his feelings for me.

He's so hot and cold I can never get a good read on what's going through his thick skull.

Maybe that's something I can talk to Willow about if I ever get the opportunity to meet with her again. She does have four husbands after all, and I'm confident things weren't always this simple.

Sydney speaks of Deghan in a good nature, and Cameron does the same. There doesn't appear to be any bad blood between them—but there's another husband I haven't heard anyone refer to. Is he the troublesome one of the bunch or is it happenstance that he hasn't been brought up yet?

"Don't be a stranger," Cameron adds. "You're an Oliver, which means you're one of us."

My heart clenches in my chest. Does he realize how much of an impact his words have on me?

"Thank you," I tell him. "I appreciate that more than you could know." I hold the muffin out toward him. "And for this, thank you. It smells divine."

"My pleasure." Cam places his hand over his chest and looks at Willow. "My love." Another buzzer rings through the air and captures his attention.

Willow tilts her head, nodding toward the opposite side of the kitchen. "This way," she says while peeling back the paper on her muffin and taking a bite.

No longer wanting to hold back from devouring this warm thing in my hand, I do the same and follow her out. I suppress a moan and swallow the soft decadence he created. "I can't imagine this tasting better."

Willow grins. "He really is an incredible baker. Cam may create some wild concoctions from time to time but there isn't anything that man makes that isn't delicious."

It's sweet to hear her speak of him so highly but she's not exactly lying, and this muffin is proof.

We go down another hall that is almost identical to the other ones weaving their way around this expansive house. Any other person might have lost sense of direction, but this kind of thing has always come naturally to me. That's a surefire way to get yourself into unnecessary danger. One can never be too sure if they're being led to their death, even if it's by a newfound family member.

"Sydney tells me you're staying at the old estate?" Willow keeps her strides matching mine and bites off another bit of her muffin.

"Yeah, we sort of stumbled upon it and didn't really know where else to go."

"Well." She glances over at me briefly. "I believe sometimes we find ourselves in places we're supposed to be without understanding how. I can't imagine how my life would have turned out had I not gone to Harper Academy."

"You weren't always planning on going there?"

"Honestly, I was at a crossroads. I had been caring for my mother most of my life and didn't think I could take the time away to do something that would mean abandoning the role of caretaker. It was hard allowing myself that chance to stretch my proverbial wings, but it was something I felt called to do. I knew I wouldn't be far, and my uncle agreed to step in temporarily while I figured things out. Had he not pushed me, I don't think I would have. From the second I stepped foot in that academy, my entire life changed. Nothing was ever the same, and as difficult as the next few years of my life would be, I'm grateful for every second of it."

"The curse, that's right. Sydney mentioned you had great obstacles to overcome to break it."

Willow nods, rounds a corner, and continues walking. "Yes, to say the least. But in doing so, not only did I liberate myself, but so many others. And had I not, I wouldn't know the true nature of who I am. Every struggle, painful and traumatic as they may have been, brought me here today; I wouldn't have stepped into my power, met my mates, my friends, my family, or been able to help others without everything unfolding the way it did. It may have been a simpler life, but us Oliver's..." She nudges me with her elbow. "We're not much for taking the easy way out."

Every word she says speaks directly to my soul. My life has been chaotic from the start. Ripped from my mother at an early age, I spent every day after training to become the best at what I do—killing. I harnessed and tapped into my anger to unleash the ultimate soldier who fought in a war that never should have been waged.

Willow reclaimed her power and fought a similar evil.

I'm not convinced she'd still want me as her family if she knew the truth about who I was and what I had done.

Would I still have become that person if my mother wasn't brutally slain? If my father had been involved? What if Prania had never been overrun by hunters who wanted to eradicate every demonic creature in existence? The plethora of possibilities and what-ifs do nothing to change the fact that I am the person I am, and that I have done the things that I've done.

But as Willow said, each painful reality is what made her who she is today. Had I not gone through every single thing I did, would I be standing here with her? Maybe this is all part of the plan that brings me to whatever purpose I'm supposed to have. Maybe I have more suffering to endure before I can step into the next chapter of my life.

I cling to the hope that one day, perhaps my life will be as grand as hers.

And if it isn't, I'll die trying to make it happen.

"I'd love to talk to you more sometime," she says to me while slowing her pace. "I'm afraid my schedule is rather full at the moment, but in the coming months, I may be able to carve some time out."

I swallow down the lump in my throat. *Months.* I can't wait that long for answers. I didn't expect every one of my questions answered today, but matters are still pressing, and I don't have the luxury of time on my side.

"I do hope that Sydney can give you a warm welcome in my absence though, and as Cam said, don't be a stranger." Willow lingers near a door which I'm guessing leads to wherever she must be off to. Given the circumstances, it could be the outside world or a whole other realm entirely.

"I...I need your help," I blurt out. "I wouldn't ask if it weren't necessary." Requesting aid from anyone has never really been my strong suit, and the sinking pit in my stomach is a reminder of why I'd like to never do it ever again.

"Sydney is a master scholar, if there's any research you need done, he's the most equipped for the job."

"He said he already did and couldn't find anything." I grow angry at the weakness in my voice—at the hopelessness blooming in my chest.

"I understand how frustrating it can be to struggle to find the answers you're looking for." Willow breathes in deeply and exhales. "I have a meeting with Headmaster Walker later. I'll see what I can figure out..." She seems to lose track of where her sentence was going.

I wait for her focus to return and plead with the Angels to bring with it good news.

"Have Sydney bring you by the academy around 7:00 p.m. I have an idea."

An idea—that's surely better than nothing at all,

and regardless of how vague it may be, I cling to the prospect of its possibilities.

Willow pushes the door open but doesn't leave just yet.

"Thank you," I tell her.

"Don't get your hopes up, it's a long shot, but back when I was searching for answers, it was something I did that helped me." She shrugs. "Maybe it will work for you, too."

And if it doesn't, at least I'll get some more time with her—my family.

"I'll try anything," I say truthfully. Whatever might help uncover the secrets of Prania and potentially provide a solution to save those that were left behind.

I can't stay in Arthlia and pretend my entire homeland isn't falling completely apart.

"Can you find your way back?" She nods in the direction we just came.

"Two lefts, a right, through the kitchen with these." I hold up what's left of my muffin.

"A sucker for details." Willow nudges me. "We're more alike than you may think." She smiles softly. "If you ever get lost, here or out there. Just close your eyes, ground yourself to the universe, and ask for the way. You'd be surprised what answers are waiting if you remain patient."

How can I stay patient when so many are dying back home because Parla still rules over Prania? I must find a way back to avenge those lives I've taken and put a stop to any further damage she may cause.

"I'll see you this evening." Willow slips through the door and it latches shut behind her, leaving me here at the end of this corridor with nothing but my thoughts.

Taking a second to let out a breath and relax my tense shoulders, I shove the rest of the muffin in my mouth and quickly savor the taste of such a creation. Bo would lose his mind if he could get his arrogant lips around one of those muffins. Maybe on my way back I could barter with Cameron to bring one back to him.

Perhaps bribing Bo with something edible will convince him to drop his guard and let me in enough to figure out what's going on in his head. And even if it doesn't, the look of satisfaction that will no doubt be on his face will be enough of a reward.

Turning toward the open hallway, I'm brought to an abrupt halt. I nearly slam into another body, and my feet instinctually move to take a step from this person suddenly appearing.

"Angels," I gasp while clutching my chest.

His sort of purple gaze stares down at mine, his jaw clenched and his shoulders broad. A white T-shirt does a half-ass job of covering his tattooed body and ink spills over the exposed parts of his wrists that his black leather jacket doesn't cover.

He's...beautiful, in an almost too-perfect kind of way.

"Willow?" His lips part only slightly to mutter the one word.

I tilt my head in the direction she went, and when I blink, he disappears from in front of me and darts through that same door.

With an exhale, I shake off the awkward interaction. "I guess that would be her *other* husband," I whisper to myself. "Either freakishly fast or definitely supernatural."

12

WES

I don't hate it here.

There's damn good food. Comfortable lodging. And much less danger than where we came from.

It's not that I don't enjoy a battle or two here or there, but the constant fighting for our lives thing was a bit exhausting.

Not to mention, Wren being in a safer place is a huge perk, too.

My hound worries a lot less, and so do I.

She's tough, to say the least, and without enemies looming around every corner, I have fewer doubts that she can and will remain unharmed.

"You're really okay with this?" Bo mouths off from his spot leaning against the counter. He throws his arms toward the door exaggeratedly. "She's Angels knows where and you're fine playing house."

Shut him up, my hound tells me.

I sigh and shake my head. "You're overreacting."

Bo's dark gaze widens. "You're *under*reacting."

"What's this really about?" I ask him while drinking my third glass of orange juice. I'm not sure what they put in this stuff, but it sure is tasty.

Simple pleasures, Sydney calls it.

Whatever it is, it's reason enough to want to stay in Arthlia for as long as I live.

"It must be nice." Bo folds his arms over his chest. "Knowing that no matter what, she's coming back to you."

"What?" I lower the glass and stare at him.

"The fated mate bond. It's like a fucking guarantee that you two will always find each other."

"You're jealous?" I try my hardest not to laugh.

Bo's jaw tenses and the vein in his forehead bulges. "No."

I let out a chuckle. "You're jealous."

"Well, at least I gave her a choice in the matter. Who's to say she isn't with you just because of the stupid bond? She may be your mate but at what cost? Her free will? No." Bo kicks off from the counter. "No, I'd rather die than force her to be with me."

He storms out of the kitchen, leaving me behind with the unraveling thought I do my best to keep concealed.

Bo might be an arrogant asshole, but he's right.

The mate bond that Wren and I share is unbreakable. Our connection will overcome any obstacle. It is sure and steadfast, and nothing could hinder our loyalty to one another. There isn't anything me or my hound wouldn't do for her, and if I had to take my best guess, I'd say that she feels the same.

But as certain and secure as it may be, is that really the best thing for her? A love she cannot choose to escape. A love that would chase her to the ends of the universe and not once stop until it found her again. I would traverse hell and back to worship at her feet. Even in death, I would come for her. I would die a thousand deaths just to be near her.

I knew it from the very moment I laid my sights on her.

My hound growled deep within my chest, claiming her as his—as *ours*.

I did what I could to resist the carnal desire to be with her but I was no match for what fate had in store for us.

Would my love be that powerful without the magical bind that ties us together?

Would she still choose me if given the chance?

I thought I was doing the right thing in allowing the bond to tether us, but was I a fool for following through with allowing her to link herself to me permanently? I wanted it—Angels, I needed it. Perhaps I was blinded by the visceral plea my soul had been screaming out to make her mine.

Have I doomed her to a worse fate because I couldn't defy what was already written in the stars?

Jade waltzes into the kitchen and plucks an apple from the bowl on the counter. "What's got Bo's panties in a bunch?"

"You know, typical Bo." I drain the rest of my juice and rinse the glass out in the sink. "I've been meaning to ask you." I turn toward her once I've placed the glass in the dishwasher. Another mysterious and magical creation of this realm.

"Oh Angels, what is it?" She bites into the crisp apple and wipes at her mouth.

Fruit from back home doesn't even remotely compare to that of Arthlia.

"Do you and Everest have plans for the future?" I rest against the wall and do my best to come off as less overprotective brother as I can.

Still, I can't help but want the best for her, especially now that she's gone through what she has. I'll never begin to understand what it was like to be held captive in Rockbridge for such a long period, but if my short stint there was any indication, Jade deserves the best life has to offer. And what kind of person would I be if I tried to prevent that from happening?

Do I want her to go off on her own with some random man? No, absolutely not. But he was one, if not the main reason for her survival, and if he's what brings her joy, I support that.

Any good brother would.

"Um, I mean, not really." Jade presses her hands behind her on the counter and scoots back until she's sitting on the hard surface. "Do you?"

I draw in a breath and exhale slowly. "I'd like to stay here, in Arthlia. I don't know what that entails, but I don't want to leave."

Jade bobs her head up and down while chewing another bite. "Me either. Ev and I want to stay, too."

Her face lights up and her gaze shifts to Everest as he walks into the kitchen and joins us.

"What about you?" I ask him. "You going along with whatever she has to say or do you actually want to stay?"

Everest strolls over to Jade's side, kissing her cheek and gripping her thigh. "I'm all in wherever she is."

I grin. "Didn't answer my question."

"I don't have anything anywhere else." He glances up at her before focusing back on me. "She's it for me. I'd be an idiot if I left her now. And the thought of ever going back to Prania—I'll pass. There's nothing left for any of us there. It's a wasteland."

It turns my stomach to think about what we escaped from, but he's right. There's no going back. What remains of our homeland will burn to ashes in time and if it doesn't, it will be overcome by hunters and the entire demon population will be eliminated. Why return there when it's a hopeless cause?

"You mentioned your brother is no longer with us."

"Wes," Jade snaps at me.

"No, it's okay," Everest reassures her. "He died a few years ago."

"I'm sorry for your loss." I shouldn't press, but I can't ignore the nagging that he isn't divulging the whole story. "Casualty of the war?"

Everest nods and his gaze falls to the floor. "Yeah. You could say that." Just when I'm sure he won't say anything else, he opens his mouth again. "It was random, his death. No explanation. Only a letter that came to his house stating if next of kin wanted to pick up his body, they could show up at Rockbridge to get it."

Hunters paint a picture that demons are cruel, but that lack of consideration is cold-hearted and unforgiving.

"Of course, I did," he continues. "I showed up demanding answers, but when they had none to provide, I infiltrated their operation in an attempt to figure it out for myself." Everest laughs dryly. "They never expected me to not be on their side. Few non-demons ever go against the natural way. Because my brother was respected and had made a name for himself, I got preferential treatment. I refused to work in the field so they gave me a higher-ranking guard position. I thought I could lay low and uncover the truth."

"Did you?" I ask him.

Everest averts his gaze again. "Only took about a month to learn what had happened."

"A month? And yet you stayed there for years?" That's when it hits me, he went there for the truth of his brother's death, but he stayed for something else entirely.

"I was assigned sector eighteen." He grips Jade's thigh, and she wraps her fingers over his. "I found what I was looking for and then some."

"You saved me," she mutters to him.

"We saved each other," he whispers back to her.

"I'm grateful you found her, Everest." I can't fathom the possibilities had he not been there for her when she needed him the most.

We may have lost Mother, but thank the Angels that Jade was spared.

"I am, too." Everest forces a smile.

"I hadn't spoken to anyone since Mother." Jade's eyes glisten with each word spoken. "It was Everest who finally broke through to me. I was a shell of a person left there to rot, and somehow he saw something in me that I thought I had lost forever. He was kind, and patient, and eventually, I started to trust him. He's the one who insisted I use a fake name. He didn't want me to lose anything else to that place than I already had."

"And so, Franny was born," he says.

"I never lost hope," I tell her. "I never quit trying to get you two back. I'm so sorry for all that wasted time. I should have come sooner."

"It wasn't all wasted." She tugs Everest toward her,

positioning his back to her chest, between her legs. Jade hugs him close, kissing the top of his head and resting her chin on it.

"And what of your brother? You said you uncovered the truth." My heart swells at seeing the two of them find comfort in the darkness together.

Maybe powerful love can come not just in fated mates.

"I discovered that the hunters, the true hunters, were somehow harvesting demonic power after their kills. And they were ordered to return to Rockbridge for some kind of ritual to extract that power. Most hunters only made it through one or two of these rituals before their life force gave out, my brother included. He was the last to die before they put a stop to it. They expanded the prison and changed the orders. Instead of being told to kill the demons on sight, they were informed they must bring them in alive. I think they were biding time until they could figure out how to start extracting again without losing hunters in the process. They couldn't afford for their numbers to keep dwindling so they had to do something."

How is it even possible for a hunter to harvest demonic power from a kill? Does Wren know anything about this? What would they do with that power? Both the hunter *and* the organization calling the shots? I thought eliminating us was their sole mission, but apparently, it was something more complex. Was she participating in said rituals and stealing the power of those she killed? She would have been doing the same thing that had been done to her bloodline for centuries. Stealing and suppressing someone else for unjust reasons. Would there even be a *just* reason at all? Surely, she wouldn't do something *that* unbelievably wrong.

But when my thoughts bring me back to that room, that day I thought everything was going to end, isn't that what Parla was trying to get Wren to do to me? She wanted Wren to kill me and said if she did, she would allow Wren to live. Is it possible that Wren, and whatever magic she holds, can do the ritual without meeting the same fate the other hunters did?

Because Wren isn't a hunter at all, she's a witch—one descended from the Angels themselves.

I want to question more, to learn what else Everest knows of this heinous act, only the second my mind slows down long enough to ask, the door opens and Wren walks in.

Her smile distracts me, something bright and beaming about her that wasn't there a few hours ago. It tugs at my heart, and without meaning to, I gravitate toward her, my soul being called to hers.

"Oh, what do you have there?" Jade hops off the counter and goes toward Wren.

"The most incredible muffins in the entire world." Wren sets a box on the counter and flips the lid open. She pulls one out and gives it to Jade. "You have to try, seriously." She raises a brow but gives me no choice to say no. She shoves one toward me, too, and then takes another.

I kiss her cheek and bask in how her sheer presence alone can soothe me.

"Where's Bo?" she asks with a muffin still in her grasp. "He has to eat one of these."

I crane my thumb in the direction he stormed off not too long ago. "That way somewhere."

Sydney enters through the same door Wren had come from. "I have another box of them, so feel free to have as many as you want."

My attention flits to him, and in that split second, Wren moves out of the room in her pursuit of Bo. Her absence leaves a chill in her wake and grants the space for my concerning questions to rise back to the surface.

13
WREN

Taking the stairs two at a time, I rush up to the second floor of Sydney's home to locate Bo.

Certainty that I'm on the right path fills me with each step closer to him. Is it the mark on my neck that allows me to sense him? Maybe the hunter nature in me kicking in? Or perhaps it's something else entirely that makes me sure he's nearby.

I bolt through the door to our shared bedroom, and my heart drops when I don't see him.

Was I wrong in thinking what he and I share is anything more than nothing?

"What's the rush, Birdie? House on fire again?" His gruff voice calms my aching soul.

"You," I say while spinning on my heel. "Have to try this."

"What is it?" He raises a dark brow but doesn't move from his seat in the corner of the room. Instead of sleeping in the bed with the rest of us, he slumbers uncomfortably upright in a chair. And that's if he sleeps at all, knowing him, he probably lurks in those dark hours.

"It's a muffin." I stalk toward him. "Blueberry."

"Did you poison it?"

"What?" No. Why would I do that?"

"You're entirely too excited. You must admit, it's rather suspicious."

"Fine," I pout. "Don't eat it." I peel back the paper surrounding the still-warm muffin and bite off a huge chunk of it, way more than I normally would have.

But I'm brought to a halt when Bo grabs my waist and tugs me toward him. He positions me between his legs and grips my chin. "Open up." He tilts his head to where his lips are just a breath away from mine.

I do as he says, the muffin falling from my mouth and into his. Heat swells between my legs.

How is it possible to be turned on by such an act?

Bo's eyes widen. "Damn birdie." He keeps his one hand around my waist and says, "More."

I break off a chunk and plop it into his mouth; my fingers grazing his lips only heightens my desire for him. I continue until there's nothing left for me to give him.

"Tasted better straight from your mouth." He relaxes into the chair but doesn't take his hand off me.

And because I can't miss the open opportunity, I plop myself onto his lap. "Was that so hard?"

"You keep pressing your ass up against me and I'll show you what's hard."

I wiggle on him and laugh. "You wouldn't."

He pokes me in the side. "Keep messing around, Birdie. You're going to be sorry."

Why can't he be like this all the time? Fun, playful, cocky. This side of him is temporary and fleeting and makes me wonder which version of him is actually real.

Bo slides my legs sideways over his and keeps his arm draped over them while his other remains wrapped around my torso. He leans back and stares over at me, his resolve softening. "You really brought that up here for me?"

"What?" I settle into him and rest my head on the high back of the chair.

"The muffin. You got that for me?"

But there's something about the way he says *me* that tugs at my heart.

"Of course, I did." This time it's my finger that jabs him in the ribs. "I believe my exact thought was *Damn this is delicious. I have to get one for Bo.*"

"Really? You thought about me?"

"Are you serious?" I melt into him a bit more. "Aside from wondering what the fuck we're doing here, you're on my mind a lot, you big idiot."

"Why?" His dark gaze steadies itself on mine.

I swallow down the intensity of his stare. "Because...I...care...about...you."

"Why?"

"Did you hit your head or something?" I pinch my brows together. "I know the concept is foreign to you, the whole *caring* thing, but it's not just me. Wes and Dash and Jade care about you, too."

"Oh," he says.

"And do you care about them?"

Bo blinks, his attention faltering as if I asked him to solve the hardest riddle. "I mean, I don't want them to die."

"That's not the same, Bo, and you know it."

"I don't know what you want from me." His palm tenses on my thigh.

"Do you care about me?" I shouldn't ask, but I do anyway.

"It's complicated, Birdie."

"You've said that before. It's a simple yes or no."

"It's not simple, Wren, and you know it."

"Are you mocking me?"

"No."

"You can answer that, but you can't admit whether or not you care about me." I scoot away but he keeps his hold tight on me.

His jaw constricts and his nostrils flare. He lets out a breath. "Is that what you want? For me to say I do?"

I shake my head. "Not if you don't mean it."

"It's just words, Birdie." Bo skims his hand along my leg. "This," he whispers and continues moving his touch up until his rough palm is resting against my cheek. "This is..." His fingers spread, encapsulating my entire cheek and dipping into my hair. Bo swirls his thumb gently, so very unlike who he typically is. Bo is harsh, violent, and commanding. The man touching me is everything but.

"What is it, Bo?" I mutter, practically begging him to finish his train of thought.

But as quickly as he became this soft version of himself, he blinks and it's gone.

"I can't do this." He stands and in one swift motion, drops me onto the chair he was in and rushes out the door.

I pinch my eyes shut and bring my hand up to rub my temple. "Great, that went great," I mutter to no one but myself. The warmth from his body on the chair does nothing to replace what it felt like being that near him.

He was so fucking close to saying *something*. What stopped him? Why is he so resistant to letting me in? If he truly didn't want me, surely, he would just say it. I can't imagine Bo ever doing *anything* he didn't want. If it were a no, he would admit it. Unless the only reason it feels like a yes is because of this stupid fucking mark on my neck. What if Bo truly isn't interested but the mark is what ties him to me?

More reason to remove the thing and free himself for good.

Am I forcing an issue on something he doesn't want at all?

"You okay in here?" Wes pokes his head into the

room. "Saw Bo leave in typical Bo fashion."

"Yeah," I lie. "I'm good." Leaving the chair Bo and I intimately sat in together behind, I stroll over to the edge of the bed and plop down onto the mattress, patting the spot beside me for Wes.

"Those muffins were to die for." Wes comes over, his body filling the void Bo just created.

I've never been the type to need anyone near, but now that I've gotten a taste of what it's like, I can't stand being without any of these three men for long. Even simply having Dash with me today was a comfort I didn't realize I desired until I had it.

"They were, weren't they?" I only meant to bring the one home for Bo, but Cameron was kind enough to send me with a whole batch of them. I offered to repay him somehow, and yet he insisted I take them without anything in return. This world is strange, and with each interaction, it becomes even more bizarre.

Back home, nothing is given without something being taken. It's a familiar exchange and something I could rely on. Unless it was stolen, there was always a swap of some capacity.

A favor for a favor. A barter of sorts. Everything had a balance.

Here, people do things for others without the need for them to be reciprocal, even if it costs them time, energy, or money. Or at least, that's what it seems—there very well could be a price down the line that one party is unaware of until it comes due.

"What are you thinking about?" Wes asks me.

"This place," I say. "It's too good to be true. Don't you agree?"

Wes drags his bottom lip into his mouth and rakes his teeth over it. "Perhaps we're used to things being harder than they need to be."

"A lifetime in Prania and you're so willing to accept that things can really be this good?"

He shrugs. "Why not? What do we have to lose?"

"What does he think?" I press my hand to his chest.

Wes's hellhound hasn't come out since we've been in Arthlia. Is it possible he has abandoned us again?

But when Wes's irises glow, I'm reminded that he's very much here with us now.

Wes pushes his palm into my hand. "He said he likes it wherever you are."

"He *said*?" I tilt my head.

"Mmhm."

"What does he think about this?" I climb onto his lap and straddle him.

Wes hides a grin. "He wants you to continue."

"Does he?" I slide my hands up his chiseled chest, his muscles bulging the fabric of his shirt. "What about this?" I rock my hips and weave my fingers through his hair, tugging on it gently.

Wes latches onto my waist, his eyes igniting that familiar red that has me completely captivated. He pushes down and pivots himself upward. "He wants you."

I swallow and gently move over his growing erection pushing the space between us. "And what about you? Do you want me, too?"

His fiery gaze stares up at me. "More than anything." Wes finds my lips with his, kissing me with an intensity that sets my soul ablaze.

I moan and dig my fingers in deeper, desperate for every bit of him I can get a hold of.

He tugs me tighter and spreads his hands over my back, my waist, my hips, my ass.

I barely notice when he stands, my body not daring to separate from his.

How had I been so fucking oblivious to how badly I wanted him until this very moment?

With my legs wrapped around his torso and my arms on his neck, Wes grips the waistband of my bottoms and rips them off me, the fabric shredding along with my panties as they fall away from me. He unbuttons his pants and frees his cock, gliding it over my soaked entrance before lining himself into place.

Wes sits on the bed and shoves me down onto him, my pussy spreading around him.

"Fuck," I whimper. "You're so big, I can barely take you."

He draws my lip into his mouth and looks into my eyes. "You were made for me, Wren." Wes thrusts deeper. "Every inch of me was made for you."

I shove the weight of my body down and revel in the pain that mixes with pleasure.

"That's it," he whispers as he holds onto my hips. "You're taking me like such a good girl." Wes lies back on the bed but moves his hands to the nape of my shirt, ripping it down the center and exposing my bare breasts.

I adjust to fit this new angle of him and sigh at the fullness.

He squeezes my tits before trailing one hand back to my waist. Wes brings his thumb to his mouth, licking it and returning it to my center. Pushing it against my clit, he swirls it with the perfect amount of pressure.

"Angels," I sigh.

"That's it," he says. "Come for me."

I climax around him, reaching back to grip his thighs as pleasure consumes me.

He slows his hips but moves his thumb through my orgasm, not stopping when I've finished. Instead, in one swift movement, he stands, throws me onto the mattress, and continues rubbing my clit while pumping into me once again.

I bring my knees up, spreading myself wide for him to give me everything he has.

He complies, fucking me harder and wrecking my pussy in the most beautiful way. Wes pinches my clit and sends me over the edge, his cock still thrusting into me through the second orgasm. Shoving both my legs to one side, he keeps his pace while deepening his strokes.

The new sensation heightens my pleasure even more.

I drag my hair out of my sweat-lined face and take in just how fucking beautiful this man is. I barely make it from his chiseled jawline to his perfectly plush lips before I get distracted by his grin.

He licks his lips and lowers himself down, scooting me up onto the mattress to climb more on top of me. Wes slows his movements and stares into my eyes.

I want to open my mouth, to say something, but nothing could ever be said to make him realize just how much he means to me. He was the catalyst that set my entire world on a different course. The person who finally made me feel alive for the first time in my life. He is one half of my soul, and not a single thing could ever make me love him any less.

Love.

My heart stutters at the thought.

I've never *loved* anything, let alone *anyone*.

Cheese is probably the only thing that comes close, but that doesn't count.

We haven't been together long, and most of our time has been spent running for our lives. Is it possible to love someone that soon? How else would I explain the feeling that courses through me when I look into his blazing eyes? We're fated mates, doesn't that give us a free pass to fall deeply and fast?

I plant my hands on his cheeks and study the man that stares back at me.

His lip twitches, and his mouth parts slightly. "I love you, Wren."

A smile breaks across my face and a laugh bubbles out of my chest.

"You think it's funny that I love you?" Wes frowns but keeps pumping himself into me, his desire to continue having sex with me stronger than his pride at thinking I'm laughing at him.

"I think it's funny that you said the very thing that was on my own mind." I drag him closer to me, my lips a hair from his. "I love you, too, Wes." I press my mouth onto his before he can say another word and kiss him with a renewed passion.

He matches my force and dances his tongue along mine.

My core tightens and his cock throbs in response, filling me even more.

We orgasm in tandem, both of us crying out into each other in a wave of pure bliss.

Another moment passes, our bodies not quite ready to be apart just yet.

Wes stays inside of me but collapses beside my shuddering form. He presses a kiss to my forehead, my nose, and finally, my lips, while dragging my leg over his to lay atop him. "I mean it, Wren. I love you."

I prop myself onto my elbow and drag my fingertip along his forehead. "I meant it, too, Wes. With everything in me." I smile at him. "Plus, I know you can't lie."

"Right. How could I forget?" He lets his head fall

back but then quickly returns his attention. "I didn't hurt you, did I? I was rough, I'm sorry."

I bask in the soreness and appreciate the fullness he still provides even though his erection has softened inside me. There's something incredibly intimate about staying this close even after we've both finished. If only there was a way to get nearer without cutting our bodies open and sewing them together.

What a morbidly romantic and disturbing thought.

"No," I tell him. "It was perfect, really."

"If only you couldn't lie either." He rolls his eyes but doesn't push the issue more.

"How can you not see how completely content I am?"

"Content. Hmm. I should really strive for something better than content."

"I am supremely satisfied." I bring my leg off him and kick at the loose fabric still clinging to my ankle. "Although, I owe Sydney some new clothes."

"I could set them on fire, and we could pretend they never existed."

"Good plan. Maybe we could do that with all the food Bo has eaten, too." What was meant to be a lighthearted remark somehow feels like a swift kick in the gut. I should have known better than to bring Bo up so soon. Leave it to him to always get under my skin, literally and figuratively.

As if Wes can sense the shift, he pushes up onto his elbow to face me. "He'll come around. Don't worry."

I chew at the inside of my lip. "And you're not mad about that?"

He narrows his gaze. "What would I be mad about?"

"I don't know. For starters, the whole sharing me thing. Being a possessive hellhound and all, you're both sure taking that pretty well."

"We would never do anything to hurt you. Not intentionally. And making you choose, that would hurt, wouldn't it?"

I let the thought run through my head, it only needing about half a millisecond to rip a hole through my chest.

"See," he says. "That right there, it goes against our very nature." Wes sighs. "Do we want to share you? No. But will we do everything in our power to make you happy and keep you safe? Absolutely."

"Because of the mate bond."

"Because you are our person. Is it the bond? Maybe. I don't know, I don't care. All I know is this." He grazes his hand over my cheek. "Us." He leans in closer. "You're my world, Wren. My entire universe." His lips caress mine. "I'd die to prove that to you."

"Can you not die? That would be great." I kiss him and smile against his mouth when his cock hardens inside of me again.

My entire life might be up in the air right now, but at least I have this, I have us.

And that counts for something.

14
WREN

Twirling my finger through the hair on Wes's chest, I lose myself in the comfort of him.

"What are you thinking about?" I ask the burly man.

His eyes flutter open, that familiar shade of glowing red flashing through as he settles his sights on me. He smiles softly. "You."

I rest my chin on his stomach and look up at him. "I'm right here, doofus."

"I like to consume myself in you. Bathe in all things Wren, if I may. It's simply not enough to be near you, I want my every waking thought to revolve around..." He pokes me on the tip of the nose. "You."

"Obsessive much?" I tease.

He shrugs. "Guilty as charged."

"How do you feel about Everest?" I change the subject.

"Well, he's not nearly as good-looking as you."

I let out a laugh. "Ha. Ha. Very funny."

Wes drags his arm behind his head to prop him up and rubs the other over my bare shoulders. "He's a nice guy, from what I've gathered. Was there for Jade when I wasn't."

"That's not your fault," I tell him. "It was out of your control."

"Doesn't make it any easier to stomach. I should have tried getting to her sooner. Maybe I could have—"

"Wes," I cut him off. "It's not your fault."

"Yeah." He lets out a breath.

"He does seem like a good guy. I guess I'm just confused about why he was at Rockbridge."

"Oh." Wes repositions himself slightly. "He was there to investigate his brother's death. And after he figured it out, he stayed for Jade. Said he didn't want to leave her behind and was biding his time until he could figure out how to free her. I'm glad someone was there to give her hope."

"What was the cause of death?"

"Everest was certain that hunters were harnessing demonic power after their kills, and when it was harvested from them, it killed them in the process. Few hunters made it past a couple sessions before it would end their lives."

My heart stutters and I wish there was a way to turn back the clock and guarantee none of this ever happened. The killings, the theft of magic, the curses.

So many died for a hopeless cause on both sides of this pointless war.

And for what? For the power-hungry bitch named Parla to gain some kind of advantage over the demons. She's never going to win. It's been centuries and Prania is still descending into the abyss. If only hell would swallow her whole and rid us of her reprehensible ways.

No one else has to die and if I have to kill her myself to make that happen, I will.

"Did you know anything about this?" Wes stares right into my eyes, his focus intense.

"I..."

But I don't get a chance to answer him, and even if I did, I'm not sure what I would have said. The truth? Parts of it? How do I tell him that I was doing the very thing he's referring to? Would he forgive me if he knew how much I hated myself for it? If I told him that I wasn't aware, not fully, of why I was doing what I was doing? I was going off orders—doing what was commanded of me, but that doesn't make what I did any less wrong.

I'll never forgive my actions and that burden alone is a weight I carry through each day. Can I handle the pressure of his judgment, too?

Dash comes into the room, not at all bothered by me and Wes lying here intimately. "Hey," he says. "Sorry to interrupt, but Sydney is downstairs waiting for you."

"Oh shit." I jump up from my spot on the bed and point to a pile of clothes on top of the dresser. "Throw me something to wear, please."

Wes props himself onto his elbows. "Where are you off to? And should I be concerned about this *alone* time you're spending with another man?"

I roll my eyes, rushing around the bed to press a quick kiss to his lips. "Jealousy looks cute on you."

"Here." Dash hands me a few items from the stack —all shades of black or dark grey.

I toss the sweater over my head and step into the leggings.

"Sit," Dash says, kneeling in front of me with a pair of socks in his grasp.

"You don't have to—"

Wes grabs my waist and tugs me onto the edge of the mattress. "Listen to the guy." He nuzzles his head against my side while Dash slides a sock onto each of my feet.

"Thank you," I tell Dash.

It's strange to allow someone to do such a simple task, but it doesn't fail to warm my heart at the thoughtful gesture. This isn't the first time they've made it a point to do little things for me. Even in Bo's frustrating way, he does, too. Like when he serves my rations first instead of just helping himself, or when he steps aside to let me walk through a doorway in front of him. Maybe it's so he can get a better look at my ass, but I choose to believe it's for something else entirely.

Bo is more subtle than Wes and Dash are in their displays of affection, yet still, I feel his consideration whether he refuses to admit it's there or not.

And maybe that's something that I'll have to get used to—how Bo chooses to give himself only in longing stares and those soft fleeting moments. Or even in the smile of a victory won together after a brutal battle. I could learn to love him in the manner he prefers, because isn't that what love is about? Give *and* take, not just take. I can't expect him to change for me but perhaps I could change for him. Or at the very least, meet him somewhere in the middle.

I slide into my boots and give Wes one last kiss, leaving him lying there like he was sent here by the angels themselves with his hair wafting onto his forehead. His sleepy gaze follows me out of the room.

"You coming?" I call out to Dash, taking a departing glance at the closed door across the hall from ours.

Tremont. Another one of life's mysteries that has yet to be solved.

He hasn't made a commotion or tried to escape. Sometimes I expect him to be gone, but he remains imprisoned in the room of his enemy. Is it possible that he's familiar enough with captivity that he doesn't desire being set free? Or have his wrongdoings finally caught up to him and made him realize that he deserves the punishment? Either way, I'm no better than him. I killed without question and stole power that was not mine for the taking.

I even enjoyed doing it and took great pleasure in becoming the most lethal of my kind.

I should be locked away the same as him.

Dash catches up to me on the stairs and distracts my mind from imploding.

"You're coming with me, right?" I take in his gentle but masculine features and try not to lose my footing and fall down the stairs.

"You want me to?" He does a poor job hiding the grin that forms on his handsome face.

"Obviously." I cup my hand around his biceps and continue descending.

My relationship with Dash hasn't always been easy, but it's never been challenging either. There have been times when I worried or had doubts or grew frustrated. He's been a constant support and goes above and beyond to show his fondness of me. Even when I didn't deserve it. He has been kind and optimistic despite having everything taken from him. He never gave up hope that there was something better out there, and I adore his persistence to persevere. Part of me wishes I could be more like him, but I'm not foolish enough to think my darkness wouldn't immediately drown out that light.

Maybe that's why Bo and I can't seem to get things right—because we're too much alike. Both of us forged in the depths of our despair and fueled by the continued rage pumping through our veins.

Sydney glances up from his spot in the kitchen and

shoves that tiny device of his into his pocket. "You ready?"

"What is that?" I ask him. "That thing you're on all the time."

He slides it back out and holds it in front of him. "This? It's a cell phone."

"Oh," I say, moving in his direction. "What's so special about it?"

"Um, well, nothing and everything, I suppose." He pokes the front of it, and it lights up. "You can call people, text them, email. Um, there are social media apps. The weather. Games. News. Pretty much any information that you could possibly want is at your fingertips." He pushes it another few times and points it at me. "It has a camera." Sydney turns it around to show me the picture.

"Ew, I look like that?"

"What are you talking about?" Dash gawks at me. "You're beautiful."

I pat the sides of my head to tame my hair. "I look like I fell off a wagon and got sat on by a scruni."

"Do not." Dash elbows me in the ribs.

Sydney touches the screen again. "Here, I deleted it. That better?"

"Yeah," I tell him. "Thanks."

"I'm sure you'll all get one of your own at some point once you've established yourselves in our realm. It's easier to stay connected that way. I was just talking to Silas about upcoming plans." Sydney snatches his keys off the counter and makes his way toward the door.

"Silas." The memory of that attractive man popping up out of nowhere at Willow's house comes back to me. "Is that another one of Willow's husbands?"

"Yep." Sydney continues down the hall and opens the door to the outside world.

"He's, uh, interesting." I breathe in deeply and savor the freshness of the air.

"You two met?" Dash stays close to my side without being overly into my personal space.

I urge to yank him toward me but refrain from the intrusive thought.

"He sort of appeared out of thin air. Right after I shoved half a muffin in my mouth, too. I probably frightened him."

"There isn't much that can scare him. He's been to hell and back."

"Haven't we all?" I reach for the handle on the car door, my body already falling in line with the ways of this world.

"No," Sydney says from the driver's side. "Literally."

"Oh." I climb into the passenger seat and buckle myself in before I'm told to. "That explains why he's so broody."

Sydney chuckles. "He was like that prior, actually. That's just how he is." He turns the key in the ignition and backs us out of the parking spot. "We've had our differences, we still do, but he's a good man."

"So you two didn't always get along?" I glance over at him, wondering how much I'm allowed to ask without coming across too overbearing. I can't help but want to learn everything I can about Willow and her men. *My family.*

"Not for a great while, really. We hated each other." Sydney turns onto the main road and accelerates to get ahead of the car he pulled out in front of.

It grows smaller in the mirror behind us.

"Was it because of her? Like you were fighting over Willow?"

Sydney shakes his head. "No, not really. Although, that didn't make the beginning of our relationships any easier." He puts the blinker thing on and switches lanes. "Witches and vampires are natural born enemies."

Silas was freakishly fast and able to sneak up on me without drawing attention to himself.

"He's a vampire," I say out loud, confirming what Sydney already said. "So you and Willow are witches, Deghan is a werewolf, and Silas is a vampire. What's Cameron?"

The one I haven't quite figured out yet. I had a hunch that Silas was *something* in line with vampires or dhampirs but Cameron leaves me with a big ol' blank in the supernatural department.

"That's a great question." Sydney reaches for the bottle of water in his cup holder, takes a swig, and then puts it back in its place. "Cam is Cam. He's no one thing."

"That's…"

"Not the answer you wanted?" Sydney glances over at me.

I snort. "Something like that."

"Cameron's kind of the glue, if that makes sense. Which I'm guessing it doesn't. It will over time, the more you learn of your ancestry and how your partners play a role in your magic."

"You keep mentioning my magic, and I keep doubting it exists." I swirl my index finger over my thumbnail and consider that maybe we have this all wrong. Maybe I'm not really an Oliver. Maybe I don't have magic. Maybe I'm an imposter who is clinging to the hope that she's something that she isn't.

"You've had hidden magic your entire life. It may take some time for it to come to fruition. I wouldn't worry."

I pray to the Angels that he's right, that there's more to me than a washed-up assassin.

"What did you mean about her partners and her magic?" Dash asks from the back seat.

Sydney briefly meets his gaze in the rear-view mirror. "The Olivers are fueled by love. Their magic made more powerful by it, which is no surprise that Olivers are drawn to have multiple mates."

"Willow mentioned a mother and father. Does she only have one partner?" I cross and uncross my legs, unsure of what to do with them. Why am I suddenly so fidgety?

"Yes, but that was from before. Ancient textbooks linked back to the early days suggest that the original Olivers had many partners prior to the curse. It was the cursed magic that put a stop to Oliver's being with their love. A fail-safe of sorts. If the Olivers are powered by love, they are weaker without it, meaning those that wish to steal their magic have a greater probability of doing so."

"That's fucked up," I blurt out.

"It is," Sydney confirms. "And it will never happen again. Willow made sure of that."

We turn down another long lane, this one narrower than the last. It takes a minute before a structure comes into view, but when it does, my eyes widen.

"What is this place?" I inch forward in my seat to study the beautiful architecture of the building. Stone walls with vines wrapped up and down them. The circled pathway out front leads to a lush garden that's concealed by an iron gate.

"This is Harper Academy, or as the supernaturals know it, Harper Shadow Academy." Sydney pulls his car out of the way and puts it into park. "Most of the human faction is on spring break, but there are some that remain." He pivots his body toward us and glances between us. "I'm taking a risk bringing you here. Please don't make me regret it."

I press my hand to my chest. "I promise, I won't."

Dash puts his palms into the air in front of him. "I don't have any magical powers, I'm just weird."

"Aren't we all?" Sydney smiles and reaches for the door handle. "Let's do this."

Carefully, I follow suit, stepping out of the car and stepping onto the gravel. It crunches beneath my feet and distracts me temporarily from my racing heart. I don't move any farther until Sydney approaches and waves us over.

"This way." He strolls through the gated area at a much quicker pace than I prefer.

I want to take my time and consume every detail of this astonishing place. Maybe if things go well, this won't be my last visit to the Harper Shadow Academy.

The door to the massive building creaks when Sydney opens it.

I go through the threshold, something tingling within me at the atmosphere of this place. My eyes desperately scan the contents in their attempt to take it all in. They stop and widen, my head tilting up to admire the enclosed garden smack dab in the middle of the open area. A tree grows right in the center with lavish shrubbery and flowers surrounding it. I step closer, cautiously and wonder how such a thing is possible. Upon further inspection, the roof to the garden seems to also be glass, and doubles as the floor to the second level of the building.

"This is...magical," I whisper. That would be the only explanation of how it would work.

Sydney appears at my side. "It is, actually." He winks and turns around. "This is sort of the main floor common area." He points in the direction we came where extravagant furniture speckles the grand area. "People hang out here between classes. There are stairs to the dorms there and there." He continues to move his hand around to signal to new things. "Down that hallway is the west wing, this is the east, and I'm sure you can guess the north and south are that way."

Sydney waves us over like he doesn't realize how incredibly amazed and entranced I am. "Infirmary is through there." He taps gently on a door that he walks by. "Women's restrooms are there, along with stairs that take you to their dorm." He shifts his body. "Headmaster's office that way and this is..." He leads us away from that grand display in the main area into a large room filled with empty tables. "The dining hall."

The space is vast and open, with windows that line the far wall and allow copious amounts of natural light to rush in. Orange and red echo off the floor from the sunset.

I spin in a slow circle and consider what it might be like when the students are here. Who sits at what table? What kind of food do they eat? Is it loud with chatter or quiet as they keep to themselves? Do the humans and supernaturals co-mingle? How can the supernaturals be so close yet remain hidden? Are humans that oblivious? Or are the supernaturals just that good?

Dash smiles and stays by my side.

"What are they doing out there?" I ask when I spot Willow and someone else out through the windows.

They're standing against the rail of a large patio attached to the back of the school. There are a few empty tables scattered about, and it leads to a grassy area that's encased by a tree line in the distance.

Willow rests her head on a person nearly half a foot taller than her, and from a simple process of elimination, I assume it's her other husband, Deghan. The only one I haven't met yet.

The sun dips out of view in the distance, and the sky changes into a darker shade of orange with pink swirls cascading through it.

"Watching the sunset." Sydney comes near me, his arms crossed over his chest but not in a closed-off kind of way. More like he's admiring the view, too. The one of two people he deeply cares about. "It's kind of his thing." He glances over at me. "That's Deghan, by the way."

I nod and watch Deghan stand from his bent-over position at the rails, his height growing even more. He snatches Willow into his arms and twirls her into a circle before slowly lowering her to the ground. Both of their faces beam with happiness and somehow it warms my heart to witness such a simple, yet intimate interaction.

They share a brief kiss and lock hands, turning and stalking toward us together.

I feel like we should look away, do anything other

than stare at them, but Sydney remains in wait, so I do, too.

"Syd, my man," Deghan says the second he walks through the door. "How was your day?"

"Eventful, to say the least. And the pup training?"

Deghan laughs sharply. "Kept me busy, that's for sure." His gaze trails from Sydney to me, to Dash, then back to me. "And who do we have here?"

"Deghan," Willow begins. "This is Wren, Wren Oliver."

His brows curve up as he continues toward me. He releases Willow, and before I can react, he's wrapped his arms around me into a body-crushing embrace. He lets go, holding me at an arm's length, his gaze scanning my face. "Oliver, ey? I think I see the family resemblance."

I force a smile.

"Pleasure to meet an extension of the family." Deghan turns his focus to the red-headed man beside me.

"And this"—Willow steps close—"is Dash."

"Dash," Deghan tries out on his tongue. He spares no expense, wrapping Dash into his arms and pulling him to his chest. He slaps his back and Dash seems to do the same, not bothered by the smothering affection this stranger is giving him.

"Nice to meet you," Dash says under Deghan's stronghold.

"Deghan's a bit of a hugger, if you can't tell," Sydney mentions all too late.

Willow chuckles and tugs Deghan away from Dash. "You're going to scare them away, Deg."

"It's fine, really," Dash reassures them. "It's a heck of a lot better of a welcome than what I'm used to back home."

"Where is home?" Deghan asks him.

"Prania," Dash says.

I tilt my head in the direction we came from and grow suspicious of how much information we should be confessing so publicly. Are there humans nearby that might hear and question what we're discussing?

"Never heard of it." Deghan flits his gaze to Sydney.

Sydney shrugs. "Me either."

"Weird." Deghan scratches at his scruffy beard. "Have you asked Walker?"

"That's the plan." Willow tilts her wrist toward her to check the time. "He should be back shortly." She looks at me. "In the meantime, I have a theory I want to test. You in?"

I point to my chest. "Me?"

"Yes, you. Mind if I borrow her for a minute?" Willow asks Dash.

"Uh, sure, yeah. As long as she stays safe."

His misplaced concern warms my chest. If anything, I'm the one worried about him going off on his own.

"Without question," she tells him. "We won't be far, just going to go down to the library."

"I'm starving," Deghan announces and latches onto Dash's shoulder. "You hungry? We can raid the kitchen." He tilts his head toward a set of closed doors at the far side of the dining area.

"I could eat." Dash shoots me a wary look.

"I'll be fine," I tell him. "You be careful though." I don't enjoy the idea of leaving him behind, but I won't be gone long, and Deghan doesn't exactly come across as a threat. If anything, he's the nicest out of Willow's husbands, and that's saying a lot considering Sydney has been nothing but gracious—outside of his initial interaction when he found us crashing at his place. And Cameron gave us two boxes of those delicious muffins and offered to bring us more.

Silas isn't in the running, with the whole one word he spoke to me, but even still, I can't imagine he would harm any of us either. Not unless we posed some threat to Willow, and that is something I would never do. She's my family. My *only* family. I would die for her.

Sydney reaches out to gently grasp Willow's arm. "I'll let you know when Walker arrives."

"Thanks, Syd." She steps toward him, standing a bit taller and pressing her lips to his cheek. "And you." She turns toward Deghan. "Stay out of trouble."

Deghan averts his gaze and feigns innocence. "I don't know what you're talking about." He throws his arm around Dash's back and moves him toward the kitchen. He mumbles something to Dash, but I can't quite make it out.

Dash laughs and I know with certainty that everything is going to be okay.

At least, right now, in the short term, it will.

"Follow me," Willow says as she heads in the original direction we came.

Sydney comes with us, but takes a seat in the common area, pulling out his phone and poking the screen to life. "I have some emails to answer."

"Evening, Professor," a round-faced girl mumbles with her face buried in a book as she walks.

"Clara," Sydney acknowledges.

Willow continues forward and walks us down a set of concrete stairs. "That's Clara. Second-year witch."

"Interesting."

"She's a bit of an overachiever, but I can't say I blame her."

We go through a doorway into a room that lights up upon our entry.

"Was that magic?" I whisper, unsure if there's anyone else around.

Willow shakes her head. "No, just a motion sensor. It's to preserve electricity."

"Sounds like magic."

"So, what you see here." Willow extends her arm and motions to the shelves full of books lining the walls and the tables in the open area. "Is the human side of the library." She continues through the space, walking around more tables and past a few rows of shelves. "But this…" She steps through a threshold that appears to be a dead-end to nowhere.

I trail her, but once I'm on the other side, a long, seemingly endless hallway with doors on both sides appears.

"This is magic." She winks at me and goes in a bit farther. "This is the supernatural library, which houses a plethora of ancient and new text covering all things supernatural. There are sections for basic witchcraft, the origins of werewolves, history of most creatures, whatever you can think of, there is probably a book in here *somewhere* covering the topic."

My heart constricts in my chest at the idea that the answers I've been searching for my entire life are under one giant roof.

"It's…incredible," I whisper and press my fingers to the mark on my neck that seems to warm with the growing distance between me and Bo.

Does he feel that distance, too?

"I want you to try something." Willow turns toward me. "I want you to close your eyes, take a deep breath, and allow the angels to guide you."

"The Angels?"

"I know it sounds silly, but just trust me, please."

"What's the worst that could happen?" I say, not expecting an answer. I drop my arms to the side and shake my fingers, releasing the tension within me.

Drawing in a lungful of air, I let it out slowly and pinch my eyes shut.

A quiet humming plays a backdrop to the steady thumping of my pulse.

I stand there and consider whether Willow has this all wrong. Has me all wrong.

Am I wasting her time when she clearly has more important things she needs to attend to?

It's selfish of me to demand her help, especially the more I learn how important she is to this world. I should give up, let her go, and stop bothering her and her mates with my woes.

"Do you feel that?" I ask her with my eyes still shut.

"Let it guide you," she says softly like she understands this strange tugging in my core.

I take a cautious step forward, a sense of relief gently washing over me like a reassurance that I'm going in the right direction. Blindly, I walk foot by foot with my hands out in front of me. Turning down a corner, and then another, I must go for two whole minutes before I feel called to stop.

Blinking myself back to reality, I open my eyes to find a doorway in front of me.

"I believe this is Angel archives," Willow says while stepping into the room.

Why would I be drawn to this room? What information is waiting for me here?

Willow strolls the wall, her fingertip grazing the shelf as she goes by. "I think I studied here years ago when I first came to the academy." She pauses at a shelf, skims the spines, and then latches onto an old dusty book. "This one, yes." She blows on the front, exposing the faded letters, and cracks it open.

I examine the shelf opposite of where she's standing, my gaze trailing the old tomes. Nothing sticks out any more than the last. They're all interesting and my gut begs for me to scour them each, but not in a magical kind of way. More general curiosity than anything else.

That is, until I find my hand hovering along the spine of a larger text, my fingers itching to pick it up. I swallow harshly and give in to the craving, sliding the book carefully out of its home tucked among many others.

With great caution, I walk the thing over to a nearby table and set it on the surface.

"What did you find?" Willow shuts the book in her grasp, returns it to its spot on the shelf, and comes over beside me.

"I don't know," I tell her honestly. "I don't see a title."

"Hmm." She wipes at the cover but doesn't reveal anything other than the leather encasement. "Well." Willow tilts her head toward me. "Ready to find out what's inside?"

My jaw clenches and I grow increasingly unsteady. I've never both wanted and feared something so much in my life. What if this book holds information that will make things worse? What if it uncovers a truth that I'm not prepared to face? What if I really am the monster I believe myself to be, and Willow is there when I find out? What if she rejects me and I lose everything I've gained here in Arthlia?

I've already lost my home, what if even more loss is yet to come?

But before I can choose to succumb or overcome my fears, a figure appears in the doorway. Large, older, and masculine but with a sort of non-threatening aura.

"Headmaster Walker." Willow immediately greets him, rushing around the table to wrap her arms around him.

"Willow." He hugs her back and steadies his inquisitive attention on me.

"Walker." She releases him. "I have someone I want you to meet." Willow points toward me. "This is Wren Oliver. Wren, this is Headmaster Walker."

I nod politely. What are the formalities in this world? Everyone sure does hug a lot, but that isn't exactly how I've grown used to greeting strangers. Do I bow? Shake hands? Offer him something? I don't want to offend him, but I have no idea what I'm supposed to do. I shall make a mental note to ask Sydney once I've departed this magical place.

"Oliver?" The headmaster rubs Willow's shoulder before leaving her side. He glances down at the book in front of me. "Arcane Angelic text."

"You're familiar?" I ask him, my interest getting the best of me.

"May I?" He approaches and points to the book.

"By all means, it's kind of yours anyway." I scoot it toward him.

He flips over the thick cover, exposing a pale beige page with faded, unreadable text. And not because of the condition, but because it's in another language.

"I've never had it translated." Walker fingers through a few pages.

Of course, I would be led to the one book in the room that no one can read. How is that supposed to help answer any of my questions? Including why this book is even of any relevance to me.

"Was there something specific you were after?" He side-eyes me while continuing to move through some of the pages.

I shrug. "I don't know." Glancing at Willow, I silently pray for her to have some input.

Like she could read my mind, she opens her mouth to speak. "Remember when I was struggling at the beginning of my magical journey?"

Walker gives her his attention.

"I came down here, and I was guided toward various texts. I believe it was the Angels leading me toward what I needed to find. That's how I learned more about the Oliver curse, the Harlow curse, the hell dimensions." Willow dips her head to the book none of us can read. "This is where Wren was led. There must be something in there for her."

Walker takes a breath in and runs his hand through

his dark but speckled grey hair. "I see." He rubs his chin. "I can see about having it translated, but it may take some time."

Time. Something I both do and do not have.

I am no longer running for my life, but how can I remain here when I know the truth about what's happening in my homeland? There is no luxury of time regarding Parla and her mission to kill every demon she can get her manicured hands on.

"I would very much appreciate that," I tell him. Because even if it takes forever, it's something he's willing to do. "How can I repay you?"

He shakes his head. "Not necessary. I'm happy to help."

"Speaking of help," Willow says. "I wanted to ask you something."

"Shoot." Walker closes the book and focuses on her.

"Are you familiar with a realm called Prania?"

Walker blinks stiffly. "Why?"

"That's where Wren is from. And Sydney can't find any literature on it. He's scoured the archives, and he came up empty. We figured it's worth a shot to see if you know anything about it."

I chew at the inside of my lip in anticipation of what could be another dead-end.

"That's impossible." Walker's serious gaze rakes over me.

"Do you know something?" Willow questions him.

"I know enough to tell you who you need to talk to."

He hesitates before saying, "But you're not going to like it."

"Why?" Willow and I say at the same time.

"Because Prania is a demon realm." Walker stares at Willow as if that should be enough.

"What does that have to do with anything?" I shift my gaze between them, desperate to read something on their faces that would give me more insight.

Willow's body goes tense. "No."

"Yes," Walker answers her.

"Someone please tell me what's going on." I grip the edge of the table.

"If you want answers about Prania," Walker says. "You're going to need to talk to Balial."

Willow cringes at the very mention of his name but I don't quite understand.

Balial is one of the princes of Hell. What does that have to do with Willow? Why is she so turned off by the idea of speaking to him?

She shakes her head. "No. Not happening."

"I can do it, you don't have to," I suggest. "I wouldn't want to put you out."

"I doubt he would willingly give you information, Wren." Walker adds, "No offense. He's just not the most communicable person in existence."

"And what makes you so sure he would for Willow?"

"They have...history."

Willow grimaces again at that last word. "I'm sorry, Wren. I can't help you."

I get one step closer, and another obstacle is thrown in my direction.

"There must be some other way. I'll go myself and see if he will. How do I get there? I don't know how to realm travel." I'll get down on my knees and beg if that's what I have to do. If there's even a slight chance I can learn about Prania enough to free it from the hold Parla has on it, I'll do anything.

Walker raises a brow. "Then how did you leave Prania to begin with?"

"I, uh." I shift from putting all my weight on one leg to the other. "I had help."

"Help?" he presses.

"Before you freak out, I assure you, the situation is contained." My heart pounds so loudly that I swear it's going to leap out of my ears.

"Who helped you?" Walker asks and Willow stares, both waiting for my answer.

"Tremont." I don't know which one of them to focus on.

Willow folds her arms over her chest. Walker takes a step back.

"I didn't know what he was to you," I insist. "Not until we were already here. Sydney is the one who told me."

"Sydney knows about this?" Willow tightens the

hold she has on her body, her voice growing more frustrated.

"He spelled him to a room in the house. He can't come out. I swear, he seems harmless, really," I spit out every bit of the truth I can to convince them.

"No. You don't know what he's capable of," Willow tells me. "He's a monster."

But if that's how she feels about him, there's no doubt she'll have the same reaction when she finds out what I've done.

Tears well in my eyes, and I blink them away. "I'm sorry. I didn't mean to upset you. I'm not with him. Or on his side. You have every right to be upset. I shouldn't have said anything."

Walker sighs. "You told the truth, Wren, and that means something in my book." He reaches toward Willow, his hand lingering in the air between them. "There has to be some reason Sydney didn't tell us yet. If he thought it were an immediate threat, he would have. We have to trust that he has the situation contained like Wren says he does." He looks over at me like an idea just struck him. "He's confined to a room where?"

"Sydney's estate," I answer without hesitation.

"That means the barrier spell wore off." Walker picks up the angelic book and tucks it under his arm. "I should have stayed up on ensuring it was in place. I'll double-check the wards but it'll require your help." He looks to Willow.

She nods. "Yeah, of course. Whatever you need to keep the academy safe." Willow avoids my wandering gaze. "As far as Balial goes. I'm sorry, but I can't help you."

Her declaration is heavier than being crushed under a passed-out scruni.

"I don't expect you to do this out of the goodness of your heart," I tell her. "I will pay whatever the cost. And I'm willing to do it myself if someone would just teach me how."

Willow lets out a long breath. "This has nothing to do with my heart, Wren. I *want* to help. Probably too much. That's why I'm spread so thin as it is. It's simply a matter of impossibility. There are only so many places I can be at one time, and I'm already overextended on my list of obligations. Unless I can figure out how to clone myself, there isn't enough of me to go around." She pauses and reaches out to grab onto my hand. "I promise you, I'd love to help if I could. Even as much as I loathe that man, I would. But it would require an immense amount of my power to travel there, and I wouldn't be able to fulfill my obligations here."

"What if..." I rack my brain to figure out a solution. "What if I help you? With your *obligations*? There has to be something I can do for you."

"I'm sorry, these are things that only I can do. I can't..."

"Wait—I have an idea." Walker cuts Willow off. "Wren is of the Oliver bloodline."

"And?" Willow says as if she doesn't understand his train of thought.

Although, it's not like I do either.

"Your tasks, while some of them are truly only things that *you* can do. Some are things that require an *Oliver witch*, not necessarily *you*," Walker explains.

"So what you're saying is I *can* help?" Even if it was to simply repay the kindness they have shown me since being in Arthlia, I would do anything.

"If your blood is a close enough match, then yes, it's possible." Walker looks to Willow. "It's worth testing, and honestly, might take some pressure off of you in the meantime."

"I don't know. I..." Willow rubs her hands together and cracks her knuckles. "I'll need to think about it."

It might not be the answer I was hoping for, but it wasn't the one I was dreading. And for now, that will have to be enough.

15

BO

I sit outside by myself on a hard wooden chair not nearly big enough for me to rest comfortably.

Being uncomfortable is something I've grown used to, though.

It's my normal.

The human world is vast, but everything is built for small creatures. Their furniture, their ceilings, their fucking food portions. I have to consume at least five times the *suggested* serving size to feel remotely satiated.

Not that I should complain. Especially when Prania is set up to favor anyone but demons.

No place has ever felt warm or inviting or remotely like home. But Prania is all I know. It's what I was used to. And despite it massively fucking sucking, I can't help but yearn to be back there.

Because in Prania, at least I knew where I stood. I

was the hunted. But in that, I hunted the hunters, and in a way, I enjoyed the sick little game of cat and mouse. The roles reversing each day made my time there a bit more interesting—especially when compared to sitting here and doing nothing.

The chair creaks when I adjust myself, and I worry for a moment that the whole thing will collapse out from under me.

"What are you doing out here?" Wren asks with her arms tucked tightly across her chest.

"Admiring the view." I stare out into the dark abyss of the forest beyond Sydney's house.

"It's pitch black."

"I have night vision."

"What's that like?"

"I'm guessing where you see black, I see shades of grey."

"That's cool." Wren kneels beside my chair and puts her hands on the armrest. "Can we talk?"

"About what?" I don't look at her because if I do, I may lose the ability to restrain myself from taking exactly what I want.

"I need a favor."

I cave and turn toward her. "What?" Can she sense how desperate I am to do anything I can for her?

"I need you to come with me somewhere."

"Where?"

"Balial's hell realm."

"Have you lost your mind?"

"He has answers, Bo. About Prania."

My hand tightens into a fist, but I refuse to let my anger unleash itself. "You don't know that."

"Neither do you," she spits out. "You hate it here. Why wouldn't you jump at the opportunity to go somewhere else?"

"I don't hate it here."

"You're miserable. More so than usual."

"Am not."

She sighs. "Whatever. Fine." Wren stands. "I'll go without you."

I latch onto her wrist. "No, you won't."

Wren tries to yank herself free. "I'm going one way or another, Bo. You can either go or don't, but you can't stop me."

"Let me rephrase then. You're not going without me." The mark on her neck would surely light up if she were *that* far away from me. The distance between here and the academy today was enough to flicker it to life. There's no fucking way I'm allowing her to go to a realm filled with demons with that marker blaring on her neck.

"Was that so difficult?"

"When do we leave?" I ask her while ignoring her own question.

"Tomorrow morning." She pulls herself from my loosened grip and turns to walk away.

"Birdie?"

Wren stops in her tracks. "Yes?"

"Did you ask me because of the mark or because you want me to go?"

"Does it matter?"

"No," I lie. It matters more than anything, but I won't tell her that.

"Then you can decide for yourself what the answer is." She marches away, leaving me here where I began —alone with my thoughts.

I stand in a classroom at Harper Shadow Academy with Willow, Wren, and Sydney.

Willow was strangely nice considering I'm a demon living in her husband's parents' estate. She's prettier than I thought she would be, too. There's something familiar about her, like there are pieces of Wren inside of her because of their bloodline connection. Her presence isn't threatening, but it is powerful. I can sense the magic rippling through her veins at a sheer volume, unlike any other witch I have ever come across.

The witches from Prania were weak compared to the strength of this vibrant woman standing before me. Is that what's in store for Wren when she comes into whatever magic Sydney keeps claiming she has? I don't doubt that there's something hidden under the surface, but I'd be surprised if it's as vast as Willow's.

I could taste the heavenly power upon sinking my fangs into Wren's flesh. There was nothing as sweet as her blood on my lips, but within a split second, I knew the gravity of the situation and that if I didn't restrain myself, I would suck her dry.

I've craved her every moment after but have done everything I can to withstand that hunger. Yet with it, I have deprived myself of blood altogether. Since I tasted her, I have not been drawn to consume another even though it's in my very nature. If I can't have her, I don't want it. I'm not so sure that I could. The thought of draining someone else repulses me.

Biting Wren changed me, and I don't know how I'll ever recover.

It's like her blood in my system somehow altered my entire DNA.

"Are you ready?" Sydney glances at each of us.

I nod while Wren says, "Yes."

"You sure you want to do this?" Sydney asks Willow. "I can come with you."

"I'll be fine. He won't hurt me. It will be better for me to go alone."

He's the prince of hell, how is she so sure he won't harm her?

I've been told that this little mission is harmless, that we aren't actually traveling through the fold the same way we did to get to Arthlia, but we're doing a sort of astral projection that will send us there while our corporal forms remain without putting us in danger. It doesn't really make sense, the whole being in two places at once, but they assured me it's the less strenuous of ways to get there and back quicker. If we fully traveled there, it would require more power and put us all at a greater risk.

Sydney remains rooted in place in the classroom and will be our anchor to Arthlia.

When we wish to return to our bodies, we either say the phrase, *"Copeth trebum,"* or push this little button that all of us got. A failsafe in case we're not able to speak for whatever reason.

"Okay," Sydney speaks. "I need all of you to lie down and hold hands."

"Does it matter who is where?" Wren asks.

"You should be in the middle since you have a strong tether to both Willow and Bo."

We lower to our respective areas, and I reach for Wren.

She weaves her fingers between mine, my entire world rocking despite everything being so incredibly still.

It's just her fucking hand, you idiot.

But when I've deprived myself of her for this long, it's that much more. I want to be fully consumed by her. I want to hold on and never let go and force her to realize just how much she means to me.

I'll never do that though, because it wouldn't be fair to her.

Wes might be able to be selfish enough to allow his hound to claim her, but I care enough to allow her to keep her free will.

Even if it fucking kills me.

"Close your eyes," Sydney tells us. "And don't let go until you're there. If possible, come back at the same time, too." He mumbles something I can't make out. A blur of words that don't sound anything like our language.

My body feels heavier, and then lighter. I keep my eyes shut, noticing the brightness that's quickly replaced with darkness. Heat swells around me, and all I can seem to truly focus on is the small hand wrapped tightly around mine.

"We're here," Willow says from her spot on the other side of Wren.

I blink a few times, allowing my vision to adjust to this new place. It's dark but somehow light at the same time, flames flickering over the barren land. Lava flows like a creek near us, and steam rises from crevices scattered about.

I stand, keeping Wren's hand in mine, not yet ready to let go of her.

She doesn't bother releasing me, either. "It's warm here."

Sweat beads on her brow, and I salivate at the idea of stepping toward her and licking it from her forehead. Anything to taste her sweet essence. Against my growing desire, I restrain myself.

"I've tried getting him to turn the temperature down, but he's rather persistent on keeping things hot." Willow looks around her. "This way."

"You two are like friends or something?" I ask her.

"We aren't friends," she says.

"Or something. Got it." I guess I shouldn't be surprised that a powerful witch has even more powerful connections with people from the underworld.

My boots crumble against the rocky ground, and if I didn't know better, I'd never expect my entire being to actually be here, in this Angel-forsaken place. I *feel* here. The heat covers my body like a cloak, and the stench of rotting flesh and charred ashes greets me. The desolate expanse calls to me—almost welcoming me home.

We follow Willow in a single-file line over an embankment and across a thin walkway surrounded by flowing lava.

Wren moves with ease behind her, never once faltering along the sketchy terrain. She is elegant and covert and if I had to guess, this is a result of her many years of being a hunter.

I do what I can to not stare at her plump ass as she walks, but it grows impossible when it's right in front of me.

"You okay back there?" Wren calls out to me over my shoulder.

"Yep." I give her a thumbs up and look anywhere but her rear end.

My shoe slips and I lose my footing. I slide toward a steep cliff overlooking a seemingly bottomless pit.

But instead of falling, Wren catches my arm and prevents me from tumbling over the edge.

"What the fuck, Bo?" She yanks me onto solid ground. "Did you do that on purpose?" Wren plants her hands on my shoulders and stares up at me. "Bo. Answer me."

Raising my hand, I skim it across her cheek and tuck her hair behind her ear.

"You two good?" Willow pauses to ask us.

"Yeah, we're fine," Wren tells her then focuses on me. "Don't you dare throw yourself off a cliff to get away from me. I can handle you being an asshole, but I can't handle you being gone forever. Okay?"

My attention falls to her lips, soft and plush and begging to be taken.

"Do you hear me?" She shakes me.

"I hear you, Birdie. Loud and clear."

"Good." Wren releases me. "Now go ahead of me so I can keep an eye on you."

My cheeks turn up. "Not a chance."

"Then promise me you won't mess up again." She narrows her gaze.

How can I make that promise when that's all I seem to be capable of doing?

Not just here, but in every facet of our relationship. If it's not one thing, it's another, and everything I do only drives her away from me.

But if that were true, would she be standing here before me asking me not to die? Maybe I haven't lost her after all. Maybe there's still hope that I can fix this. Maybe I should tell her why I am the way I am, and then she could understand why I push her away every chance I get. Why I can't get too close. Why I can't be what she wants me to be.

In doing so, I would have to confess things that I've never told anyone before. And I'm not so sure I'm ready to admit, even to myself, what I keep locked inside.

Instead of giving her the response she wants, I say, "I'll try."

Her chest rises and she lets out a breath. "I can work with that."

Wren returns to her spot in front of me, and Willow and I exchange a nod to signal that we can keep moving forward.

It's only another minute until we step into a foggy clearing. Through the haze, a throne sits in the distance, covered in skulls and bones.

A man rises from the throne, standing tall and peering in our direction. He comes closer, his entire form gliding over the ground like he's hovering about an inch above it. His all-black outfit matches his fully black eyes.

Without meaning to, I kneel and bow my head.

"You may stand," he declares once he's right in front of me. He crosses his arms over his brawny chest and steadies his intense gaze on Willow. "My love. Have you come back to haunt me? Or have you realized you cannot live without me?"

"You wish," Willow says.

"Then you're back for another attempt at torture."

"I'll figure it out one way or another."

"My love, not being with you is torture enough, don't you see?"

"I'll never be with you." Willow shakes her head. "This isn't a social visit, Balial."

"Ah, they never are, are they?" He floats near her and then turns his attention to Wren. "And what do we have here?" Balial closes his eyes and breathes her in deeply. "Another Oliver." He licks his lips. "Bring me a consolation prize?"

A growl leaves my chest, and I step between Wren and Balial.

Balial grins, his extremely white teeth bared. "I see this one is claimed, too." He points to his neck. "Still an alpha mark though." He focuses on me. "What are you waiting for?"

"Bal." Willow steps forward and presses her hand to his chest, immediately snapping him out of his trance on me.

"What can I do for you, my love?"

Screams sound in the distance, followed by the sound of dogs barking.

Wren takes a step forward, her body gravitating closer to mine. "We came to ask you about Prania."

"Prania. Hm." He presses his long finger to his chin. "Doesn't ring a bell."

"Tell the truth." Willow stares at him, her gaze unwavering despite him being who he is.

My demonic nature kicked in the second I saw him, my body betraying me and submitting before him. I might be at the top of the food chain in any other realm, but here, he is superior.

It's not something I'm quite fond of. Although, unlike Arthlia, I know where I stand here.

This hell dimension is much more a home than Arthlia ever could be.

"And what do I get in return?" Balial tilts his head to the side.

"Nothing," Willow retorts without hesitating. "You owe me a lifetime of favors. Don't act like you don't."

What could he have possibly done to get this type of response out of her? The prince of hell owing someone else something? And a multiple something?

"Please," Wren adds.

"Fine," the big bad king of darkness huffs. He hovers back and with his hands out in front of him, he begins. "Once upon a time, there was a great war. One that spread millennia. Sides were chosen, lives were lost. Magic was stolen." He looks to Willow. "I'm sure you're familiar." He pauses for effect and continues. "Realms fought each other, until one day, things got out of hand. The..." He scratches his chin. "Hunters, I believe they called themselves, vowed to eliminate all demonic creatures."

Wren tenses and hangs on his every word.

"This one immortal bitch spearheaded the whole thing. And so, the Angels and some of the princes got together and closed her off into her homeland. The end."

"The end?" Wren blurts out. "That's it? Really? You left an entire realm to fend for themselves even knowing what she was capable of."

Balial turns his hand over and studies his nails boringly. "Mmhm."

Willow shoves him. "Why? Why would you do that?"

"She needed to be contained. This was the only way to make that happen."

"You could have just, I don't know, killed her?" Wren grows angrier and steps around me, but I put my arm out to stop her from going any farther.

"We tried. She kept evading us, and the threat to other realms was too great." Balial shrugs. "You should be thanking me."

"Why not open the realm, give the demons a chance to escape? You left them there to die." Wren shoves my arm. "Don't touch me right now, Bo."

"Prania cannot be opened until Parla is dead. What happens to those demons is no concern of mine, not in the grand scheme of things. Eventually, she will run out of demons to feed on and her immortality will fail. It's only a matter of time until there is nothing left of both Parla and Prania."

"And if I kill her? Then you'll lower the barrier?"

Balial hovers toward her. "You know." He takes another breath. "I thought I caught a whiff of something else on you."

Wren holds her ground, not moving with his advance.

"You're an Oliver...but you're also a...hunter." Balial latches onto her neck and yanks her toward him.

I lurch forward and am met with a powerful force-field keeping me glued to the ground. "Let her go," I yell at him.

Willow plants her arm to the side, a ball of magic forming in her fist. "Don't make me hurt you, Balial. Release her." She readies herself to throw it at him.

But Balial complies and drops Wren from his grip.

She clutches at her neck and gasps for air. "What the hell," she mutters.

Willow rushes to her side, holding her shoulders. "Are you okay?"

I remain stuck in place.

"There are many secrets between you. Ones that will tear you apart. You cannot withstand neither the truth or the lies. Both will be your demise." Balial looks directly at me. "You are not fit for that world, son. You have a place here." He motions to the vast expanse around him. "An endless supply of flesh to feed on. Whatever you want is yours for the taking. Under my command, obviously."

"No one wants to join you here, Balial. Give it a

rest." Willow stands. "Why do you think you're alone? You're a bully."

"My love, what sweet words your delectable lips mutter."

"You're an asshole."

Balial grins. "Like music to my ears."

Willow glances back at me. "We're done here."

"Ah, yes," Balial says. "Such a short visit." He snaps his fingers and Willow and Wren disappear, leaving me here with the prince of hell. "Now that it's just us boys, we should chat."

"I have nothing to say to you," I tell him.

What's the phrase I'm supposed to say to get home? If I could break the hold he has on me, I could reach into my pocket to press the button on the device.

"That's very well." Balial hovers closer. "You know, that marking was quite clever."

"Where did you send them?"

"Your concern is misplaced. I would never harm a hair on Willow's beautiful head. Not again, at least."

"That doesn't answer my question. Where are they?" I grit my teeth.

"Back with the witch that cast the spell to send them here, I suppose. Sydney? Unless they've already abandoned you and moved on from casting another to retrieve you. That's the sinking pit in your gut right now, am I correct?" Balial exhales. "You sure are insecure for such an influential creature."

"You know nothing about me."

"No?" he taunts. "Not even that you're afraid she will no longer desire you if you remove the mark? But that if you do rid her of it, you'd ensure she'd be yours forever. What a predicament."

I swallow harshly. How can he be aware of such things? The things I keep hidden deep within me.

"You'll never have her. Not the way you want her. You're too much like me. And despite her darkness, she'd never accept you for yours. Need I mention, she's marked by a hellhound. That mate bond is already forged and cannot be reversed. Perhaps it was one of mine. I'll leave that to determine later."

Wes never should have succumbed to the pressure of the bond. He should have been stronger and let her go. She deserves much better than what he and I have to offer. She deserves someone like Dash—who is kind and patient and does not pose a threat to her.

"There's another way." Balial touches my chin with his finger. "A way to remove the mark without doing the very thing you fear. She would never forgive you for putting her through that."

"What is it?"

"I would gladly remove it for you."

"At what cost?"

"No cost you wouldn't benefit from."

"Tell me."

"You'd remain here, with me. You'd get the life you always wanted. And you'd free both yourself and her of that heinous alpha marker on her neck. At this very moment, the thing is lighting up brighter than ever before. The distance between the two of you is greater than ever. Any demon near the academy will surely be racing toward her, to end her life with great haste. All you have to do is say the word, and I will eliminate the threat you pose to her."

Wren is at a school for supernaturals, where there are no doubt creatures of the demonic variety. Hell, even Deghan and Silas have enough demonic blood to send them into a frenzy to kill her. And depending on Sydney's origins, he might feel that desire, too. The only one capable of withstanding that urge is Willow, and there's no way she would put herself between one of her mates and some girl she's only just met.

Every second I'm away, the danger rises to an unbearable level.

"Let me go," I yell at him and strain against the magic holding me in place.

Why can't I just remember the stupid fucking words that get me out of here?

"This worry of yours, you wouldn't have it if the mark weren't there."

"I swear to the Angels, I'm going to—"

"You're going to what?" Balial laughs. "I am more powerful than you'll ever be. Where do you think you get your strength?" He comes closer. "It's that demonic blood coursing through your veins." He lowers his voice. "The same that Wren harbors inside of her."

I stop craning against the magic keeping me secured in place. "What?"

Balial covers his mouth. "Oops. I wasn't supposed to say that, was I?"

"You're lying."

"The truth is much more entertaining in this case."

"She's descended from the Angels. I've tasted her, she's pure."

"Yes, you are correct, Wren is very much an Oliver at her core, but you fail to see what's right in front of you. She was a hunter. The most feared of Parla's assassins. She has strength unlike any other yet has never come into her true power. Why do you think that is? Because of her good looks and tenacity?" He shakes his head. "No."

If what he's saying is true, and Wren really does have demonic power inside of her, there's only one way she could have obtained it.

And if that's the case, she's no better than the witches who cursed the Oliver bloodline, or the sadistic bitch who plagues Prania to this day.

"It can't be true. She wouldn't," I tell him.

"Then maybe you don't know Wren Oliver as well as you think you do."

16
WREN

"Where is he?" I yell and jerk Bo's limp shoulders. "He was right there with us, why isn't he back?"

Sydney leans against the wall.

Willow rushes over to him. "Are you okay?"

He nods. "Took more out of me than I thought it would. I underestimated the power it would take to send all three of you."

Willow grabs a chair and drags it over to Sydney. "Here. Sit."

"What's taking so long?" I take in Bo's rugged features and smooth the hair from his face. "Come back to me, Bo," I whisper.

"I'm sorry," Sydney says. "I can't send you back. Not yet."

"Tell me how to do it," I demand. "I can do the spell. I'm a witch, right?"

Sydney shakes his head. "It's too advanced. If you get the slightest pronunciation wrong, there's no telling where you'll end up."

I shift my attention to Willow. "You can do it, can't you?"

"I'm sorry, Wren." Her sad doe eyes don't make it hurt any less.

"Fuck," I blurt out. "Bo." I continue to move his large body. "Can you hear me?"

"What happened?" Sydney asks.

"He attacked her," Willow tells him. "Then started on about secrets." She looks at me. "Do you know what he was talking about?"

"No," I lie. Is it possible Balial can sense the demonic power coursing through me? Is he aware that I'm the worst monster of them all? Is that why he kept Bo behind? To tell him about what I had done and convince him to end my life before I can continue killing demons for Parla.

"Clara." Willow jumps up from her spot next to Sydney and rushes toward the door. "Nothing you need to see in here."

But Clara doesn't listen. Instead, she pushes through into the room and steadies her gaze on me. Dark, threatening, and determined. She heaves her arm in front of her, a blast of green magic flowing from her fingertips and shoving me away from Bo.

I slam into the wall and gasp for breath. An invisible

hand wraps around my throat, tightening and constricting my airway. I scrape my fingers against it but there's nothing there for me to grab onto.

"Clara!" Willow yells as she rushes over to her. She throws herself in the line of the attack but it's no use, the spell is already latched onto me.

My vision blurs and I struggle through the fog to stare at Bo's lifeless body still lying on the floor. Tears well in my eyes. "Bo," I mutter.

In my final moment, I swear I witness him rising to his feet, and with that, I slide comfortably into the darkness.

But instead of death, I'm caught by a stronghold.

"I've got you, Birdie." Bo scoops me into his arms.

"I'm..." Clara's voice fills my ears. "I'm so sorry. I don't know what came over me."

"Is it really you?" I weakly reach up to touch his face.

"I'm here." Bo holds me closer to his broad chest. "I'm here."

"The infirmary," Sydney says. "Down the hall to the right. I'll be right behind you."

"It's not her fault," Bo tells them. "As long as I'm near, she won't have that urge again." He walks us through the room. "Just means she has demon blood in her veins."

Someone gasps but I'm not sure who. If I had to guess, it was probably the sweet and innocent second-year witch who just tried to murder me for no reason other than the demonic pull this stupid marker on my neck has when the alpha who bit me gets too far.

I had a hunch that would happen when visiting Balial's hell, but I was hoping given the nature of our travel, that those same laws wouldn't apply. Now we know astral projection is off the table unless I want any demon around to be alerted to kill me.

"I have to remove this mark from your neck, Birdie. I can't keep putting you at risk." Bo carries me out of the room.

"I can walk," I mutter through my tender windpipe.

"Good for you."

This isn't the first time he's insisted on carrying me when I told him I was fine. And I'm sure it won't be the last. He might pretend he doesn't care, but this is just another instance of him proving himself wrong.

Bo continues around the corner and opens another door, nudging it shut behind him. He flips on a light switch with me still in his grasp and brings me over to a table covered in a thin layer of paper. "If Wes were here, he could fix this for you."

I sit up and scoot myself to the edge of the table while rubbing at my neck. "I'm fine." Between the hold Balial had and then the one Clara did, I am rather sore. "You got back in the nick of time."

"Had I been a moment later, she may have succeeded." Bo lowers his head.

"Don't act like this is your fault. You couldn't have

known Balial would keep you there. It's just as much my fault."

Bo slams his fist into his chest. "I'm the one who marked you, Wren. *Me*. I'm the only one to blame here."

Sydney comes into the room like he promised and makes his way over to us. "I have something that should help." He fumbles with a few vials in a large glass cabinet and plucks two of them out. "Here. Drink this." He hands me one of them and consumes the other himself.

The color returns to his cheeks within seconds and the energy he had lost seems to return.

I drain the one he gave me, the taste bitter on my tongue. Warmth spreads through me, and despite really understanding how, the pressure on my neck subsides. It's still there, but not half as bad as it was seconds prior.

"It will take some time to take full effect, but it should take the edge off." Sydney glances at Bo and then at me. "I'll give you two a minute. I'm going to find something for you to eat."

"I'm not hungry," I tell him.

"It's a witchy thing. You should always replenish after a spell that big to counteract the impact it has." Sydney doesn't bother waiting for my protest. He strolls back the way he came and leaves Bo and me behind.

"Bo." I press my palm on his shoulder. "Will you talk to me, please?"

He clenches his jaw. "I should see if he needs any

help." Bo makes his way across the room but stops when he turns the door handle and it doesn't budge. He tugs and twists it. "It's locked."

I hop off the table. "From the outside?"

"That bastard locked us in here." Bo slams his fist against the door but it doesn't flex in the slightest.

"Let me try." I shove him out of the way.

"Yeah, like you're going to be able to get it if I can't."

I narrow my gaze at him. "Rude." I close my eyes and latch onto the handle, willing whatever power I have within me to rise to the surface.

But no amount of strength will get us through this door.

Sydney didn't *just* lock us in this room together, he sealed us in with magic.

"Well, I guess you can't run away like you always do." I stalk back over to the table and sit back on the crumbled paper.

"I don't run away." Bo crosses his arms over his chest.

"You do, too. Every time you almost say something that might actually let me know what's going through your thick skull, you bolt." I scoot farther onto the table and let my legs dangle over the edge. "What are you so afraid of?"

"I'm not afraid of anything." Bo stays near the door. "You don't know what you're talking about."

"Oh? I don't?" I let out a laugh. "At least Wes can't

lie to me, and Dash has enough respect for me that he chooses not to."

"Is that what you want? Me to be more like Wes and Dash?" Bo throws up his arms. "That's never going to happen."

"I'm aware." I huff. "Angels forbid you have a shred of decency in you."

"Whatever."

"Whatever," I repeat.

We sit there in silence, my heart pattering in my chest the only sound I can make out.

I lie down on the table and stare at the ceiling of this unfamiliar yet sterile room.

How long will Sydney keep us in here? I can only imagine he did it on purpose, but why? Did he know something was going on between me and Bo? Or maybe it was Willow that could sense our tension based on what happened when we visited Balial's hell?

I recall the fear that coursed through me when I woke up and Bo wasn't in that room. He was there, his body, but not him, his soul. The part of him that matters the most. I had no way to get back to him and I was terrified that something had happened in those fleeting moments.

"I was worried about you," I admit.

"When?"

I chuckle. "Always. But I'm referring to when you stayed behind."

"Oh."

"What took you so long?"

Bo sighs. "Balial propositioned me."

I rise onto my elbows. "Sounds kinky."

"Pretty sure he's into Willow, not me."

"Pretty sure he's *obsessed* with Willow. But what did he want with you?"

Bo walks over, drags a chair across the floor, and sits in it backward, facing me. "He offered to remove the mark on your neck."

I sit completely up and return my legs over the edge of the table. "What?"

"Yep." Bo nods.

"I don't get it. Why do you act like that's a bad thing?" That's when it hits me. "What did he want in return?"

"My eternal allegiance."

"What does that mean?"

"He said he would do it in exchange for me staying in his realm. Permanently."

"That's not fucking happening," I tell him.

"It would get the beacon off your neck."

"And what good would that do me if you're stuck in fucking hell? I said no. It's my body, my choice. I'd rather keep the dreaded thing. Besides, didn't you say you can remove it yourself?"

Bo rubs his hand over his jaw. "It's worse than me being in hell, Birdie."

"I'll be the judge of that."

"No."

"Bo, so help me, Angels,...if you don't tell me what it is." I climb off the table and stand in front of him. "How bad could it be? No one has to die. You don't have to spend eternity with that creep of a man. And I wouldn't have the beacon anymore. I see zero downsides."

Bo looks up at me, his lip quivering in the slightest. "I won't do it to you, Birdie."

I grab his face and force him to keep his gaze on mine. "Tell me what it is, Bo. Tell me what you're afraid of."

"I can't."

I lean in closer, my breath mingling with his. Our noses graze and I realize this is the closest our faces have ever been. Despite our few intimate times together, he's never once kissed me.

"Please," I beg him. "What are you feeling right now?"

His intense stare bores into me. "I'm scared. Is that what you want to hear?"

"Bo," I whisper. "Why?"

"For the first time in my life, I feel vulnerable, torn apart at the seams. I finally have something, some*one* to lose that I cannot recover from." His voice is the quietest he's ever spoken. "I'm afraid that the only thing I'm good at is making you hate me, and I'd rather have you hate me than feel nothing at all. If you won't love me, at least you could hate me. I could live with that."

"Why would you ever think I couldn't love you when that's all I've been trying to do?"

"You don't mean it, not really." He reaches up to cup my face in his hand. "It's just the mark."

"I don't believe that." Tears fill my eyes. "This is why you keep pushing me away, because you think the only reason I like you is the mark connecting us?" I let out a laugh. "I was starting to think you actually hated me."

"Oh, Birdie." Bo grazes my cheek. "I could never hate you, not in any lifetime."

"Remove the mark then, please. And then I can show you that it has nothing to do with my feelings for you. Let me at least try to prove it to you."

Bo softly rocks his head back and forth. "The only way for me to rid you of that mark, is to..." His sullen gaze tugs at my heartstrings.

"What is it, Bo? What do we have to do? I'll do anything. Just tell me what it is."

"That's the thing, Birdie. I know you would. And so would I, that's why I can't."

"You have to help me understand, Bo. You're killing me. Is that what you want? To hurt me?"

"Never."

"Please, I need to know."

"I have to replace it."

"I don't understand. Replace it with what?" I scan

his features, desperate to find the answer he keeps hidden from me.

"With a fated mate mark."

I blink and register his words. "I..."

"I won't do that to you," he tells me. "I won't take away your right to choose."

"My right to choose? Isn't that what you're doing now?" A single tear rolls down my cheek. "You dislike me so much that you refuse to be with me? You'd rather go be in hell with Balial than be stuck with me because of some mark?"

"That isn't what I said." Bo rises from his seat, his stature towering over me.

"Then explain it to me." I wipe my face and sniffle. "Why won't you do it?"

"Because Wren, don't you get it? There's no going back from a fated mate mark. Ask yourself this, could you walk away from Wes?"

"Well, no. I wouldn't do that."

"Wouldn't, or couldn't? There's a difference there. It's one thing to be with a person because you *want* to, and it's another to be forced to be with someone because of the mark. I don't want you to be with me because you have no choice in the matter. How do you not realize that I can't be selfish with you? As much as it fucking kills me. As much as I want nothing more than to give in to every fucking desire I have to make you mine, I withstand that urge because it's not fair to you. Wes may not have had the willpower to withstand it, but I do. And I won't do that to you."

"You think...you think the only reason Wes and I are together is because of the mate bond?"

"Can you honestly tell me otherwise?"

"I...I'm not fated to Dash, and I want to be with him."

Bo sighs. "It's Dash. He's the perfect guy. He's the one you should be with. Not me. Not Wes."

"You want me to choose?"

Bo puts his large hands on my shoulders. "I want you to *have* the choice, Wren."

"Then I choose all of you."

"You don't get it. Not when your head is clouded with the marks. And the only way I can make you see what it's doing to you is to take Balial up on his offer."

I take a step back. "You're going to say yes?"

"I have no other choice, Birdie."

"So you get to make the decision for me, under the pretense that you're doing what's best for me? That's not fair and you know it."

"This is the only way."

"No. I refuse to accept that."

"I already told you...I can live with you hating me."

"If you leave me, you can guarantee that I will."

"If that's what it takes, Birdie. I'd give you that."

"That's not what I want, Bo." My shoulders tense and my hands ball into fists. "You'd rather leave me than face the possibility that we might have actually had a chance." I turn on my heel and march away from him and toward the door. I grip the handle and yank with all my might. It's strong and the hold is firm but it's no match to how fucking determined I am to get away from him.

17

WREN

Bo ignores me more than I ignore him.

He sleeps in the chair in our bedroom but doesn't come in until he's convinced I'm already asleep.

I'm not.

No, I stay up all night, unable to fall into a slumber, and I consider what I could have done to make him prefer spending eternity in a hell dimension instead of staying here as my mate.

He says he's doing it to give me a choice in the matter, but what actual choice has he allowed me?

Is life in Balial's realm more appealing to him than staying in Arthlia? I wouldn't be surprised if that would be the case, but is he really ready to give Wes, Dash, and Jade up, too?

Jade will remain with Everest, wherever they end up —that much is given.

Wes and I won't leave each other, and Dash doesn't seem like he's wanting to go off on his own. The only person hanging in the balance is Bo, and he's made his decision to accept Balial's offer.

The thought of him leaving cuts like a hot knife through my chest. How did I go from wanting to end his life when we first met to not being able to imagine a world without him?

Is leaving that easy for him?

Wes and Dash sleep soundly at both of my sides. Wes with his arm thrown over my stomach, and Dash with his freckled face buried in his pillow.

Carefully, I peel Wes off me and sit up.

He stirs but goes right back into his peaceful slumber.

Without making a sound, I scoot from under the covers and inch to the foot of the bed. Then, I hop over and onto the floor.

I hug the loose sweater around my chest and tiptoe through the room, the door creaking on my way out and almost giving me up. The hall is quiet and desolate, and it welcomes me with its solitude. My footsteps silently descend the stairs, and once I'm at the bottom, I release the breath I had been holding. Sydney's house is vast and has an eerie ambiance to it that only comes with the memories of something terrible.

Growing up the way that I did, I'm familiar with tragedy.

Every single person in this house has their own trauma.

Maybe that's why we get along, because we share in the agony of what our past has dealt us. The real test is what we choose to do with our suffering. We can inflict that same pain on others in an attempt to settle the score, or we can overcome the hardships we've experienced.

Dash is a perfect example of someone who perseveres despite everything that's happened to him. And Bo and I are the opposite, we have taken our past and allowed it to shape us into the murderous psychopaths we are today.

I want to do better. Be better. But it's hard when that innate desire to kill still remains.

At least now I've channeled it into wanting to end Parla and free Prania from her hold.

But how will I be successful if I'm here, in Arthlia?

My entire life, I've never thought it was possible to escape Prania. People talked about it in hushed conversations or drunken moments. It was a fever dream that could never come true. Yet I am living proof that there is more out there than the forsaken remnants of my homeland.

"Couldn't sleep?" His deep voice nearly makes me jump out of my skin.

"No." I shut the fridge, empty-handed, and consider snatching a banana off the counter. I don't. "You?"

Bo leans there in the doorway, his arms crossed

over his chest. The grey sweatpants he's wearing leave little to the imagination. "No."

I stalk toward him with every intention to go right by and back up the stairs.

"Can we talk?" he says when I'm inches from him.

I pause in the doorway but don't look up at his ruggedly handsome face. "Now you want to talk?"

"Yes."

"What's left to say, Bo?"

He slams his hand up on the doorframe, caging me between it and him. Bo takes his other hand to grip my jaw and tilt my head toward him. His dark gaze darts between mine like he's trying to say something without words.

But doesn't he know I can't read his fucking mind?

"You don't get it, do you?" he whispers.

I swallow at his nearness—his breath that kisses my cheek. "Explain it to me."

His thumb grazes my bottom lip. He leans in closer and inhales, his eyes widening. "You're bleeding."

"What? No, I'm not." I turn my hands over in front of me and examine my arms. "I'm fine."

Bo drops to his knees, his hands on my hips. He drags his nose over my crotch. "Birdie." He stares at me through his thick, dark lashes. "I want to taste you." Bo clutches the sides of my bottoms. "I need you to stop me."

But how can I do that when it goes against every desire consuming me?

"No," I tell him. "I won't."

"You're giving me permission?" The defiant alpha doesn't move, not even when I nod. "I need you to say it, Birdie."

"You have permission."

His chest rises and falls dramatically, and he yanks my sweats over my ass, along with my panties, exposing me to anyone who might walk by. Bo inches closer and grinds his nose against me, only this time, I'm no longer covered by clothing. "Fuck," he moans.

My body gravitates toward him, a traitor to the early version of me who was trying to avoid the man who would rather abandon me. But it's the furthest thing on my mind when he's swirling his long, split tongue over my clit and dipping it into me.

I've never been one to shy away from a little action while on my cycle, but no one has ever practically begged to go down on me while I was actively bleeding.

And never in a million years did I think I would be *this* turned on by it.

Bo grips the back of my legs and digs his fingers in. His claws prickle but do not quite penetrate my flesh. Only a small taste of the pain heightens my already rising pleasure.

I shouldn't give in to him, but it's hard when he's this fucking tempting.

"Birdie," he breathes against me. "I don't think I can..." With my fingers weaved through his hair, he glances up at me in the dimly lit space. "I want you so fucking bad."

"Then what are you waiting for?" I nearly pant in anticipation for him to keep going.

"I'm afraid I won't be able to restrain myself." He licks at his lips. "You taste...divine."

"I trust you," I tell him, the words surprising me probably more than they do him.

"You shouldn't."

"That isn't going to stop me."

Just when I think he might actually end things, he moves forward and presses his lips to mine. His tongue darts out, coating and swirling and tasting every drop of me. His fangs gently scrape my skin, and I do everything I can to remain upright and not melt into a puddle on the fucking floor.

"Angels," I moan and spread myself wider to give him better access.

He slides my leg over his shoulder and cups my ass with his large hand, pulling me closer. Bo takes his hand and slides his finger along my soaked entrance.

With no warning, I climax the second he pushes into me, my orgasm rattling through me and shattering on his hungry mouth. I bite down on my lip to suppress my moans as he laps me up.

He keeps going, long after the tremors have stopped. Bo shoves another finger inside of me, the width of him spreading me open. My core tightens and my pleasure builds under his influence again.

He rocks himself deeper inside of me and tilts his grasp up, hitting me in just the right spot to send sparks flying in my eyes. I whimper and thrust my hips against him.

Heat swells between my legs, and I can no longer withstand the sudden urge to come yet another time. It's no surprise that I'm hornier than usual when I'm on my cycle, but Bo seems to know his way around my body better than I do.

Better than anyone else ever has.

How infuriating that it's him, though, when he would rather leave than be with me.

Bo slows his movement and draws out his hand. He licks every bit of me off his fingers before rising to his feet, pulling my bottoms up on his way. He towers over me, his dark gaze melting into mine.

"I'm still mad at you," I say.

"I know."

"This doesn't change anything."

"I know."

I want to yank him by the collar, pull him toward me, and kiss him, while also wanting to slap his face and shove him away. Both equally vying for my attention. But I do neither. Instead, I stand here, desperately wishing for things to be different. For him to see me for who I am and what I have to offer and accept that maybe the possibility of a future together is something worth fighting for. That will never happen though, and if I've learned anything from Bo, it's that changing his mind once he's made it is an impossible feat.

But considering we started out as complete enemies, maybe hope isn't entirely lost.

"You didn't kill me," I announce.

"I guess I have more control than I thought I did." His tongue glides across his lips. "That doesn't mean I didn't want more, though."

I recall the first moment we met. Bo had rushed toward me and sank his fangs into my neck, marking and solidifying our connection. I was lightheaded but a euphoric feeling coursed through me, and I'd be lying if I said I hadn't missed that strange and unfamiliar sensation. There was something incredibly intimate about his fangs penetrating my flesh and my blood pooling in his mouth. I never understood the appeal of the blood sharing we were taught about in our training, but now, the attraction is very much there.

I want Bo to drink from me.

No, I *need* Bo to drink from me. The desire is far too visceral to be a simple want.

Does he have any idea just how badly I want to be entangled in him? Body and soul.

Maybe it's the mark making me crave him that much more, but whatever it is, no amount of hate for him will deter me from not giving up. I have every reason to put that final boundary between us and call the death of our relationship before it's even begun, but

I can't bring myself to stop chasing after something that I think, deep down, he really wants, too.

I skim my fingers over the scar on my neck. "Do you want to bite me?"

"No."

"Are you lying?" I move my hair off my shoulder and expose the area to him.

He clenches his jaw. "No."

I tilt toward him. "You know you want to."

"Wren." He uses my name like a threat but it doesn't have the impact he wants.

No, it only tells me just how badly I'm getting under his skin.

I grab his hand and force his fingertips over the mark. "Just a little taste."

Bo snarls, his fangs showing. His gaze flits to my neck, to my eyes, and back down. "I can't." He pauses and adds, "I shouldn't."

I stand a bit taller and tug him toward me. "What's the worst that could happen?"

"I could kill you."

I shrug. "I'm not scared." At this point, I'd say anything to get him to follow through.

"You should be." A low growl leaves Bo before he leans down and presses his lips around the scar. He hesitates for what feels like an eternity, and my flesh snaps as he sinks his teeth into my neck.

Ecstasy cascades through me, and immediately, I feel faint.

His strong hold keeps me upright as my blood flows into his mouth. There is no agony, just sheer pleasure of his intimate nearness. I melt into him and bask in this moment for fear that it will end too quickly. That maybe *I* will end too quickly. But death isn't what scares me. No. What I fear is losing this moment with him. Not experiencing it fully. I'm overwhelmed with wanting it to last, to slow time and be here, in this temporary heaven with him.

Bo bites down harder, his teeth penetrating me deeper.

I grow cold despite his warm embrace. I need to feel him. To be enveloped by his entire existence and allow him to swallow me fucking whole.

Both literally and meta-fucking-phorically

I don't want him to stop, not now, not ever. If this is what it takes to be close to him, I'll take whatever I can get. Even if it results in my death. Because what is love without a little sacrifice?

Bo releases me quickly, his gaze frantic as it scans my face. "Birdie," he breathes, the scent of my blood lingering. "Oh Angels, what have I done?"

My body, still and paralyzed, remains in his grasp. I part my lips but nothing comes out.

I am weak, tired, but so content.

"Fuck," he blurts out. "What have I done?" Bo scoops me into his arms, lifting me from the floor. He rushes out of the room and up the stairs.

His jaw tenses, his face so fucking beautiful from this angle. He holds me tighter than he ever has.

Bo darts through the doorway of our shared bedroom and rushes over to the bed.

My heavy eyes close, and there isn't anything I can do to keep them open. Here, I am home in his embrace.

"What's wrong?" Wes mumbles, his presence growing near, too. "What the fuck did you do to her?"

"I...I..." Bo lowers me onto the mattress where Wes must have just risen from.

I tuck into myself and lie there, still and blissful.

Don't they see that their concern is misplaced? There is nothing wrong.

Wes leans in. "Wren, baby. Can you hear me?"

"Mmhm," I mumble.

His voice grows quiet but more intense. "I'm going to fucking murder you."

"I didn't mean to," Bo responds with a hint of concern unlike I've ever known from him.

"Stop arguing," I manage to spit out. "I asked for it."

"What's going on?" Dash says sleepily.

"Be quiet," Wes snaps.

I try to sit up but my body won't seem to cooperate with any of my normal commands. Everything is somehow heavy and light, all at once, and no matter what I do, I can't get anything to function properly. What I'd really like is to fall asleep—to drift off into the abyss and savor this decadent release from reality I'm consumed by.

Wes comes toward me, his lips hovering next to my face. He moves lower, mumbling something I cannot make out, and then comes closer again. "Come back to me." He lets out a soft breath. "Give me your pain. I accept your suffering. Allow me to carry that burden."

But what he doesn't understand is I'm not in pain. And the suffering I'm experiencing isn't physical. It's something internal I can't quite get my hands on. It's discouragement mixed with helplessness at not knowing how to fix everything I've broken.

If I could end Parla, maybe I could make things right. But until then, how can I play pretend that anything is okay? People are dying and it's my fault. I gave her too much power, and she ate up every bit of it.

Even with Bo's euphoric venom coursing through me, I can't ignore the truth of what's really happening. That I must kill her if I stand a chance at ever moving forward in this life. No matter the distance between Prania and Arthlia, I cannot escape or forget what she's doing.

And when I regain the strength to control my bodily functions, I open my eyes and declare the one thing I cannot get off my mind, "I must murder Parla."

"You're okay." Wes tucks my hair behind my ear, his eyes glowing softly as he watches me intensely. "You're going to be okay."

"I have to kill her, Wes. There's no other way."

"Shh." He's soft and gentle despite his dominating exterior. "You should rest."

I sit up in my attempt to convince him that I'm fine. "I'm not joking, Wes," I say with a bit more conviction. I shift my focus to Bo, who remains like a statue, secured in place with a concern still lining his brow. "I'm going back, I have to go back."

"To Prania?" Bo speaks, his voice strained.

"You're not going back there," Wes says.

But I don't look at him, I keep my gaze on Bo, because he might be the only other one in this room that truly understands how fucking badly I hate Parla. Regardless of our differences, at least we have a common enemy.

"I'm with you, Birdie." Bo takes a small step forward, almost like he's testing the distance between us.

"This is not up for discussion tonight." Wes turns toward Bo. "You need to watch your mouth."

Bo crosses his arms over his chest, the one that I had been pressed against not too long ago. "Don't tell me what to do."

"I shouldn't have to, Bo. You're a fucking adult. But here I am, cleaning up yet another one of your messes. You're a child and you must be stopped." Wes stands from the bed and positions himself between me and Bo.

"Guys, come on." Dash yawns and pushes himself onto his butt. "Is this really necessary?"

"Yes," Wes and Bo mouth off at the same time.

I scoot off the bed, throwing my legs over the side, the weight of them heavier than I remember them being. With Bo's venom no doubt still in my body, the effects of his bite linger.

Bo reaches toward me, but Wes shoves his arms away.

"Don't touch her." Wes's hound side surfaces, his entire body glowing. "You have no self-control."

Bo laughs loudly. "Are you fucking serious? I don't? Who's the asshole who fucking marked her because he couldn't keep it in his pants?" He steps dangerously close to Wes, not daring to back down from him. "You're a coward. You couldn't fathom the idea of her not choosing you so you took that choice away from her."

"Did not." Wes pushes his torso against Bo's.

Bo shoves into Wes. "Selfish prick."

Wes burns brighter, his fiery self becoming more present.

"I'm not afraid of you." Bo stares directly at Wes. "You want to burn me, burn me. Doesn't change what you did."

I slide off the bed, wedging my weak body between them. "Both of you"—I look briefly at each of them—"need to grow up." I push past them and march toward the door, not bothering to look behind and witness whether they've decided to murder each other.

Crossing the threshold, a chill washes over me, and my attention locks onto the small opening in the doorway across the hall. A shadow appears in the illuminated space, his body moving around the door to come into view. "My apologies," he says. "I was having trouble sleeping and heard the commotion."

"It's fine." I fold my arms over my chest and stand there, a few feet away from him.

He remains in his room because that's his only option. Tremont cannot escape the confines of that small space—not until Sydney decides what he's going to do with him.

Tremont doesn't seem bothered by it. Mostly, it's as though he's accepted his fate and realized there's nothing that can be done to rid him of this confinement. He hasn't begged for his release or tried to convince anyone to let him out. He takes the food Sydney brings him and leaves the empty plates in the doorway. The room he's in has a bathroom and more accommodations than Rockbridge, so he hasn't exactly lacked in comfort at all.

After having endured what he has, I'm not convinced I would put up much of a fight either. Especially knowing how similar our paths were. He's not in the wrong for feeling defeated. There's a part of me that pities him, but I recognize that's the same part of me that wishes there was a way to make amends for what I have done. Perhaps I wouldn't sympathize with him as much had I not realized that my heroic acts only turned me into the villain in someone else's story.

"I don't blame you for wanting to go back," he says.

"How much did you hear?" I ask him.

"Enough."

I nod and avert my gaze while remembering the conversation. My head is still fuzzy, and I'm going to need to sleep off the venom high, but one thing is certain, I wasn't lying when I said I needed to kill Parla. It's the only scenario where contentment remotely finds me. Every other alternative leaves me with a sinking pit in my stomach.

"I don't know how I'll get there," I admit. Cross-realm travel wasn't in the teachings during my hunter training, and until recently, I had no knowledge of the hidden magic within me. I'll have to consult Sydney and see if he is willing to assist me on my final assassination mission.

Dash joins me in the hallway, his body gently pressed behind me. He rubs gentle circles on my shoulders, and it melts away some of the tension overwhelming me. "Hey, you." He kisses the side of my face.

"Evening." Tremont nods to Dash.

"Sir." Dash's manners have no bounds.

Tremont focuses back on me, his gaze strangely more serious than before. "When you're ready, I can help you." He pauses only slightly and then disappears back into his prison.

"What was that all about?" Dash continues skimming his arms over my biceps.

"Nothing," I lie and weave my fingers through his. "I'm going downstairs. Want to come?"

"Duh." He yawns and swoops the hair off his brow

with his free hand. "You know I'd go anywhere with you."

I don't respond, not when my mind runs wild at the possibility that maybe Dash could come with me to Prania. It's not that I want to put him in danger, but if he *is* a phoenix, what's the harm in having someone who supports me there? I'm not particularly sold on inviting either Wes or Bo, and after everything that's happened to Jade, I would never ask her to return to such a place. Sydney and his family have been gracious, but I could never put them in danger, not in the way that Prania would. It's not their fight and it would be careless of me to involve them any more than I already have.

Dash and I walk down the stairs, the creaking of his steps a bit louder than mine.

It isn't until we're in the large living room some distance from the kitchen that I finally speak. "Would you ever go back to Prania?" Relaxing into the couch, I turn toward Dash, who settles in, too, opposite of me.

Dash sucks in a breath and exhales. "I mean, I can't say it sounds very enticing. I didn't exactly fit in, but I'd be lying if I said I felt like I fit in anywhere. Why? Is that why you've been on edge lately? You want to return to your homeland?"

"I've been on edge? How so?"

"I don't know." Dash extends his arm over the back of the couch and finds my hand. He swirls his finger along my skin. "Nothing major. I've just felt it. Something different. A shift. A sort of unspoken internal struggle. Whatever it is, you can tell me. Or you don't have to. That's okay, too."

"Dash…"

"I hope you don't think that's weird. I care about you, so I notice things."

My heart constricts. "It's not weird. It's…unfamiliar. I've never had someone look out for me before. Not the way you do."

Dash forces a smile. "I don't plan on stopping, so get used to it."

"How are you, Dash?" It's my turn to focus on him for a chance. He's been going through his own things lately, and I've been consumed with my own bullshit that I haven't checked in. "How's your back?"

"It's fine. I'm fine. Don't worry about me."

I narrow my gaze. "Look at you being all evasive."

Dash chuckles and his eyes sparkle with that beautiful Dash-like twinkle. "I'm good, sweetheart." He leans in closer and kisses my hand. "When are we leaving?"

I blink at him. "What?"

"You want to go back. When are we leaving?"

"To Prania?"

He nods stiffly.

"Oh. I—I would never ask that of you." Even though having him there with me would be equal parts great and terrible. I don't want to put him in danger, but there is a silver lining to his phoenix abilities. Perhaps I'm being selfish for desiring his presence.

"You're not asking, I'm offering. I want to go with you. I want to be there. Whatever you need. I'll be there for you." He pauses and adds, "Do you plan to stay, or is it something more short-term?"

I let out a breath I hadn't realized I had been holding. "I have to kill her," I whisper, the declaration barely audible.

"I understand," he says.

"You do?"

"What she did to you, to Wes, to Jade, to everyone in that realm—it was wrong. She deserves to be punished. Death is too kind for what she deserves."

I would love to torture her. To make her pay with every ounce of pain I could potentially inflict. But the only sure way to stop Parla from hurting anyone else is to slide a blade straight through her cold heart.

"Tremont said he could help," I admit.

"Do you trust him?"

"Not really. But he got us here, didn't he?"

"Why not ask Sydney or Willow?"

I shake my head. "I don't want to bother them any more than I already have. They've done enough. More than enough, really. This isn't their battle."

"Well, I support whatever decision you make." He sighs and leans back, extending his arm to invite me toward him. "In the meantime."

I smile softly and scoot into his embrace, the

warmth of him swallowing me whole and encasing me in a sea of comfort.

He drags the blanket off the back of the couch and covers us up. Dash kisses my forehead. "Get some rest, we'll come up with a plan in the morning."

Everything might be up in the air, but at least I can count on Dash to be with me to see things through.

I just hope going back to Prania, especially with Dash, isn't a grave mistake.

I would never forgive myself if something happened to him.

18

DASH

"And you're sure we'll be back by tonight? I told Willow I would help her." Wren asks Tremont from her spot leaning against the wall in Tremont's bedroom.

According to the information Wren gave me, she did some kind of test to determine that her blood was a close enough match to Willow's to ensure that she could act as Willow to help take some things that only Willow could do off her plate. Supposedly they are not threatening in any capacity, just time-consuming when Willow has many obligations to maintain. Wren was eager and willing to help.

"Yes," Tremont tells her. "If you haven't returned on your own, I will pull you out myself."

"I don't like this," Bo announces.

But Bo doesn't exactly ever like anything, so it

comes as no surprise he's not thrilled about me and Wren taking a quick trip to Prania without him.

Wren side-eyes him briefly but doesn't give him any more attention than that. "What do you need me to do?"

"You and Dash need to lie down and hold hands. You'll have to open yourself up to me again. Do you remember what that was like back in Prania? It gives me access to your magic. I won't need much since this is simply astral projection, but it will make penetrating the barrier into Prania easier than with my magic alone."

She nods. "Okay, yeah. I can do that." Wren tilts her head in my direction. "You ready for this?"

"I am if you are."

Wren makes her way over to Wes, who has remained quiet through this whole interaction. She stands taller and presses a kiss to his cheek. "I'll see you soon."

Wes wraps his arms around her and tugs her toward him. "I'm not a huge fan of this either," he whispers to her. "So hurry back."

Wren didn't want Bo to come, mostly because she wants the alpha beacon to engage. I'm sure it had something to do with their constant disagreements, too. And with Wes's immense authority, it was too much for Tremont to manage, leaving me as the most viable choice. I kept it to myself that I had already asked Wren about coming with her in my attempt to not make them feel any less important than they really are to her.

I might be aware that she's capable of caring for us all, but that doesn't mean they've wrapped their heads around it yet.

Bo exhales dramatically and storms out of the room.

Wes points to Tremont. "I'll make you suffer if something happens to her."

Tremont nods. "I'd expect nothing less."

"Keep an eye on him," Wren tells Wes.

"I will." He pecks her lips quickly with his and leaves in the same direction Bo had gone in just moments prior.

Wren makes her way toward the center of the room, lowers herself onto the rug on the floor, and pats the spot next to her. "Let's do this."

I follow her over, repeating the same movement, and lie next to her. Weaving my fingers through hers, I close my eyes and wait for what comes next.

"Just relax," Tremont says. He mumbles a few words under his breath, the language unknown.

Wren holds me tighter and rubs her thumb along my hand.

Tremont continues chanting and within another few seconds, it's like I'm being sucked into a vacuum and spit out.

The air is thicker, heavier, and filled with a stench I had hoped I'd never smell again.

"We made it," Wren declares while rising to a sitting position.

I blink through the dense fog and take in my surroundings. It's familiar and foreign all at once. Most of Prania looks the same with its murky atmosphere and lack of lighting. It's nothing like Arthlia.

"What's the plan again?" I ask her, the details of it blurring in my head now that we're actually here.

"Everest said there's a group of insurgents in the north that we could rally. The goal is to make contact with them." Wren pulls a compass out of her pocket. The little dial moves and rocks, but then settles itself into position. "This way." She rises to her feet and reaches down.

I latch onto her and allow her to help me up. "Thanks."

"Of course." She presses her fingers to the wound on her neck. The one that was reopened last night. "It's hot so I'm guessing it's on."

"Are you in pain?" I hadn't considered what else that mark entailed outside of it alerting demons to her whereabouts. Perhaps I would have been more hesitant about Bo not coming along had I known it would cause her pain.

"No," she says. "It's fine."

The same thing I had said to her when she asked me how I was yesterday.

I wasn't lying, but I wasn't telling the truth either.

Is that what she's doing now?

I couldn't have answered her truthfully even if I wanted to. I don't know how to explain how I am. Nothing is technically wrong. But I keep having these vivid nightmares that feel more like long-forgotten memories than dreams. Some of them cause actual physical discomfort, and some tear at my heartstrings more than others. They've made me question reality a bit more, but overall, it isn't anything I can't handle on my own. Wren has enough going on, and my bad night's sleep is nothing she should concern herself with.

"You still have the button Tremont made for you, right?" Wren dusts her legs off and examines the compass again.

"Yeah, do you?"

She pats her pocket and nods. "This way." Wren navigates us through the wooded area we're surrounded by.

A chill creeps up my back at how strangely eerie and quiet it is here.

Prania has never been a place of much commotion, but generally, there are other demons or hunters making some kind of noise.

We walk side by side for a few minutes, our footsteps crinkling against the ground. Wren's are softer than mine—her stealth hunter nature doing what it can to conceal her presence.

I do what I can to match her movements, but I'd need years of training to be as sly as her.

"What if we come across demons first?" I whisper.

"We reason with them." She continues forward. "There will be no more demon bloodshed."

I never thought I'd see the day when a hunter as fierce as Wren would put a stop to the unjust killings. This life is all I've known and for my entire time in Prania, there wasn't a single hunter that didn't want to kill either of my friends. And they would have done the same to me the second they found out I wasn't on their side. There was no reasoning with them. The only thing they were capable of was ending demons and nothing else.

Wren throws her arm out in front of me, stopping dead in her tracks. Her intense gaze meets mine, a silent warning to not make a sound. She looks past me, turns her head, and stares behind her. "Something is coming," she mutters enough for me to hear.

I barely have time to blink when a blur flashes across my vision, tackling Wren to the ground many feet away from where she just was.

Her scream pierces through my chest, and I can't possibly move fast enough to get to her.

A large, off-white wolf-like creature pins her to the ground, its teeth snapping at her neck as she holds it off the best she can. She keeps her arms extended and her head to the side to avoid its ferocious bite.

I run toward her and do the only thing I can think of —I leap toward it, hoping the weight of my blow will knock it off her and give her a chance to escape. The beast can tear me to shreds but I refuse to allow it to hurt another hair on her beautiful head.

I throw my arms around the wolf's torso and pull with all my might.

The two of us spin and hit the ground hard, dust flying up around us.

"Run!" I yell at Wren before the thing tosses me aside and sets its sights back on her.

It bears down, scraping at the dirt with its claws as it snarls at her, its mouth salivating.

Wren throws up her arms. "I'm not here to harm you. Please see that."

But this creature does not care; it wants to end her life.

I gasp for breath and rise to my feet, scurrying quickly to position myself between her and the animal. But it's no use, the thing leaps toward her at a rate faster than I could ever manage.

I watch in horror, her arms lowering and shielding herself from impact. But the impact never comes.

Seconds before the thing makes contact, another creature barrels through the clearing and slams into the wolf's side, tossing it away. Just when I think the worst has yet to come, Wren's savior turns toward her and releases a heavy breath.

"What are you doing here?" the familiar person asks.

Wren takes her in, her eyes scanning the dull-blue

woman standing in front of her. "Pippa," Wren sighs and throws her arms around the person. "You're alive."

Pippa hugs Wren back, her trunk wrapping around Wren's small torso. "Barely."

Wren releases her and holds her at an arm's length. "Where's Lo?" She scans the direction Pippa just came.

Pippa slowly shakes her head. "He didn't make it."

The wolf that Pippa tackled whimpers and struggles to get to its feet.

I rush over, my sights settling on the claw marks on Wren's arm. "You're hurt."

Wren shrugs, not at all bothered by the bleeding wound. "It's fine."

No doubt another lie. But because things could have been a lot worse, I decide to let it go for now.

I rip at the bottom of my shirt until I've pulled off a long, thin strip of fabric. Without Wren's consent, I secure it around her biceps to stop the continued bleeding. Wes can tend to it once we have returned home.

"I'm so sorry, Pippa," Wren tells her but glances over at the wolf. "Who's the mutt?"

"That's Gary. He's a bit of a hot head." Pippa points to her neck but looks at Wren's. "That thing is sending out a massive signal."

Wren grazes her fingers over it briefly. "Yeah. That was kind of the point. I guess I just didn't think it through fully." She scans Pippa's dirty face. "What's stopping you from tearing me apart?"

Pippa forces a smile and reaches out to touch Wren's shoulder. "I know you're not the enemy."

Wren puts her hand on top of Pippa's. "I just need to convince the rest of the demonic population of that, too."

Pippa steps in front of Wren when Gary saunters over. "I'll snap your neck if you touch her again." Pippa glances behind her. "I owe Wren my life, and if you're going to make me cash that in today," she turns back toward the wolf. "Then so be it."

Gary whimpers and lowers his fur-covered head in submission.

"Fill me in," Wren tells Pippa. "What's happened since I saw you last?" Wren glances down at her compass. "Mind if we walk this way while we talk?"

"Sure." Pippa steps past Gary but remains at Wren's side.

I lead up the rear, keeping myself between Wren and her attacker. I won't be too much of a diversion, but maybe it'll be enough to allow Pippa to save Wren if Gary decides to go after her again.

"Things have worsened," Pippa says. "Many demons were killed in that poison fog at Rockbridge. Those of us that escaped sought refuge together, but it wasn't long until Parla and her soldiers sniffed us out. It was like she could track us somehow."

"I wonder if she put trackers in the prisoners without their knowledge. Or slipped something into the food. We had to eat at some point, so it would almost guarantee that she could slip it into our system."

"There's no telling but I wouldn't be surprised." Pippa steps over a log and continues walking. "They keep taking us out. One by one. It won't be long before they've won." She laughs dryly and puts her hands out in front of her. "What a prize."

Wren lets out a breath. "She's sick and twisted. Parla won't stop until she's killed every last person who disagrees with her way of life." She glances over at Pippa. "Speaking of, where can I find her?"

Pippa's shoulders rise and fall. "Beats me. I tend to try to avoid her. You know, the whole self-preservation thing."

"Understandable."

"Where have you been hiding out?"

Wren flits her attention back at me before opening her mouth to speak. "Arthlia."

Pippa stops and I nearly run into her. "That's impossible."

Wren pauses, too. "It's not. We left the day after Rockbridge. We've been there about a week."

"A week? Honey, the last I saw you was over a month ago."

"A month?" Wren meets my gaze.

Pippa points to the compass. "Where are you heading?"

"North. I was told there's a group of rebels hiding out that we could align with."

"There isn't much left of the north. It's a wasteland."

I swallow the lump that forms in my throat. There's already been so much loss, when will it ever stop?

"I have to try." Wren continues moving in the direction we came here for. "If we can get help, maybe some intel, we can eliminate her."

"Is that why you came back? To kill her?"

Wren nods. "I never meant to abandon you." She moves a branch out of the way and walks past it, holding it long enough for me to latch on before it snaps me in the face. "I would have come sooner if I could have."

"If it's been a month, there's no telling when he'll pull us back. We may have more time than we think," I tell her.

"What do you mean?" Pippa asks.

"We're not actually here," Wren explains. "We're astral projecting. Our physical bodies are on Arthlia. This was an impromptu recon mission."

"You appear here."

"Yeah, I don't really understand how it works. I didn't think I could get hurt, either, and well…" Wren holds out her arm. "This blood is very much mine."

"And that alpha beacon is very much engaged, too."

"That I knew would happen. When I traveled to Balial's hell dimension, it went off."

"You went where?" Pippa's footsteps thunder against the ground.

I thought I was the loud one, but mine are whispers compared to hers. Gary doesn't seem to make much noise but I'm not that thrilled about that considering I can't tell how far or near he is to me at any given time unless I'm looking right at him.

"According to Balial, Prania was sealed off ages ago to keep Parla contained. If I can kill her, maybe they'll reopen the realm and those that remain can be set free."

"Why didn't they just kill her themselves if they were capable of sealing off a whole realm?" Pippa asks the same question we all wondered, too.

"She kept evading them. It made the most sense for them to do what they did. Can't say I agree with their methods, but apparently, it was for the greater good. She had planned on eliminating all demonic creatures, no matter how big or small their demonic nature was."

"Sick bitch," Pippa says.

"She has to be stopped." Wren pauses and puts out her arm before pressing her index finger to her lips. Her gaze flits to each one of us, even the wolf that attacked her. "This way," she mouths.

We follow her slowly into a bit of overgrown shrubbery. She kneels on the ground and peers through an opening.

I step closer to her and look for myself, noting the smoking structure ahead of us.

A group of at least six soldiers surveys the place. All wearing identical outfits with matching buzz cuts. I recall walking into hunter territory and stealing those provisions, not entirely sure if I would make it out of there alive. I escaped with more than my life and almost lost it again moments later. Bo and I struggled to stay alive while trapped in Rockbridge's territory, but we did everything we could to rescue Wes and Wren from that hellish prison. Even if that meant bombing the place until we could locate them.

Nothing felt as good as seeing her across that field, and the second I wrapped my arms around her, I knew I never wanted to lose her again. Bo experienced it, too, and even though he denies his feelings for her every chance he gets, I'm certain he was just as concerned about her as I was when she was locked away.

My sights adjust to another person that walks out of the building ahead. A woman, middle-aged, with clothing unlike anything other women wear. It's too formal, too rigid, and too uncomfortable looking. Something in my chest tugs, and my stomach turns over.

"That fucking bitch," Wren whispers but doesn't move toward her. She might be hot-headed, but she's rational, and marching herself up there right now would not be the safest thing to do. Wren wants to make sure she succeeds in her mission, not fail before she even gets started.

"I'd love to..." Pippa doesn't continue her sentence but leaves the rest to our imagination. There's no denying what it is she'd like to have said.

Gary growls low and his furry shoulder rubs against me.

I glance down at him, the strange urge to pat his fluffy head is strong. But I deny my urge in fear that he'll bite my entire arm off. I might be a phoenix who can be reborn in death, but I'm not sold on my limbs regenerating. If I'm not mistaken, my body does no supernatural healing aside from bringing me back from the dead. Which explains the scars on my back that are only visible to me when I look in the mirror. I would have never known they existed had Wes and Bo not seen them. They don't hurt, at least, they didn't, not until recently. Lately, though, they've been aching like they're fresh. It makes no sense at all.

But as I stare through the haze at the woman in the distance, something inside me tugs at the seams.

"Leave no survivors," she orders the soldiers around her. "And then clear out."

Her voice floats back to me, smacking me dead in the chest.

I avert my gaze and try to recall a memory that's been hidden from me.

It's right there, but just out of reach. That outfit. That voice. That cruel demeanor.

"What's she doing?" Pippa whispers, drawing my attention to the unfamiliar yet familiar woman.

"Knowing Parla...something nefarious." Wren sighs and waits for the scene to unfold.

I can only imagine how hard it is for her to not run

out there and drive a knife straight through her heart. Or maybe she would snap her neck in one swift movement. Regardless, Wren came here to see Parla's death through, and being this close to her without acting on it is a difficulty that is not lost on me. I press my palm against her shoulder in an attempt to reassure her that I understand and that I am here for her.

And when the time is right, I will stand by her side to see this through.

A portal appears in front of Parla, green and blue with hints of shimmering orange.

In my state of distraction, I don't notice the figure that towers over me from behind, the one that latches its grimy hand over my mouth and yanks me a few feet away. I gasp but it's no use, the sound is muffled under the clutch of this thing holding me hostage.

Wren spins on her heel and crouches down, her mesmerizing eyes going wide. She's frozen in place, like her mind is trying to run possible scenarios through her head and decide which of them has the best outcome.

I try to shake my head, to tell her not to act, but I can barely move.

I'm brought back to when the wendigo had taken me from her once before. Sheer panic coursed through me at the idea of never seeing her again. I'm not sure who was more surprised upon my rising from those ashes, me or my loved ones. Either way, I was thankful that I wasn't a complete anomaly of this world. That finally, I fit in. Even if my only magical trait is dying.

I recall the rancid smell of his grasp, the one matching that of the thing holding onto me now.

It groans, the sound matching that of the wendigo from once before.

It isn't just some random creature who has found me, it's the wendigo.

"Do you want to be caught?" Wren whisper-shouts at him and throws her thumb toward Parla and her cronies. "Because if she doesn't kill you today, it will be tomorrow. Or the next day. You're never going to make it out of here alive. Not without me." Her gaze flashes to mine but darts back to the wendigo.

She's attempting to appeal to his desire to survive. Instead of threatening him, she's telling him the truth.

"I always finish what I start," the wendigo says, his voice deep and gravely.

I stare through the small gap in the brush at Parla. She glances around, and for a split second, I swear she's glaring in our direction. But instead of coming toward us, she steps into the magical thing and disappears. Her men follow her through, and within a few short moments, they're all gone.

"This one doesn't want to stay dead." He tightens his hold and moves back a few inches, dragging me farther away from my love.

Pippa remains with her hands sort of in the air in front of her, almost like she's waiting for Wren to make a move. Gary has taken his spot next to Pippa.

If he would just hurry up and kill me, Wren could

attack him and end his life. Then she wouldn't have to worry about me getting *hurt* in the crossfire. I can heal myself from death, but not from being injured. That much she's aware of, too. If I had a knife on me, I would drive it straight into my heart. With his hand over my mouth and his suffocating grasp, I can't say the word to bring me to Arthlia, and I can't reach for the button, either. Both fail safes fail epically. Who could have prepared us for me losing my ability to speak and move all at the same time?

Part of me wishes I could tell her to run, to use the means to get back to Arthlia, and that I would be right behind her. But I can't even do that. No, I'm stuck at the mercy of this arrogant and idiotic asshole who refuses to let go of some random vendetta.

If he kills me, surely the three of them can end one wendigo. Suddenly, the thought of being dead while Wren must fight for her life unsettles me. What if she's unable to escape? What if I'm burning into ashes while she dies her own, very permanent, death? I thought it was a good idea for me to be here, but perhaps I was wrong. Wes would have been the better person, because at least then, if she got hurt, he could heal her. Not to mention, his natural ability to kick ass is a major bonus, too. They probably wouldn't even be in this position if he were here.

But I can't change that now, and being mad at myself for making a poor decision won't serve me in this moment.

I mumble under his strong hold and wiggle in his grasp. If I can get him to release his hand on my mouth, I can blurt out the magic word to bring me home, and Wren could follow suit. Both of us finding safety in Arthlia and leaving Pippa and Gary behind.

The battle with the wendigo is between us, surely, he would leave those two alone, wouldn't he?

And on the off chance that he wouldn't, there's no way that Wren would leave knowing those two would be in danger.

Fuck.

"You don't need to hurt him," Wren says, her gaze pleading with the cautious step she takes toward us.

He matches her in the opposite direction. "Now, now."

"Fine." She throws her arms up like a white flag. "What do I need to do to convince you we're on the same side here? This war, it doesn't have to be between us. We have a common enemy."

The wendigo laughs sharply. "You are a hunter marked by an alpha, my dear. You are ripe for the taking."

Wren shakes her head slowly. "He's my partner," she explains. "I came here without him to engage the beacon. I wanted demons to find me. I wanted to convince them that we should be fighting together, not against each other."

"There are not many that remain."

"Then what better reason to join me, to join us." Wren motions to Pippa and Gary.

"I don't believe you." The wendigo grips my face tighter, his rough fingers digging into my flesh.

Pippa stands taller. "Then believe me. I am with her." She shoots her stare at Gary.

He hesitates but bows his head down in submission.

"You've convinced a couple demons, so what?" The wendigo leans in closer and breathes deeply. "And whatever this is."

Wren puts her hand to her chest. "I have made mistakes, okay? More than I'm proud to admit, but my pride doesn't prevent me from knowing that something must be done if Prania stands any chance of being saved."

"What makes you the hero of this story?"

"Someone has to do it." Wren swallows harshly. "I don't want to be labeled as the good guy. I just want to do the right thing for once in my life."

"And I want to escape this realm, but we can't always get what we want now can we?"

"What if I could make that happen?" Wren's chest heaves. She extends her arm toward me again like if she reaches just a bit farther, she'd snatch me from his vicious embrace.

My vision blurs from his hold, and I wish nothing more than to be out of here, to be with her in the safety of Arthlia once again. But like the wendigo just said, we don't always get what we desire.

"You wouldn't be here if you could." The wendigo wastes not another moment when he moves swiftly and snaps my neck for the second time.

It only hurts for the shortest second, the pain of leaving her worse than that of death.

19
WREN

"What is taking so long?" I pace around the living room.

Dash's body lies on the floor in the center of the large space, unmoving, unbreathing, lifeless.

Was I wrong to bring him back here?

We weren't supposed to be able to get hurt in astral projection, and yet I have gash marks on my arm, and Dash is quite literally fucking dead.

I should have listened to my original instincts and charged the wendigo the second I saw him, but I thought I could try a new tactic and convince him that we should align.

I did, ultimately, convince him, but it was too late.

As I crouched to the ground with Dash in my grasp, tears welled in my eyes and I told him that in seconds, I would confirm to him that cross-realm travel was possible. I pleaded with him and made him promise that if I were speaking the truth, he would leave Pippa and Gary alone.

He assured me the feud was with me and my mates, not with them, so either way, I felt somewhat sure that their safety would remain. At least, there would be no threat from him—I couldn't stop the wrath that Parla insisted on inflicting on them.

I explained that I had traveled to Arthlia and found refuge there with others. I went on to confess what I had learned from Balial, and that the only way Prania would be a free realm is if Parla was eliminated. I vowed to return, to see things through, and despite him laughing at me, he gave his word that he would fight on our side if given the opportunity. He claims he would rally those that remained in my absence and await my beacon once I have returned.

But how can I go back there when Dash still hasn't resurrected?

Have my worst nightmares come to life with the final death of this beautiful and broken man?

"According to this text"—Sydney says from his spot on the couch with that ancient book from the library at Harper Shadow Academy in his grasp—"the phoenix is made from the death of two very specific angels. Their DNA, and theirs alone, combined, is what created the phoenix. Their death would result in them rising from the ashes to be reborn again, a result of the potent angelic blood running through their veins. They are said to be a myth, and that they do not exist."

I stare at him, blink, look at Dash, then back to Sydney. "Are you telling me Dash isn't a phoenix?"

He shakes his head. "No. I'm telling you Dash is *the* phoenix. The only one in existence. There are no others like him. There is limited information on the subject, at least from what I have gathered."

"Does it say anything in there about their resurrection?" I stalk over to him and attempt to read the foreign text on the page. "A limit? Something that kills him? How can I protect him if I don't know what his weaknesses are?"

Sydney shrugs and lets out a sigh. "I don't know. I wish I could be of more assistance. This is all new information to me. I'll try to continue to decode the text and fill you in every step of the way."

Wes enters the room and walks right over to me. He grabs my shoulders, steadies me, and looks into my eyes. "He's going to be fine. It's Dash."

I glance behind him. "Where's Bo?"

He infuriates the ever-loving shit out of me but I crave for him to be near, especially in times like this, when so much is uncertain.

"Off stewing." Wes slides my hair off my face and tucks it behind my ear. "He was fuming about the mate bond."

"Right, yeah. He'd rather go live in hell with Balial than be with me."

Sydney perks up from his textbook. "Wait, what?"

I lean into Wes's embrace but turn toward Sydney. "Yeah, Balial told him he'd eliminate the alpha mark on my neck if he pledged his allegiance to him."

"I thought you were with all three of them." Sydney flits his attention between Wes and Dash.

"Bo claims the alpha mark is the only reason I like him and said the only way he can prove that to me is to remove it. Because apparently if he does it himself, the removal, he must mark me as his fated mate, and he'd rather die than be stuck with me." I ignore the tugging of my heart at saying this all out loud.

It's no secret that Bo and I have a futile relationship. What's the point in hiding the truth that he would rather run away than be fated to me?

"Balial is so desperate for company he'd do anything to procure it." Sydney runs his hand through his hair, the pencil he was holding, still in his grasp. "So let me get this straight. Bo marked you, and because he's an alpha, it became an alpha mark. Bo thinks you only like him because of the mark, and refuses to replace it with a fated mate mark, because he thinks you both would have no control over your feelings for each other?"

I nod and point to Wes. "He thinks the same about me and Wes, too. That the only reason we love each other is because of the mate bond."

Wes stares down at me, his eyes glowing a bit redder than they were. "You love me?"

I smile up at him. "Duh."

Not being bothered that Sydney is right here, or that Dash is still lying motionless on the floor, Wes presses his lips to mine.

He breaks away, resting our foreheads together. "I love you, too."

I knew it, for a long time, really, perhaps even that first moment I locked eyes with him across that building. He changed the entire course of my life that day, and despite its tumultuous nature, I am grateful for where it brought us.

Although, having this war behind us and finding true safety might be an even better outcome.

"I hate to break up such a sweet moment, but it's worth sharing that mate bonds don't work that way." Sydney positions himself toward us. "There is a definite pull toward your fated mate, but that's not all that factors in. It can be rejected."

I stare at him and let his words wash over me. Could what he's saying be true? That I was right and my feelings for Bo really are mine and mine alone, not forced upon me by the mark he left on my neck.

"There are obvious magical influencers of lust and desire. That is not what you're experiencing though. Trust me, I went down a very deep rabbit hole when I found out the love of my life had four love interests of her own. I wanted to understand it, to figure out its complexities. And back when Silas and I hated each other, a strong part of me wished that their fated mate bond was the only thing that drew her to him."

"And it wasn't?" I ask him with bated breath.

"As a matter of fact, no. It's what brought them together, but it isn't what sealed their fate. Ultimately, it was their decision, their choice, their own free will, that secured their love for one another." Sydney takes a sip of his coffee. "There are things that come with the fated mate bond, supernatural things, but those are merely perks or extras, not the whole package. Willow and Silas share another supernatural bond, too, although it's far too complex to get into today. As do her and Cameron."

I want to ask him more questions, to find out every last detail about the mate bond and revel in how very wrong Bo was in thinking that what we shared wasn't real, but when Dash *finally* starts to molt, my every waking thought falls to him.

"This is so interesting," Sydney says from the couch.

Dash does his thing, molting and burning and his entire form becomes encased in a hard shell of ash. It's a beautiful process once it's started, but the moments leading up to it are brutally painful. To think that it's ever his last life drives a serrated blade straight through my heart.

After a small eternity, Dash shoves his fist through the center and emerges from the rubble. He blinks a few times, the debris falling over his long lashes, and settles his sights on me.

I rush over to him, my hands finding his face, my thumbs rubbing circles on his renewed flesh. "Took you long enough."

The corners of his lips turn up. "Sorry to keep you waiting."

Wes walks over and reaches down. "Glad to have you back."

Dash latches onto him and allows him to pull him onto his feet. Dash dusts off his body and steps out of the remains of his process. "I remembered something."

"What is it?" I ask him.

"That woman." Dash pats his arm. "Parla."

"Yeah?" The very being I can't wait to end.

"She's the one who tortured me." Dash reaches back to slap his back. "My scars. They're from her. I don't remember all of it, but there are fragments that keep coming to me. I think my mind was trying to uncover it with those nightmares. To show me the truth of what happened."

My blood boils—my hatred for that evil bitch growing with each passing second. I thought I couldn't hate her anymore, but I was wrong. It's one thing to fuck with me, and something else entirely to hurt any of my men.

I will make her pay for what she's done, one way or another.

And the sooner I can return to Prania, the better.

Time moves much quicker in Prania than it does in Arthlia. Tremont said we hadn't been gone long before we abruptly came back. And if that's any indication, there's no telling what else Parla has done in her extended time in Prania.

I promised Pippa and Gary that I would return, I gave my word to that wendigo.

What kind of person would I be if I went back on that now?

"I will make her pay." I plant my hand on Dash's shoulder.

"We both will," Wes chimes in. He glances over at me. "I'm not letting you go without me."

Sydney sighs. "If you're both going, I'm going to have to help Tremont with the spell. It's the only way to ensure enough power to send you."

"You'll help us?" I turn toward him, not quite believing how easily he volunteered.

"If I've learned anything from being married to an Oliver, there isn't any convincing her of something she's set her mind to. I'd rather assist and greater your chances of survival than let you go off on your own. She'd say the same thing."

"I...I don't know how to thank you." My eyes glisten.

"Try not to get yourself killed, that would be a start. Willow will be pissed if I let someone die."

I study the ticking clock at the far side of the room. "In theory, I still have enough time to get there and back before she needs my assistance later." Letting her down is not a part of this plan.

Neither is losing.

Bo's heavy presence makes itself known as he comes into the room and leans in the doorway. He takes in the most current version of Dash. "You're alive."

Dash chuckles. "Don't sound so disappointed."

Bo keeps his attention on Dash. "How was it?"

"Death? Kind of boring, really. A lot of darkness until I catch on fire."

"Prania. How was Prania?"

"Devastating." I interrupt Dash before he can begin. "We're going back immediately."

"What?" Bo stops leaning and stands up straight. "I'm coming this time."

I shake my head. "Can't."

"Why the hell not?" Bo looks to Wes.

"I need the beacon to engage," I tell him. "The plan doesn't work without it."

"And how did that work out for you last time? You got hurt and Dash died."

"I am very much fine, and so is Dash." I pause and consider my next words carefully, deciding that there is no gentle way in telling him the truth. "Plus, Wes is coming."

"You're kidding me." Bo rakes his hand over his face. "Everyone gets to go except me?"

Sydney clears his throat. "I'm, uh, going to get Tremont." He slips out of the room, and I wish I could follow him out and avoid Bo's seething glare.

"Not everyone," Wes says. "Jade and Everest are

staying here. As are Sydney and Tremont. You'll barely even know we're gone."

"They don't count and you know it." Bo tightens his hand into a fist. "This is bullshit."

I step toward him, my head tilted up at the tall, broody man in front of me. "You know what's bullshit? You trying to leave because you don't want to be with me."

"It's the only way," Bo mutters through a clenched jaw.

"It's not actually, and when I get back, we need to talk."

"Talk?"

But before I can continue, Sydney and Tremont come into the room.

"I've extended the barrier for Tremont to the entire house, this will allow him to assist in the spell." Sydney walks to the center of the open space, near the spot Dash and his phoenix powers were activated.

I follow him over and stand at his side. "Thank you," I whisper.

He nods. "I must warn you, astral travel this frequent comes with risks. If you notice any uncomfortable side effects, you need to return immediately."

I had a feeling this type of thing didn't come without a cost but that isn't going to stop me from completing what I said I would do.

Parla must die.

Not tomorrow. Not next week. Today. Right now. As soon as fucking possible.

"What should I be on the lookout for?" I ask him.

"Headaches, fatigue, nose bleeds, nausea. Those are all precursors to worsening symptoms."

"How worse?"

"Death." Sydney sighs. "It's incredibly uncommon, but I've read cases in which the soul of the astral traveler was stuck in the in-between, unable to reunite with its body." He looks to Dash. "Because of your regenerative abilities, you should be fine for immediate travel. And Wes, you haven't yet, so you're good to go, too."

Relief washes over me at not putting Dash or Wes at any more risk than they already are.

"Are you sure you want to go through with this?" Wes's fiery gaze meets mine.

"Without a doubt." I lower myself onto the floor and wait for my direction from the witches sending me to Prania.

Dash lies next to me, weaving our hands together, and Wes settles on the other side.

"I can't fucking believe this," Bo blurts out. "Absolutely ridiculous."

"Tell us how you really feel," I mumble.

Dash squeezes my hand and Wes rubs his thumb along mine. Having two out of three of my men being supportive will have to do, at least, for now. I'll deal with Bo when I return from hopefully what will be my final assassination mission.

With a few daggers tucked along my leather gear, I close my eyes and brace myself for what's to come. Ever since I stepped foot in Arthlia, I haven't been able to shake the thought that my work in Prania was not over. I hurt many. I made bad decisions. I was a close-minded fool doing errands for a woman who manipulates and controls anyone she possibly can. She is pure evil, and she must be stopped. And who better to do it than the person that was trained to do her bidding?

The room spins, that familiar vacuum-type thing happening as Sydney and Tremont mutter the incantation necessary to send us to Prania. I should have pushed for Dash to stay behind, but after hearing what Parla had done to him, I knew with certainty that if he wanted to come, I would be selfish for not allowing it. He deserves to watch her die just as much as the rest of us. I'll do the honors of holding her down and letting him rip into her the same way she had done to him.

Any death, no matter how brutal it could be, would still not be enough punishment for the terrible things she has done.

Once everything has stopped moving, I open my eyes and blink through the thick haze of Prania's sky. Sitting up, I notice a trickle run down my nose. I wipe at it, the crimson staining my hand. As quick as I can, I sniffle the rest of it up and drag my hand against the ground to rid myself of the evidence. I've only just got here and already the symptoms that Sydney mentioned are present.

"You guys good?" I rise to my feet and dust off my legs. There is no time like the present to get this show on the road. I refuse to leave here without following through, and I can't exactly do that if I die in the process.

"Yep," Dash joins me at my side.

Wes huffs and comes closer, too. "Can't say I'm thrilled to be back here." His eyes glow and his skin radiates heat like his hound side is already on high alert. I don't blame him for being proactive, I would probably do the same if I had those types of abilities.

I unsheathe a blade and shove the handle into Dash's hand. "If it's not a demon, kill it. And if it's a demon trying to kill you, kill it. Do not hesitate. Just because you're a phoenix doesn't mean I'm okay with you dying."

Dash nods. "Yes, ma'am."

I roll my eyes and scan the vicinity, unsure of where we landed. There's no telling where Pippa, Gary, and the wendigo went, but if my beacon is doing what it's supposed to be doing, they should be alerted to our whereabouts if they're nearby. I just hope they get here before any other bloodthirsty demon does.

I don't want to have to kill, but I will if it's what stands between us and our survival.

"Let's stick to the plan," I tell them while pulling the compass from my pocket. The dial swivels and then settles on its direction. "This way."

We take a few steps and I stop, holding out both of my arms to prevent them from going any farther.

"What's wrong?" Wes asks immediately.

"Do you see that?" I point to the ground.

"No."

"What are we supposed to be seeing?" Dash glances over my shoulder.

"That. Right there." I kneel and get a closer look at the faint but illuminated petals on the ground. They brighten, only to dim out and be replaced by another set a bit farther away.

"Are those...flowers?" Wes reaches toward them, but I grab his arm.

"Don't touch them." Something visceral within me wants to protect them, to keep them out of harm's way. I don't quite understand how I know, but I'm certain I'm supposed to follow them. Despite following a trail north, I step in between the glowing things and walk in the direction it guides me.

"Are you sure?" Wes asks skeptically.

"Yeah." I meet his gaze. "Just don't step on them." Shifting my focus to Dash, I add, "Please."

I shove the compass back into its home and put my faith in whatever magical miracle is leading me away from the north. Is it possible that I'm chasing a false hope that will get us killed? Definitely. But could this be the same divination that brought me to that book in the library at Harper Shadow Academy? I guess I'll find out.

We walk silently through the wooded area for at

least ten minutes, my heart slowing its pace with each step. I shouldn't feel this comfortable in wartime, but my body is strangely at ease. This is what I was trained for. What I'm known for. What I'm good at.

I am the furla ain, and soon, I will make Parla regret the day she ever came into my life.

The illuminating ground dies out completely, as do my steps.

"Where did they go?" Dash whispers from behind me.

"I don't know," I tell him, a strange unease trickling up my spine. "Over here," I rush over to a nearby bush and cower beside it.

They join me a second later, almost entirely too late, as a group of half a dozen soldiers march by, their formation eerily perfect and orderly. The soldiers don't look our way as they march past us like they don't see or notice us at all.

"That was creepy," Dash says the very thing going through my head.

"It's like they're mind controlled." I shift my weight and watch them disappear into the distance.

"I think they are." Wes leans in closer. "I mean, how else would she get full compliance from them? It has to be some magical mind control. Remember when…"

But he doesn't have to finish his sentence for me to recall the memory of Parla using mind control to get me to kill Wes.

"I do," I tell him, not needing the details repeated

out loud. I am ashamed I allowed her to take control and almost succeed in forcing me to murder my beloved.

"How did you break it?" he asks me.

I hadn't put too much thought into that part. "I don't know, I just did."

But that couldn't be all of it, there had to be something I did to rid myself of that influence.

"Think, Wren," Wes encourages. "You had the knife in your hand poised to my chest. I told you I'd find you in any life."

I shiver at the image of the fear that had consumed me. I was terrified, quite possibly, for the very first time in my life—truly and utterly terrified.

"It was something she said," I tell him. "She commanded me to kill the monster. But I never saw you as one. She was, at least, in my eyes. And then..." It was similar to what I felt when that magical torture device had been embedded in my skin. A flash of bright light, a welcoming and protective presence. Could that have been my hidden magic rising to the surface to save me? What else could explain what had happened?

"Wren." Dash reaches across and catches the blood that trickles out of my nose. "You're bleeding."

I rise to my feet and wipe my face. "I'm fine."

Dash looks to Wes, who steps toward me.

"Come here." Wes pulls me to his chest and mutters into my hair. He hugs me with a firm gentleness and kisses my forehead. "I need you to tell me if you're feeling bad." Wes releases me and stares into my eyes, his glowing orbs something that would have made me want to kill him in my past life, but now, all I want to do is spend every moment at his side.

"You have to promise me you won't do that again. You must preserve your energy, Wes. I'm fine, really." I avoid their pitying glances and step from around the bush that was concealing us. "We should get going. We're running out of time."

But when I take a few more strides, I smack into a large body I never saw coming.

His rough hands latch onto my shoulders and hold me firmly in place. Standing at least twice my height with antlers protruding from his bare skeleton skull, he growls. "You."

Wes immediately ignites his entire body, his flames licking everything within a few inches of him. "Let her go or I'll burn—"

"It's okay," I tell him and shake off the creepy hands of the wendigo. "He's on our side."

Dash comes into the wendigo's view. "I'd appreciate it if you refrained from killing me for the third time."

The wendigo raises its hands. "A promise is a promise. I am a man of my word."

"Where's Pippa?" I look past him and swallow down the fear that I may have been too late in my return.

What is minutes at home is much longer here.

"Waiting." He tilts his head in the direction he just came. "I gathered what I could, but there aren't many of us that remain. And those that do are in hiding. It wasn't easy to convince them of something I was skeptical of myself."

How bittersweet that my friend is alive, but so many others are not. We have all lost someone, and hopefully soon, after one final battle, the violence will stop.

"I understand," I say while following this demonic creature through the woods.

Wes hurries to join me at my side and Dash takes up the rear.

I flit my attention to Wes and dart my gaze to the semi-helpless phoenix behind me.

Wes sighs but falls back, knowing damn well that Dash shouldn't be the one left exposed.

I reach toward Dash and tug him closer to me. He's safest at my side where I can protect him from anything that may come his way. It's risky having someone else to keep my eyes on, but it's a risk I'm willing to take to give him a front-row seat to Parla's execution.

"I've never come across a phoenix before," the wendigo says over his shoulder. "Assuming that's what you are."

"The one and only," I confirm. "Sydney translated some of that text when you were taking your good ol' time molting. According to that book, you're the only phoenix in existence."

Dash's eyes widen. "Whoa. I don't know if I should be proud or sad."

I nudge him with my shoulder. "You're allowed to be both."

"We're coming up on a group of hunters." The wendigo motions to a large boulder off to the side. "We can wait it out here."

"How many are there?" I ask him, a theory popping into my head.

"Three," he says, his voice harsh.

"There's four of us." I settle my sights on Dash. "Three. You can stay here."

He frowns but doesn't protest.

"Honestly, I can take them all if you'd rather—"

The wendigo holds up his hand to stop me. "Like taking bread from a baby."

If only he knew the kind of bread they had in Arthlia. He would surely lose his creepy little mind.

"Leave one of them alive." I slide a dagger out of my pants and turn it around in my hand, familiarizing myself with the blade. It's been too long since I properly held one, and yet it feels completely at home in my grasp. Taking a steadying breath, I look at each of the men standing here with me.

The three unsuspecting soldiers march right near us, the same way the others had done. Their postures are stiff and rigid, their movements almost identical to one another. Before I can even fully step into their line of sight, the wendigo rushes toward them. He snatches two of them and bashes their heads together before tossing their lifeless bodies aside. He clutches the other by the neck and drags him over to us.

"Um." I shove my dagger back into its sheathed position. "That works, too."

Wild-eyed and panting, the remaining soldier kicks his feet to try to free himself. He opens his mouth, but the wendigo shoves his hand over it and silences his cries for help.

"What's this all about?" Wes steps toward me. "What do you want with him?"

I exhale. "I'm not sure. I want to try something."

The wendigo brings the man closer, stopping just a foot in front of me. "Haste; we must not keep the others waiting."

Rubbing my thumbs against my fingers, I suck in a breath and summon whatever power is within me. I close my eyes and will it to the surface, knowing damn well just how foolish what I'm doing must look from their point of view. That doesn't stop me from trying, from testing this possible theory that might change everything.

When nothing happens—no stirring in my chest or magical lights appearing—I bridge the space between me and this bewildered man.

"I don't want to hurt you," I reassure him. "But you're being manipulated." I close my hands into fists. "I think you're mind controlled, actually."

He tries to shake his head but the wendigo keeps

him firmly in place. I ignore the similarities of how he did the same thing to Dash, not only once, but twice.

Sometimes you have to align with your enemies if you wish to take out the even greater threat.

Extending my arm, I press my palm against the man. His heart beats aggressively in his chest, thudding so aggressively it rumbles up my forearm.

I pinch my eyes shut. "Angels," I whisper, barely audible, and pray to anyone listening to hear my call for help. If that's who saved me when I needed to be rescued, can't they assist me today, too? I push my palm into his chest and thrust any magic that may lie dormant within me to rise to the surface. My fingers tingle, my arm growing warmer and cooler all at once. I peek through my lids to witness a strange silver glow faintly illuminating my skin.

Am I losing it or is this really working?

I lock sights with the man, his gaze terrified, no doubt from the wendigo holding him hostage, but also the crazy woman in front of him.

"Wren, you're..." Dash mutters.

But I ignore him. I ignore everything except the sensation bubbling up inside of me.

I shove it forward with no real direction of how this is supposed to work and hope with everything in me that I'm doing this right.

A blast of rippling power slams the man in the chest, his eyes widening before shutting completely. His body goes limp in the wendigo's grasp.

"I didn't mean to kill him." My chest aches from the loss of a man I was only trying to help.

"He's not dead," the wendigo tells me while lowering the man's weight onto the dirt.

I kneel at the soldier's side and press my fingers to his neck, finding his slow but steady pulse. "He's not." My sights lock on Wes temporarily. "I didn't kill him."

What a strange thing to get excited about, considering my past as a trained murderer.

The man gasps for breath, his sudden movement knocking me onto my ass. He clutches his chest at the spot I blasted him and stares directly at me.

My fingers inch toward the blade at my side, ready to yank it out and throw it into his throat at a second's notice.

None of us move, like we're all waiting for the other to decide how this is going to go.

Finally, he opens his mouth. "Furla ain?"

I swallow and nod. "Yes."

"I..." His gaze trails off. "I think I've made a mistake." That distant, empty look is no longer. His shoulders are stiff but nothing of the way they were moments ago. The mind-control that Parla had been dominating him with has disappeared, along with his immediate murderous tendencies.

I did it. I broke his compulsion. And with it, it brings me hope that maybe, just maybe, we can win this war.

I had come here with the sole mission of killing Parla, not exactly working out any of the other details. I would eliminate anyone that stood in the way but would do my best to save as many innocent lives as possible. I wasn't sure if her death would be enough to break the hold she had on the hunters, but with this new ability I've discovered, maybe I can turn her own against her.

"We both have." I rise to my feet and extend my arm to him. "But it's not too late."

The soldier locks onto me and I pull him onto his feet. We stand there, at an arm's length, a heavy silence filling the space between us. I nod, and then he does.

"Very well," I say and break away from him.

"Great work," the wendigo tells me as he slaps my back, the impact rattling my entire body.

Does he think that we are friends now that we've come to a truce? It wouldn't be the worst thing to happen, although I cannot overlook that he murdered my sweet Dash on two separate occasions. I may be in my forgiving era, but that isn't easily forgotten.

Wes eyes me like he's trying to decide if I'm injured, and I do everything in my power to convince him otherwise. He doesn't need to know that my head throbs and my vision keeps blurring in and out of focus. He'd try to heal me, to convince me to return to Arthlia. Both options that I refuse to take. His strength as a hellhound is better served fighting to protect those that remain than absorbing my ailments. Not to mention, when he whispered those words to me earlier, there was no positive effect the way his healing power usually works. Typically, I feel better within seconds, but then, I felt nothing. And returning to Arthlia would be giving up on Prania completely. The amount of time it would take for me to properly recover would grant Parla the ability to eradicate the rest of the demon population.

This is our only shot and I won't waste it.

The solider stumbles, his hands darting out in front to steady himself.

I reach for him all too late.

He goes down hard with a thud. He doesn't move, he doesn't make another sound. Not a wisp of air filling his lungs, not a single heartbeat thudding in his chest.

He is simply *dead*.

"What the fuck?" I crouch next to him, grip his shoulders, and turn him face up.

Dash grabs my elbow and pulls me to my feet. "He's gone," he says with such a gentle tone.

"We must go," the wendigo tells us. "We're losing time."

"I don't know what I did wrong," I mutter despite knowing damn well that I have no understanding of how magic works. What was I thinking in blasting him with my power? It may have broken the compulsion, but it killed him in the process.

How are we going to win this war with minimal casualties if I can't stop Parla's mind control? Her soldiers don't deserve to die just because they're held captive by her mind tricks.

20

WREN

We make it to where the rest of the demons are hiding. An old, dilapidated building similar to the one where Wes and I first met.

The wendigo was not lying. There are not many survivors, at least that are able-bodied and willing to show up to fight.

I stand in front of them, a lump forming in my throat as they look at me with rage-filled stares. I'm not entirely sure if it's from the marker signaling them to kill me blaring off my neck, or the fact that Parla has done nothing but make their lives completely miserable.

Miserable doesn't even cut it.

She's threatened by their very existence; she hates them so much that she vowed to kill every last one of them despite not truly knowing any of them. I'm the first to admit that the stigma associated with being a demon is nothing but a harmful stereotype that serves only one person. How can someone hate something they don't even understand? But how can I blame her when I did the very same thing?

I blamed the demons for the death of my parents and took that same oath to rid our realm of the demons and their bringers.

"Is it true?" one of the smaller demons calls out from the front of the crowd. "You came from Arthlia?"

"I did." I nod and look her straight in the eyes. "We all did." I glance over at Wes and Dash, who stand supportively at my side. Inhaling, I scan the crowd and raise my voice. "After the bombing at Rockbridge, we were able to flee and seek refuge in Arthlia. I, personally, spoke to Balial, who told me that Prania was sealed off to prevent Parla from escaping. It was not her that created the border like she has led us to believe, yet the angels and demons who collectively decided this was for the greater good. One realm as opposed to her wreaking havoc on all of them. Until she is eliminated, none of us are safe. It doesn't matter if you have a spec of demonic blood in your veins, nothing protects you from her wrath. Anyone who opposes her is as good as dead, and those on her side, she sees them only as disposable pawns."

Wes places his hand on my lower back, almost like he could sense I needed the support.

"Today"—I stand taller with his touch still on me—
"that tyranny ends."

The crowd claps their hands, their energy fueling
me despite my already weakened state.

"Today—"I repeat—"we take back what is ours."

They roar louder.

"Today, we will kill Parla."

A collective bellow sounds this otherwise quiet and
abandoned section of Prania.

"Think that will be loud enough?" I turn to the
wendigo as the few dozen demons cheer and go wild.

"I don't doubt they could have found us without it."
His gaze floats past me into the distance. "They're
already approaching."

I breathe in deeply. "How many?"

The wendigo looks down at me, his solemn expres-
sion is more dire than ever. "At least a hundred. Maybe
more."

We're outnumbered and there's no telling what
kind of magical powers Parla and her goonies will
possess. I knew this would be a challenge, but I hadn't
realized the magnitude of it until this very instant. And
when I look out at the last of the demons, I grow
concerned of the death toll that will no doubt rise.
There will be casualties on both sides, but at what point
will enough be enough?

Parla won't rest until we're all dead, and we won't
stop until she is.

I latch onto Dash's hands and pull him toward me.

"You need to go into that building and hide. Okay? Do not come out until this is all said and done. Neither the hunters nor the demons can sense you, and we must use that to our advantage."

His gaze darts back and forth between mine. "I don't want to leave you."

"You aren't." I force a smile and shake my head. Worrying about Dash's safety will only bring more harm to me and Wes. He needs to stay tucked away, safe and sound, if we stand any chance of keeping our heads clear during battle. And I'm already struggling to do that without adding Dash into the mix. "I'll find you when it's over."

Dash kisses my cheek briefly and takes a final look into my eyes. "I'm holding you to that."

"I would expect nothing less." I unsheathe one of my blades. "You still have yours, right?"

Dash pats his side where his own knife is tucked away.

"Don't be afraid to use it," I tell him as he disappears through the chaos of the demons that swell around me.

"You ready for this?" I ask Wes, who stays silently at my side.

"You sure that you're okay?"

"I am." The energy of the coming fight rumbles through me, temporarily overriding any reservations I may have. I don't worry about Wes. He and his hound can overcome any obstacle. He can fully engulf himself in flames and catch fire to anyone who dares threaten him. He can shift into his hound form and move around this battlefield quicker than any other creature standing here today, ripping out throats and tearing off limbs. Now that he has unlocked his full form, he is unstoppable.

I've only just scratched the surface of what I'm capable of, and so far, my magic has done me almost no good. I stepped foot into Prania in a weakened state, and with each passing moment, my health declines even more. It's going to take everything I have to simply survive an extended stay, let alone fight to the death.

But luckily for me, the mate bond does not insist that *I* tell *him* the truth.

Hunters emerge from the near fog, their boisterous footsteps pelting the ground as they charge us, armed with knives and swords and magic and unrecognizable devices.

"This is it," I say to no one in particular.

As one solid group, we rush toward the hunters, erupting total chaos in the clearing in front of the building the demons were previously hiding out in.

I duck to avoid a flying knife and slice my own through the exposed flesh of a hunter as he reaches over his head to throw another blade.

His insides spill out as he hits the ground with a thud. One down, so many more to go.

Kicking my next target, I spin and drive the sharp end of my knife into the throat of the man, who clutches at the gushing wound. The air becomes thick with the stench of death and gore. I rub at my nose, more blood trickling down despite not being hit in the face.

The minor distraction allows a hunter to charge at me, his sword slicing a thin section of my armored top as I dive out of his way.

"Fucking bitch!" he screams at me.

I roll my eyes. "At least I'm not a mind-controlled puppet." I turn toward him and steady my footing. "Are you even able to wipe your ass without permission from your master?"

"At least I'm not sleeping with the enemy," he barks back.

I laugh. "At least I'm actually getting laid." I run toward him, letting him think he knows exactly where I'm going to strike, but at the last second, I slide past him and slice through his biceps. Blood splatters onto my face and provides a nice camouflage from my own dripping out of my nose.

Shoving onto my feet, I reel back my arm and slam the blade into the soft spot between his shoulder and spine. And with everything I have, I grunt and force all my weight down, cutting him wide open.

Should I have tried to save him? Probably. But this early in the battle, I don't have time to waste on something that's already failed me once.

My vision blurs and I struggle to remain upright, bodies running past and sending me spiraling. I slap my face and regain my footing. "Get it together, Wren." After a few blinks, the image of destruction comes into focus and I narrowly avoid an oncoming attack. Only this time, it's a demon, not a hunter.

"Angels, man!" I yell at him. "I'm on your side, remember?" Steadying my blade toward the wild-eyed guy with small horns protruding from his forehead, I watch him intently and hope that he will change his mind.

"I forgot, sorry." He points his dagger toward me. "That fucking beacon makes me want to kill you."

"I know," I tell him. "It makes me want to kill me too." Coming here without Bo was a great idea at first, but now it seems more of a risk than I bargained for. It helped me find the wendigo and the rest of the demon army, that much is certain. Perhaps I could have found them without it, though. Was it my magic or something else altogether that lit those leaves up on the ground and led me toward them?

Now, the alpha mark does nothing but confuse those on my side, allowing the threat to my life to continue to rise. In a way, Parla has an advantage she's not even aware of.

Not that I will allow that to stop me from following through with my mission.

That isn't to say that I wouldn't prefer Bo here, fighting alongside me like lovers dancing to their song. It's one of the few moments he lets down his guard long enough for me to see him. We come together in an unusual way and despite it being twisted, those are some of my fondest memories with him. It's as though the only time he recognizes me as an equal is on the battlefield.

I scan the crowd, locating Wes who is currently melting another man's throat with just his grasp. Pippa slams her hoof-like hand into a hunter, knocking him to the ground before stomping on his skull and smashing it with ease. The wendigo is surrounded by six hunters, but he doesn't seem at all discouraged by the number.

"Where are you?" I whisper, my sights frantically searching for the entire reason I came here today.

"On your left," Pippa screams across the way to me.

I drop to my knees and through the air soars, Gary, the wolf that had attacked me once before, only this time, he lands the weight of his blow on a hunter who flanked me.

Gary latches his razor-sharp teeth around the man's throat and rips the flesh right off him. He tilts his furry head toward me as blood dribbles out of his mouth. He growls, but this time, it isn't meant to intimidate me. Gary rushes off and snatches another random hunter that goes after that small demon who had asked me about Arthlia.

I continue to search the crowd, taking short breaks to duck, to spin, to kill.

That's when I spot her, my heart completely skipping a beat.

Parla.

She's surrounded by at least two dozen hunters and a witch at her side that's casting a glowing orb around her. Leave it to her to not be willing to fight her own battle.

Her sadistic gaze locks onto mine, and I want nothing more than to teleport into that magical bubble and slit her fucking throat.

Parla's stupid cheeks turn up into a grin and she winks at me before pointing in my direction and saying something I cannot make out from this far away.

Another person appears from behind her and casts a wand toward me.

Within split seconds, I drop to my knees, the weight of the world feeling heavier than ever. Is this from the side effects or what Parla's other witch is doing?

Wes screams and we lock eyes as his entire form bursts into flames. He takes off into a sprint, his footsteps leaving a trail of fire in his wake. But he doesn't get much farther when something flies through the air toward him and secures itself around his throat. The fire dies out immediately and he clutches the device with all his might, yanking and trying to free himself.

It's no use—whatever has attached to him is suppressing his powers, and if it's anything like what we dealt with at Rockbridge, there's no telling whether Wes will be able to overcome it without his hound side.

I try to move, to push up onto my feet. My body is too heavy, too weak, too defeated.

"No," I mutter. "This is not how I die." Not when I'm *this* fucking close to snapping her neck.

Parla and her horde inch closer, my stomach dropping with every bit of ground she covers without being able to regain my strength.

The faint whistling of a knife calls my attention, and I duck as it whizzes by, the blade slicing into my cheek but not securing itself into my skull where it was aimed. Hot blood coats my chin and drips onto the ground.

I clench my jaw and summon whatever may lie dormant within me.

This battle may have been a lot different had I learned how to use my magic like a proper witch. Although, I was not afforded the luxury of time, considering I have already wasted too much and cost too many their lives.

A strong hand wraps around my biceps, and I come to the sudden realization that this is it, this is where my story ends. Not at the hands of Parla, but some random stranger who got to me first.

But when I draw in a breath, the familiar scent of musk and rain washes over me. My eyes fill with tears and my heart swells.

"Bo," I mutter without even having laid my sights on him.

He drags me to my feet. "What are you doing down there, Birdie?"

I turn toward him, my body already feeling lighter and less under her authority. "Just hanging out."

He steadies my shoulders and studies my exterior. "You look like shit."

"Thanks." This forces a smile out of me. "What are you doing here?"

Chaos continues to erupt around us but for a second it feels like it's only the two of us standing here.

"Sorry to disappoint. Just couldn't let you have all the fun." His dark stare doesn't leave mine. "I came the second your nose started bleeding."

"That was hours ago."

"Seconds ago, in Arthlia." He releases and shoves me behind him, grabbing the knife that soars through the air toward us. Bo sends it back in the direction it came, landing straight into the chest of a hunter. He skims his attention over the dwindling crowd. "You guys are getting your asses kicked."

My lip quivers despite everything I'm doing to hold myself from falling apart.

Bo returns to face me, his hand coming up to rest against my non-injured cheek. "Hey, if we go down, we go down together."

"I'm glad you came," I tell him, because this might be my last chance to tell him the truth.

"I don't know how much longer Sydney and Tremont can hold us. Five is too many."

"Five? Who else came?" I do the math in my head.

Me. Dash. Wes. Bo. Who's the fifth?

"Everest." He points off in the distance.

Bo slams his elbow into a hunter that runs by, stopping him completely in his tracks and using the knife the man was holding against him to jab it into his throat.

Never in my wildest dreams would I have assumed Everest would return to Prania, especially when that meant leaving Jade behind. Those two have been inseparable since Rockbridge, and if I was a betting woman, I would have wagered all the cheese in the world that he'd never part from her.

"He came to help me find you. Insisted I didn't come alone." Bo wipes the blade he just killed a man with on his leg, only to drive it into another hunter that approaches. He repeats the same motion. "Angels, there sure are a lot of them."

"They're mind controlled, Bo. They don't know what they're doing." I exhale. "I was able to break the compulsion on one of them."

"Why can't you do it to the rest of them?" He motions toward the throng of people around us.

"I killed him." I keep Wes in my line of sight while talking with Bo. Despite the restraints suppressing Wes's hound side from rising to the surface, he does not lack in the combat department. He's killed a minimum of three hunters since I started watching him. Defending himself enough to lessen the worry that overtook me seeing him fall to one of Parla's magical defenses.

"Probably easier that way." Bo glances down at me. "Is that why your nose started bleeding?"

"No, it happened as soon as I got here." What's the point in lying when the chance of our survival is decreasing with each demon slaughtered?

"Where's Dash?" Bo latches onto me and spins me out of the way of an attack.

"Hiding."

"Good."

"Directly behind you," I say while picking up the knife I lost when Parla grabbed a hold of me with her magic.

"You, too."

Bo and I turn, both of us seamlessly moving in unison and forcefully implanting our knives into the people who attempted to threaten us.

"That's my girl," Bo says while a shit-eating grin forms on his handsome face. He drags his hair out of his eyes and winks at me.

Just like that, all the tension that was between us is erased, and what remains is a friendship that has grown through the strangest of ways. Bo has seen me at my worst, hated me, and wanted me dead. I have never sugar-coated the version of myself that he has seen, and despite being at odds, a relationship formed whether we wanted it to or not. Bo has always been attractive, but I didn't *truly* start to notice it until I saw more pieces of him that were uncovered. He is brutal, irrational, and a pain in the ass, but he is as broken as the rest of us. He is a lover of bread and violence, and he would do anything for the people he cares about. Bo might not let people in so easily, but when he does, he will go to the ends of the universe for them.

Literally.

And as he hovers behind me, our forms back-to-back, our knives poised to kill, I realize, I am one of those very lucky people.

He could have stayed in Arthlia. He didn't have to come. But the second he saw that something was wrong, he risked himself to be here with us.

We fall quickly into a rhythm and use the shield each other provides to slaughter anyone who dares to come our way.

I ignore the fatigue that sets in and focus on the adrenaline coursing through me.

Panting, I shove my blade into the thigh of a hunter. His screams pierce my ears and do nothing to stop me from yanking out the knife and driving it into his neck. Blood speckles my face, coating me with yet another layer of red.

Bo throws his weapon into the chest of an oncoming hunter, and reaches for another, tilting his head and sinking his fangs into his throat. He jerks back, his vicious teeth ripping a huge chunk of his flesh off. Bo spits it out and rushes over to snatch his knife from the other man's deceased torso.

"They just keep coming," he calls out to me. "Where's the bitch?"

"I…" I slam my fist across the face of one hunter and spin, extending my leg and kicking another right in the chest. "Don't know." Quickly ducking, I swipe my blade at the ankle of another unsuspecting victim. "I lost her when you showed up. I've been searching ever since."

My gaze continues to skim the crowd between every kill, but aside from being able to locate Wes and my friends, I haven't found Parla. Did she retreat when Bo arrived? Or is she planning something for him, too? There's no telling what kind of magical defense she has up her sleeve.

Most of the hunters look alike, just varying heights and weights. They're all dressed in the same attire, making them easy targets. But because of this, it's difficult to differentiate the ones that belong to Parla's personal guard. Just when I think I've homed in on them, they disperse and go their separate ways into battle. Is this a purposeful distraction or simply another advantage she doesn't even realize she has?

Four rather large hunters charge at me at once, one of them landing a blow across my jaw.

Stars dot my vision, and I lose my footing. My hands scrape against the ground as they catch the brunt of my weight. "Fuck!" I cry out.

Someone kicks me square in the back, knocking the wind out of me and cracking my spine.

I dig my fingers into the dirt and spit out the blood that's filled my mouth. "Is that all you've got?" Pushing onto my feet, I'm met with another blow, this one turning me over and onto my ass. I stare up at the endless hunters that surround me, my gaze darting to Bo, who has at least twice the number of hunters to tend to. I locate Wes, grateful to see him still standing, but that hope is dimmed quickly at noticing how many are attacking him, too. Pippa struggles with the man in front of her, and even the wendigo seems surrounded, only his antlered head poking out above the throng of hunters.

Is this it? The end? I thought I would have met my maker numerous times before, but I don't think things have ever been quite as hopeless as they have right now.

I wanted to die that day in the warehouse when Wes saved me. I thought he was going to torture me and make my final days worse than any death imaginable. But who would have thought that this, witnessing the people I care about losing a war that was never meant for them, would be more painful than the most brutal of torture? I would spend an eternity in Rockbridge to rid them of this.

My head throbs and I cough, blood spewing from my lips. The men close in, their knives and swords pointed toward me. Eyeing my empty ankle holster, hopelessness continues to hit me like a ton of bricks. My sights fall on my dagger, lying discarded in the dirt a few feet away.

It's too far.

I am weaponless and injured.

In my peak form, maybe I could have taken the lot of them on, but here, now, beaten and bloodied, I'm not so sure.

That doesn't mean I will give in without a fight, though. I size them up and quickly analyze any potential weaknesses and opportunities. Three of the men are easily twice my size. One holds a long sword, but his grip is loose, a bit unsure, as though this might be the first time he's held a weapon that massive. He's the biggest of the bunch, and somehow, the most unsteady on his feet. The littlest man's hands shake as he clutches a dagger. The other two, a tinge more confident than the others, poise their knives in my direction.

It's only been a few seconds since they knocked me onto my ass and already, I've learned more about them than their comrades probably know.

Spreading my fingers into the cold dirt, I make the decision that I'm hoping is the correct one. I shove the brunt of my weight onto my hand and force myself up, moving as quickly as I can to rush the largest of the guys and thrust the brunt of my boot into his knee.

It buckles just as I'd wanted it to, and he lets the sword slip from his grasp. It clanks onto the ground, but I leave it. It's far too heavy for either of us to use effectively and his concern is no longer on me as much as it is on his broken leg.

He whimpers and moans and clutches the awkward-shaped thing on the ground like a baby.

The two moderate fighters run toward me, their

knives aimed in my direction. The little guy follows up the rear and manages to drive his blade through the flesh on my arm on his way by. Pain, hot and steady, just like the blood gushing from my wound.

"Bleed, bitch," one of the two says.

My vision grows fuzzy again, making me miss the knife that punctures my armor top and shoves its way through my stomach.

I latch onto the person the knife is clutched by and pull them toward me, keeping the blade still buried in my body. Without even truly being able to see, I dig my nails into the soft skin on top of his hand and don't stop until his grip has released the hilt, leaving the knife up for grabs. I yank it out with a grunt and clasp the handle so hard my fingers ache. Pointing it at them, or at least, the blurry shapes in my line of sight, I press my palm to my side to apply pressure to my new wound.

"Who's next?" I scream. "Take your best fucking shot." I keep blinking and hope that will clear up my sights and allow me to finish them off.

But I'm not as lucky as I thought I was. Especially when three more blobs turn their attention toward me. Spewing blood and inching back, I keep the knife out in front of my body.

Another shape rushes over, this one tackling one of my assailants and pinning him to the ground.

"Wren, are you okay?" Everest calls out toward me.

"Yeah," I cough. "I'm good." I swing through the air, somehow landing the sharp edge of the blade across one of my targets. My sights sharpen enough for me to charge the man I hit, and I use the momentary clarity to rush toward him and slam the knife into his chest.

One, two, three blows, and his body falls to the ground.

I spin and aim for another, my hand still pressed to my side.

This man kicks me in the shin, but instead of buckling to the blow the same way the other did, I grit my teeth and fight through it. A scream bubbles up and out of my chest as I allow the pain to flow through and power me forward. Everything aches. Dull and sharp and throbbing, all at once. Between the blood of the fallen and that of my own, I can't seem to tell who's is who's.

I kill, once more, my hunter nature rising to the surface and refusing to succumb to those that try to eliminate me. *This* is why I am furla ain. No amount of pain or suffering can break me. If they want me dead, they're going to have to take the bleeding heart from my chest.

A renewed sense of vigor flows through my veins, but when I turn toward the man who rushed over to save me, my mouth falls open and another scream forces its way between my lips.

Everest takes a sword straight through the stomach, his kind eyes going wide and meeting my frantic gaze.

"No!" I yell and dig my feet into the ground to run toward him. Without hesitating, I throw the man off him and slide my own knife into his attacker's chest, aimed directly at his heart. His life ends in one fell swoop and I turn my attention to Everest, the man who is the reason I'm here today. Not only did he save me moments ago, but back at Rockbridge, too. In more ways than one, really. If it weren't for his assistance, there's no telling if we would have been able to escape that place, let alone make it out alive.

Tears well in my eyes and my hands hover at the sword, still embedded in his torso.

"I...I..." If I remove it, he could bleed out within seconds, but if I leave it in, it could continue to do more damage.

"Pu-pull it out," he mutters.

And because I would do anything to make these final moments tolerable, I comply, slowly withdrawing the sword and tossing the blood-soaked thing aside.

"I'm so sorry," I tell him. "I never meant for you to get hurt."

Everest forces a smile. "Don't be sorry." He hacks up blood, his lips coated in crimson red. "Tell Jade..." He coughs again. "That I..."

"No," I shake my head and the tears scatter around us. "You're going to make it. You're going to tell her yourself." I push my hand to his gushing wound and will him to make it. I plead and beg with anyone who might be listening to spare his innocent life. He doesn't deserve this. None of them do.

My hand grows warm, and I wonder how much

blood he can lose before he's gone for good. I sniffle and dig into my pocket and pull out the device that Sydney had sent me in with. I shove it into his palm and close his fingers around it.

"I'm going to let go, Everest. And when I do, I need you to push that button. Can you do that for me? Push the button and go home. Be with your love." I stare into his deep blue eyes. "Do not die here, do you hear me?" I rise to my feet and chew at the inside of my lip to stop the tears from coming. "Go home, Everest. Be free."

With whatever strength he's able to muster, his entire body disappears before my eyes, leaving behind not a shred of proof that he was here other than his blood that stains the ground and covers my hands.

I swallow down the sadness threatening to take hold, and channel the pain to bring me back to this reality. Everest is gone. One more lost to the twisted war that Parla waged.

I turn toward the continued chaos, scanning the crowd to find the rest of my people.

"Where are you?" I yell into the battlefield. "Come out and play, you fucking bitch." I latch onto two knives and secure them in my grasp as I run toward Bo, the closest of my friends. I fight my way to his side, returning to my position at his rear. Each footstep rattles the wound that has stopped bleeding on my stomach, but I ignore it; I ignore the exhaustion that wants to drag me under.

"Was worried about you for a second, Birdie," Bo shouts over his shoulder.

"Never been better," I tell him while gripping onto a hunter's shoulder with one hand, holding him in place, and shoving the knife in my grasp into his chest. I push him aside and settle my sights on my fated mate in the near distance. "Let's get to Wes."

Bo and I move as a solid unit, beating and kicking and slicing our path to Wes, one dead body at a time. It doesn't take us long, working better together, to make it to him.

"You good?" I ask Wes.

He grips the collar on his neck. "Could do without this, if I'm being honest."

From the blood coating his handsome face, he has claimed many victims, and without that fucking device, there's no telling how much more damage he could be inflicting. Parla was smart in launching that counterattack because if she hadn't, we might actually have the upper hand for a change.

Wes skims his gaze over my feeble frame. "You need to go back, Wren. Before it's too late."

"You know damn well I'm not leaving, not without finishing what I came here to do." If I go now, Parla will have won for good, and won't stop until she eliminates the last of the demons on this battlefield. They will not die while I run back to safety in Arthlia with my tail between my legs.

"I can't heal you." Wes tugs at the magical device again. "Not while I still have this on."

"I wouldn't let you even if you could. You need to preserve your energy for battle." I turn my back to him and wait for the next wave of hunters to attack.

"My energy"—he yells over the chaos erupting around us—"is pointless without you."

The wendigo that was once our enemy runs full speed ahead toward us, carrying two smaller swords in his grasp, slicing through the bellies of hunters on his journey toward us.

"Not this guy," Bo huffs.

"He's on our side, remember?" I give the wendigo space to join us in our growing little kill circle.

"The numbers keep rising," he shouts. "No matter how many we kill, they keep coming."

I breathe in deeply and scan the vicinity. "We have to take out Parla or this will never stop. She must be cloning them or something. I don't fucking know. But unless we get to her, we're fighting a losing battle."

Even if I were able to use my powers to break the compulsion, I don't have enough strength to do it with an endless supply of grunts at her disposal.

"Or"—Bo chimes in—"we kill the witch that's helping her."

I think back to the old man that she was using to torture me at Rockbridge. He didn't want to be used as a pawn, but he had no choice. I'm sure this new witch is in the same situation, too. If we kill them, who's to say she doesn't have another in her pocket to pull out as a replacement? How many witches must die before her arsenal runs dry?

Even if I wanted to retreat and save what's left of Prania's demonic population, I'm not capable of doing the spell to send them to Arthlia. The only reason I'm here is because of an astral projection spell that is performed by another, more powerful witch. The single path forward is the one where Parla's head is on the end of my sword.

One of us has to die—that's the only way this ends.

And as more hunters fill the gaps where their fallen have perished and surround the few of us that remain, I realize, this battle might finally be coming to an end once and for all.

21
WES

There is no greater desire coursing through me than to heal Wren.

But I can't.

Not with the device around my neck suppressing my powers.

She's stubborn. Too stubborn. And refuses to return to the safety of Arthlia.

How can I blame her when her determination and her dedication to follow through is one of the things I love most about her?

Wren is fierce.

I knew it from the first moment I saw her.

My hound locked its sights on her, and from that day forward, my life has forever been changed.

If only my hound would show the fuck up and unleash itself on every single person that stands in the way of what my beloved wants most—to free Prania of its cruel leader.

And without him, I'm not certain any of us will make it out of here alive.

There's no way Bo will leave her, not when he's more afraid to lose her than death itself.

It's a feeling both of us share, along with the phoenix who, hopefully, remains concealed in the darkness of the building near us.

This war is far from over and Wren gave him specific orders to not come out until then.

He knows better than to risk his, and her life, by exposing and putting himself in danger. Wren would easily become more distracted than she already is and potentially falter at the wrong moment in the same manner she had that fateful day at the warehouse.

Our mate bond flickered to life, causing us both to waver. I hadn't realized that's what had happened, but later, Wren confirmed she felt it, too, and that's why she was overcome by the demons that almost brought her to her death.

Love is often more disruptive than the visceral urge to stay alive.

"What's the plan?" Bo yells over his shoulder at our small group.

"Where's Pippa?" Wren calls out. "We should stick together."

We've been fighting these battles on our own, it couldn't hurt to try a group effort if we want to make it out of this alive. Individually, we've held our own, but our defenses are weakening, and there's no telling how much time we have left.

"This way," I tell them.

Gritting my teeth, I plead with my hound to return, to blast through the device clamped around my neck, and end this war once and for all. With him, I'm confident our chances of survival would greatly increase, but without him, I'm not so certain.

I slam my fist into a hunter and latch onto his shoulders, steadying him and giving Bo the chance to drive a knife straight through his chest. Discarding his lifeless body on the ground, I continue on my path toward Pippa, who is battling two hunters by herself.

If the hunters didn't continue to spawn out of nowhere, victory would have already been ours, but it seems Parla has a never-ending supply of men at her disposal.

"Are you okay?" Wren shouts overtop the chaos to Pippa.

Pippa wipes at her brow, her chest heaving. "Yeah. You?" Her gaze trails to Wren's blood-soaked body, no doubt wondering what is hers and what's her victims.

Not very convincingly, Wren nods. "We need to find and eliminate Parla, otherwise they're going to just keep coming."

"I say we take out the witch," Bo suggests before ripping the throat out of a hunter that charged him.

"No," Wren protests. "She'll only find another and

then another. We have to kill her. That's the only way this stops."

From all directions, hunters appear, knives and swords locked in their grasps, blank stares on their faces.

Our small but mighty group tightens, all our backs facing each other in a kill circle. Collectively, we rotate and wait for our attackers to close in.

I glance over my shoulder at Wren, who despite being severely injured, is powering through. My heart aches at not being able to heal her, to save her from this nightmare, to win this war for her, and take her back to Arthlia where she will remain safe.

A large part of me wants to shove the device that Tremont had given us into Wren's hand and force her to return to safety, but she would never forgive me. Her being mad sounds better than losing her forever, though.

My thoughts return to battle, my body reacting automatically to the men that charge at us. I punch, I kick, I drag my nails across throats and rip them out. I kill without hesitation, my only desire is to eliminate anyone who stands in the way between Wren and what she came here to do.

But the numbers continue to grow. One hunter turns into two. Then three. Four. Ten.

I end a life and more come—this battle endless, and the damage we inflict on them not seeming to make a dent at all.

Wren gets farther away from me, but I keep a watchful eye on her every chance I get between my own kills. She can handle herself, but with the injuries she's sustained and the fatigue hitting her harder than ever, I need to be aware of when she's hit the threshold of what she can no longer take. I want to give her the freedom and space to continue in battle, but I refuse to let her become yet another casualty in this war.

A stout hunter lands a blow across my face, snapping me back to reality.

He drives a blade forward and I jump sideways, barely evading the blade. It slices through the outer flesh of my stomach but doesn't penetrate any deeper.

The wendigo that has caused so much turmoil lurches forward and grips my attacker's head, ripping it clean off the attached body, and tosses it carelessly to the ground.

"Thanks," I blurt out, never having expected I would thank the man who killed Dash twice.

Two hunters storm him, one of them shoving a sword straight through the torso of the antlered man. The wendigo's eyes go wide, and he steels his gaze down at the blade piercing through him. He looks up at me and says, "Pull it out," before spinning his back toward me.

Trying not to inflict any more damage, I slide the knife out of him and watch in amazement as he palms both of his attacker's heads and smashes them together.

I use the darkly coated sword to slice through the next hunter that runs toward me, cutting his head clean off his body. The thud of his remains hitting the ground echoes through me somehow louder than the anarchy happening around us.

"Are you okay?" I yell out at the wendigo.

But he doesn't answer me, he just continues fighting anyone that comes within arm's reach. Black blood oozes out of the wound in his torso and makes me wonder how much longer he has left—how much longer any of us have left.

And as more and more hunters close in around us, worry overtakes me that all hope might be lost.

I once told Wren that I would find her in the next life, and I've never meant anything more. I don't know what that entails, but deep within me, I'm certain that this lifetime wasn't our first together. And it won't be our last. There's something eerily familiar about being near her. Even her scent unlocks memories I can't quite locate. Like a gentle whisper of the past to remind me that she truly is my fated mate. That no matter what, we will return to one another.

Perhaps that's the only thing bringing me any fragment of comfort as I stare down a death sentence that seems impossible to escape.

"We're outnumbered," Pippa calls out from our kill circle.

"Keep fighting!" Wren shouts.

She has the ability to leave. All she has to do is

mutter the word Tremont gave us. Bo and I have the same option. Neither of us will return without her. Pippa and the wendigo don't have that luxury, and if they did, I'm certain Wren would insist they flee. She would grant freedom to any of the demons remaining in this realm if she could. Maybe then she would return to Arthlia, if she knew they would be safe from Parla's wrath. That is not an option though, and the only way Wren will leave this wretched place is if Parla dies.

Hunters attack us from all sides, charging us at easily triple the rate. But despite their numbers, they lack the same tenacity for survival that we do. They're mindless, where we are overcome by the need to free this realm from their unfair torment.

Still, I can't help but wonder if our determination will be enough to see this through.

I yank at my collar, hoping there will be a weakness in its hold on me. But it's no use, this thing is magically bound, and my hound is not here to put up a fight. Doesn't he realize the severity of the situation? Doesn't he see that if he remains suppressed, it might be the difference between any of us making it out of here alive?

"Come on, you bastard," I mutter. "Where are you?" I skim my gaze across the foggy terrain and pray to the Angels that my sights will land upon Parla. If I could find her, then maybe this could end.

But instead of locating that ignorant bitch, I blink

and do a double take on the man who shouldn't be here.

A fist lands across my face, and I quickly regain my footing to snap the neck of the hunter who attacked me.

"Tremont," I blurt out and settle my sights on him as he runs toward us, a faint transparent orb around him and the beautiful woman at his side.

Her almost white hair flows in waves around her shoulders and for the slightest second, I'm mesmerized by the strange resemblance she has to Wren. Her features are the opposite of Wren's yet somehow similar. Wren's rugged exterior conceals the soft lines of her femininity but that doesn't mean it isn't there, hidden just under the surface.

"Willow?" Wren appears at my side, her stance wide and ready for another attack. "What are you doing here?"

Willow and Tremont come into our circle, and it isn't lost on me how Willow remains stiff at Tremont's side. She doesn't trust him, and I don't blame her. From what I've heard of their past, I'm surprised she hasn't already killed him just to rid him of her life.

"I came as soon as I could," Willow tells us, her eyes darting over the few of us that remain.

Other demons are fighting around us, but the numbers keep dwindling the more the hunters respawn in the arena.

"If you're here, who's holding the spell?" Wren narrows in on Tremont.

"Sydney," Willow tells her. She side-eyes Tremont briefly before continuing. "I didn't want him to be in charge of sending me in."

Pippa and the wendigo battle the hunters and keep most of them from us as we catch up with the newcomers.

"Where's Everest?" Tremont asks, finally breaking his silence.

"I sent him back," Wren says. "He was in rough shape. You must have missed him."

Willow steals a glance around us. "There's too many of them. You're fighting a losing battle."

"They're mind controlled." Wren steps toward Willow. "I was able to break the compulsion, but I killed the person on accident."

Willow tucks her hair behind her ears and exhales. "Take my hand." She holds her arm out between her and Wren. "I have an idea."

Without hesitation, Wren plants her palm in Willow's. "What do you need me to do?"

"Whatever it was that broke the compulsion." Willow's gaze trails up, lingering on the device around my neck, to meet mine. "Hold them off, okay?"

I nod and put my body between the two Oliver witches and the endless hunters, turning to keep one eye on them while I do everything I can to keep them from harm's way. I snap another neck with ease, the guilt of these deaths piling up on top of each other. I shouldn't care about ending their lives, but if they truly are under Parla's spell, why do they deserve to die pointlessly? If only she would stop being a coward and face us herself.

My stomach lurches when I spot that familiar red hair across the battlefield. Stepping over the rubble of the building he was supposed to remain concealed in, Dash emerges into plain sight. I swallow and dart my attention to Wren, who remains attached to Willow, a powerful energy radiating off them. With her eyes pinched shut, she doesn't see one of the men she loves walking right into the line of fire.

I want to tell her and run as fast as I can over the dead bodies that litter this land and shove him back to safety, but I can't, not when doing so would put her in danger. I must wait it out and hope like hell that Dash has a damn good reason for going against Wren's wishes.

His gaze momentarily locks onto mine and I shake my head, a warning that he shouldn't be doing what he is. Dash remains steadfast as he cautiously, but foolishly, surfaces from the safety of that building. I'm grateful he's alive, only I'm unsure how much longer that will last now that he is no longer concealed.

"It's not working," Wren tells Willow. "Something's wrong."

Tremont steps toward them. "You need an amplifier."

Willow narrows her gaze at him. "That won't work."

Tremont nods. "Yes, it will." But there's something solemn written across his face I can't quite make out. What could he be hiding? His betrayal? His next move? The reason he was drawn to us all along? The final moment when he shows us who he really is?

"It could kill you," Willow adds.

"Wren," Tremont says, ignoring what Willow just told him. "The demonic power you yield is getting in the way."

"What?" I finish killing the man in my grasp and turn my head toward them. "You said she was..."

Tremont doesn't indulge me yet remains focused on my mate. "You know what I'm talking about."

Wren swallows and dips her head slightly in acknowledgment.

"What is he talking about?" Willow asks her.

But when the tears form in Wren's eyes, I understand exactly what he means. I had worried that Wren was involved in stealing demon magic, but I hoped that she would never stoop that low and do such a dreadful thing.

Wren hasn't just been killing every demon she was sent out to eliminate, she's been stealing their essence and harnessing it within her so Parla could harvest it and grow in power. The same thing that had been happening to Willow's family, was the very thing that she has been doing to demons. Is she aware of how wrong that is? How similar to what had been happening to her ancestral line? Did she know what she was doing or was she only another pawn in Parla's twisted game? There's no way she hadn't figured this out by now, and considering how hell-bent she was on returning here to eliminate Parla, I wouldn't be surprised if she thought killing her would somehow redeem the treachery that she has done.

But getting herself killed isn't going to erase or make right any of her actions.

Wren's lips part. "I..."

I step forward and interrupt her. "There's no time," I tell them. "Whatever it is, it can wait."

Wren's wavering gaze meets mine and I've never wanted to pull her to my chest more than I do at this very moment. To reassure her that although what she did was wrong, that I understand—that I forgive her, that she shouldn't punish herself for the sins someone else manipulated her into doing. And perhaps, that's why she's gone easy on Tremont, because he was under someone else's influence when he stole the Oliver power. His crimes were not much different than hers, and with the years he spent in Rockbridge, he seemed to have learned that what he did was wrong.

"Allow me." Tremont holds out his hand toward Wren. "Please." His stare pleads with her and for the first time in a long while, I believe he means well. I've always been skeptical of him, but if my gut is right, he really does want to make amends.

"It's okay," I say. "If he hurts you, I'll snap his neck."

Wren reluctantly slides her hand into his. "What do I need to do?"

"Just let me in, I'll do the rest." Tremont flits his attention to Willow. "I know it doesn't mean much to you, but I'm sorry. For lying to you, hurting you, everything I did that played a part in the suppression of the Oliver's magical bloodline." He shakes his head. "It was wrong. I see that now. I have for a while. I should have never done the things I did. I don't expect you to forgive me, but you must know how sorry I am."

Willow glares at him through her lashes. "I don't forgive you."

"That's fine. I'm not asking for your forgiveness." Tremont, with his greying hair and tired face, focuses on Wren. "It was a pleasure meeting you."

His last statement feels more like a goodbye than anything else, and it makes me question whether I should have offered my approval.

But before I can say anything, four hunters attack, and I'm forced to react. I duck and avoid one man's punch, spinning and kicking at the same time, knocking another of the men down. I shove the sword through the chest of the tallest man, quickly withdrawing it and slamming the brunt edge of the handle into the other's face. Blood splatters and adds to the already gory atmosphere.

I catch Wren out of the corner of my eye, her body trembling under Tremont's authority. He shudders even more as a current of dark magic floats out of her and into him. Is he absorbing the demonic magic? Should I stop him from continuing whatever it is he's doing? Or should I risk the life of my mate in hopes that he's actually trying to help?

Wren's eyes pop open and she glows in a way that I've never quite experienced from her before. She's still injured and exhausted but there's something different about her.

"Now," Tremont calls out to her. "Try again."

Willow and Wren lock hands while Tremont still keeps hold of Wren.

A crackle of white light blasts out from the womens' embrace that's surely enough to temporarily blind anyone who might be looking their way.

Tremont holds his other hand toward the sky, the power leaving the girls and flowing out of him. His body stiffens and for the longest moment, a sharp and glaring brightness pours into the grim area.

The light increases its luster until all that can be seen is white.

I blink through the illumination as it fades and watch the man who was holding onto Wren collapse onto the ground.

Every single hunter on the battlefield stops their advances, some of their arms hovering in the air between them and their target.

"Stop," I scream at everyone. "Stop fighting."

For the first time in the history of my life in Prania, the

hunters and demons exist in a space without immediately killing one another. Every person, hunter and demon alike, seems dazed and confused, but none of them continue with their previous attempt at murdering one another.

"What are you waiting for?" a voice calls out, this one feminine and familiar.

I locate the source a distance away, unmoving hunters circled around her.

"Kill them," Parla commands.

I skim my attention across the many people that remain, waiting and wondering which one is going to make the first move. Have Wren and Willow really broken the compulsion or is this some fleeting moment before we lose it all?

Dash comes into my line of sight, his body inching toward the woman we came here to kill.

"Dash," Wren mumbles, her own vision locking onto him.

But when she releases Willow's hand and takes a step forward, she doesn't make it any farther. Her body collapses onto the ground next to Tremont's.

I'm at her side in a flash, and Bo joins me as we turn her lifeless body over. Blood coats her face, and I can't quite determine if it belongs to her or someone else. My hand presses softly against the wound on her stomach and tears uncontrollably well in my eyes.

"Wren," I whisper.

Bo clenches his jaw and breathes in deeply. "She's

still alive. I can hear her pulse. It's faint, but she's still in there." He meets my gaze. "It's fading fast."

I shove the person I care most about in this world into another man's arms. "Take her back. I'll be right behind you." As much as it kills me to leave her, Bo is better suited for the job. With the mark still remaining on her neck, it has to be him that returns her to Arthlia, otherwise, there's no telling the amount of danger she would face when the beacon activates, and she isn't able to protect herself.

What kind of mate would I be if I force her to return without following through with why she came here? I must finish her mission and return Dash to her unharmed. With him stepping closer and closer to Parla, I grow unsure of how much time he has left.

Latching onto Willow's wrist, I steady her attention on me. "Save her, please. I'll do whatever it takes. Just don't let her die."

Willow nods stiffly and lowers herself to the ground next to Wren. She exchanges a glance with Bo, and a moment later, the three of them disappear; my heart and soul leaves with them. Rage, unlike anything I've felt in the past, builds within me. Greater than when Mother and Jade were taken from me. More than when I found out Mother was killed. More than the time I spent in Rockbridge knowing that they were torturing my mate.

No, this is different. This feels final. Absolute.

There's an undiluted fury at being this close to the finish line and coming up short.

But I refuse to allow Wren to succumb without avenging her.

My nostrils flare and that familiar sense of warmth courses through me. I press both hands around the device still clamped around my neck. I exhale and grip it tighter, not caring at all about how it digs into my flesh as I tug each side away from the other. The metal cracks under my pressure until finally, I snap the thing clean off and toss it onto the ground.

Fire, quick and hot, licks at my flesh, my hound rising to the surface.

"About damn time," I mutter.

I could say the same to you, he growls in my mind.

I narrow my gaze across the way at the woman who is responsible for this bloodbath.

She takes a step back, stumbling over the corpse of one of her soldiers. Her arms go wide to catch herself but the phoenix is there, gripping her shoulders and holding her in place.

"You're not going anywhere," he tells her.

"For ages, Prania has been plagued," I say loud enough for anyone near to hear. "We were told that it was a feud with demons and hunters, but..." I glance to my left, then to my right. "In reality, we have one common enemy." I point a fiery finger toward Parla. "Her."

The few remaining demons follow behind me, while some of the hunters march in my wake, too.

"This stops today." I continue forward until I'm only a few feet from where Dash has Parla hostage. "Someone else hold her." I make eye contact with the wendigo and he immediately walks over to take Dash's place.

"You won't get away with this," she blurts out, desperate to say anything to attempt to threaten me. "I'm not the only one. If you kill me, you'll never find out who's next."

I laugh. "I've had enough of your fear tactics."

The mob of people stands in wait, no longer attacking each other but coming together to witness the end of an era.

I step toward her, my hand creeping closer, the fire burning a bit brighter.

Parla wiggles in the wendigo's grasp but is no match for his strength.

Wrapping my hand around her throat, I unleash some of my power. "How does it feel?"

Her skin melts under my grasp. Her scream pierces my ears. And I wish there was a way to bottle up this agony so I could gift it to Wren in the afterlife. To show her that in the end, Parla suffered.

She doesn't deserve a quick death, yet a long and antagonizing one. If I had it my way, I would imprison her in Rockbridge and expose her to the same torment she did to us, only dragging it out over decades until she withered away to nothing. I would peel every inch of flesh from her body but make sure she lived through every tortured moment just to experience that same pain over and over. I would have a witch take away her free will and force her to hurt herself and then sit back and watch her anguish and attempt to withstand the control. I would revel in the bliss of certainty that she would never hurt another person, hunter or demon, ever again.

But if I had it my way, the barrier trapping the citizens of Prania within its confines would never cease to exist. The only way to free them is to kill Parla once and for all.

I release her from my fiery grip and bask in the tears streaming down her cheeks and the sticky flesh that remains on my hand. I shake it to my side, ridding myself of her skin, and turn toward the horde that's formed behind me.

"Your entire life is a lie. You have been under the influence of this pathetic excuse of a woman right here. She convinced us that we were enemies so we would kill each other without question." I press my hand to my chest. "I have been to Arthlia. I have seen the coexistence of creatures. We do not have to hate one another. We can live in peace."

Parla spits blood onto the ground near me and chuckles. "You know nothing of peace."

I spin on my heel and face her. "You used my mate.

You convinced her that I was the enemy, and you made her kill for you."

A chilling smile creeps across her face. "That's not all I made her do."

Stepping forward, I peer down at her. "You think I don't know?" I shake my head. "You should be ashamed of yourself."

Dash comes closer and I move to give him space. "Remember me?"

Parla glares up at him. "How could I forget?"

"You killed me. Over and over again. And when you were done with me, you beat me until I had no memory of who I was."

"My only regret," she says. "Was not finding a way to kill you for good."

Dash's jaw tenses and I expect him to snap at her, to follow through with his innate desire to end her life that I don't doubt is coursing through him right now. But he doesn't. No, he remains planted in place in front of her, his form fixed to the ground.

"I thought I wanted to kill you," he tells her. "But that would be too easy. Too kind for you." Dash glances over his shoulder. "So instead, I'm going to watch as they rip you apart. *You* Parla, are the evil that must be purged from this world."

"Wh-what?" Parla's evil eyes widen.

Dash grins. "You heard me." He pops his fingers into his mouth and whistles loudly. He raises his voice and faces the crowd. "If anyone would like to have a piece of her, now is your chance."

Murmurs fill the space and without another moment passing, bodies approach from all directions, only this time, they're trained on the true villain, not us.

Dash and I take a cautious step back, leaving Parla there, secured by the wendigo who once wanted nothing more than to kill us.

"Are you sure about this?" I ask Dash.

If anyone deserves to get their pound of flesh, it's Dash. After everything he's been through, he should be able to feel the satisfaction of taking her life.

It's a shame she doesn't have resurrection abilities so we could each get a shot at ending her life repeatedly.

"I just want to go home." Dash keeps his attention focused on Parla as the crowd springs toward her.

She screams out but it's no use.

A demon claws at her back, a hunter jabs his knife through her stomach. Another demon sinks its fangs into her neck while the wendigo keeps her upright, his razor-sharp fingers impaled into her shoulders.

Parla disappears but her cries remain until eventually, they fade out among the cheers of the lasting victors. And with her departure, another burst of bright light fills the entire realm, followed by something I have never seen in all my years of living in Prania.

The sky. Blue and hazy with fluffy clouds.

"I can't believe it." I blink twice and steady my squinted eyes.

The crowd roars louder and dissipates from the woman they were descending upon. Only pieces of her remain. A twitching hand, a mutilated leg, part of her torso. The few demons that stay near her continue munching on her corpse until nothing is left of her.

I breathe in deeply, the air in this realm already seeming fresher than it ever has been.

"We did it," I say out loud to no one in particular. "Prania is free."

But with that declaration, my heart constricts, the uncertainty of whether my mate will live to learn the outcome of this war eating me alive.

Pippa appears at my side, her face covered in blood but seeming otherwise unharmed. "Is she going to make it?" Her serious gaze darts back and forth between me and Dash.

"I don't know," I tell her, because truth be told, my hound and I are terrified that Parla isn't the only one that lost this battle today.

22
WREN

I'm sitting at the table, patiently waiting for my mother to cut off a chunk of cheese and pass it to me.

"Cheese was always your father's favorite, too." She smiles warmly at me, but I can't quite make out her whole face. "I prefer bread..."

I take the piece she offers me, glancing down at my small hands.

This doesn't make sense, none of it does.

Where am I? Why am I here?

Is this a dream, a memory, or maybe a nightmare?

Commotion sounds in the distance but grows closer to our home.

My mother sighs. "Take the cheese and go hide. Don't come out until I find you. Okay, my sweet Birdie?"

A pang shoots through my heart. How could I forget that Mother called me Birdie? What else have I possibly forgotten?

I loved my mother, adored her more than anyone—how could that memory have escaped me? Seeing her now and feeling the emotions flood through me, I recognize that clear as day.

I grip the salty chunk and climb under the floorboards like we had done countless times before. My little heart patters away in my chest but I go along with my mother's orders. I would have done anything to make her happy.

Since Father left, there wasn't anything I wouldn't have done for her. I never made a fuss. Never told her when she burnt or undercooked a meal. Never mentioned when she braided my hair too tight or forgot to read me a bedtime story. I picked up after myself—and her when I could—and never asked for anything she wasn't already offering me. I could sense the sorrow, and I knew the only thing I could do for her was stay out of her hair—be a good girl.

I'm not sure when I realized Mother was sad, but perhaps I always knew.

She didn't speak of Father often, and those few times she did, it was a blessing.

So, when she asked me to hide, I did so without question. Anything for Mother.

I don't bother eating the cheese, not when Mother will soon come and tell me it's safe to come out. I wish to savor it with her because she is my favorite person.

But little did I know, that day would be different than all the rest.

And every day after would forever be changed.

Because instead of the commotion passing our shack like

it had those other times, the door flings open, and men step inside.

I peer through the cracks in the floor, my breath catching as they come farther in, closer to Mother. I want to scream, to shout, to draw their attention away from her, but I can't, not when she told me time and time again that I must remain quiet until she comes for me.

"No matter what, Birdie, you must not come out," she had said.

I hug the piece of cheese to my chest and do everything I can to steady my thudding heart. My eyes dart from person to person through the tiny cracks in the floor, and I wonder how long it'll be until they leave. I don't care if they take all the cheese, I just really want to be with Mother.

I'm frightened but I must obey her orders.

"Where's the girl?" one of the men asks her.

"I don't know what you're talking about," Mother tells him. "I live here alone."

Why would Mother lie about me being here? Is she ashamed of me?

Familiar clicking sounds across the floor but I can't quite place it.

The man presses a dagger against Mother's throat, a faint speckling of red kisses the tip of the blade. I clamp my hand over my mouth to suppress any noise that may arise.

"I'm going to ask you one more time...where is the girl?" He pushes the blade deeper, and I want nothing more than to jump through the floor and kick him in the shins. But I can't move. Not yet. Not when Mother told me to stay put.

"Kill her," a woman says.

Her voice is just as familiar as that clicking across the floor.

She comes into my line of sight, and the cheese falls from my hand, thudding onto the dirt beneath me.

The woman slowly turns in my direction but doesn't look directly at me. Instead, she continues glancing around until she's facing Mother again.

"What are you waiting for? I said kill her."

The man grabs the back of Mother's neck before she can move and slices the blade across her throat. Blood pools out and Mother drops to her knees. Her body falls forward and collapses on top of the floorboard above me, her once bright blue eyes dimming and filling with tears as she peers through at me.

"I'm sorry," she whispers, those two words meant for just me.

The scarlet pooling around her trickles down and speckles my small face, coating the piece of cheese I had dropped into the dirt.

"Burn the house down and find the girl." The woman crosses her arms over her chest, so unbothered about every-thing she's just ordered. "Then wipe her memory. Make her think demons did this. Then, she'll have no choice but to join our side."

"Yes, ma'am," another one of the men says.

I remain there, silent tears running down my cheeks as I stare into the eyes of my dead mother. How will I know when it's safe to come out if she doesn't tell me?

But when the bad people leave and many minutes pass, I wonder if I could stay down here forever?

Only, the fire that consumes my home and the smoke that fills my lungs makes it difficult to remain any longer. If I don't want to find out what happens when the flames find me and the smoke fills my lungs, I must do something.

I push on the boards above me, but they won't budge.

"Mommy, you're too heavy," I say to my dead mother. "I can't get out." I push harder and wipe at the sweat and tears on my face. Coughing, I fall to my knees and beg the universe for an ounce of fresh air. "There has to be another way."

I dig my fingers into the dirt, clawing my way under the house in a desperate attempt to escape. I don't want to leave Mother behind, but if I don't, I won't make it out either. Maybe it would be better that way. If I stay with Mother so she doesn't go into the afterlife alone. What if Daddy isn't there to help her find her way? Who will guide Mommy if I don't?

I stop digging and look back at where Mommy once was, but the smoke makes it too hard to see exactly. What if I'm too late and Mother already went without me? I don't want to be alone, there or here.

"What do I do?" I ask no one but myself.

But when a slight flickering of light appears near my fingers, my gut tells me that I must continue forward. I scrape my nails into the ground and rake out what dirt I can, frantic to find an exit from this hell.

I continue scraping away the dirt, throwing it behind me and going back for more.

Until finally, the cool night air greets me, and I squeeze through the small gap to free myself from under our burning house. I gasp for breath and wipe my nose on my shoulder as I take in the sight of the flames engulfing the house. Dirt cakes my face, and I scoot away from the fire, unsure of what I'm supposed to do.

Mother told me to wait. But now that she's gone, what do I do?

I crawl away from the house and into a shrub, hiding from anyone who might wander by. I allow the tears to fall and pull my legs to my chest. I cry until there is nothing left that remains, the waterworks disappearing just like Mother does in the rubble of what was once home.

I fall into a dreamless sleep and hope that I never wake.

But the darkness is soon replaced by a faint white light and a glowing, but beautiful creature that hovers in the distance.

It speaks to me. "You must wake up, Wren."

I rub my eyes, still in my dream, and shake my head. "I don't want to."

"Sometimes, we must do things we don't want to."

"I'm scared," I tell the creature.

"You're allowed to be afraid, but you mustn't give up."

"Mother is gone. I have no one." I sniffle. "Who are you?"

"I cannot stay." The creature flutters in and out of sight.

"I'm already being pulled from this realm. But Wren, you must wake up. Wake up. Wake up."

I shoot my eyes open, gasping for breath, and find strong hands that latch onto each side of me.

"Wren," Bo blurts out. He tugs me to his chest and practically smothers me. "Angels, I thought you were a goner."

I catch my breath and recall the terrible dream I had just had. One that felt too damn real.

No, it couldn't have been a dream, it must have been a memory.

But that isn't what I remember from that fateful day.

The version I've always known is of demons coming into my home and killing Mother.

My stomach sinks at hearing Parla tell the men to find and alter my memory.

Is that what really happened? Parla manipulated my recollection of that day in order to brainwash me into being on her side of the war? What other choice did she have? There's no way I would have joined her if I knew she was the reason my mother was dead.

I didn't think it was possible to hate Parla any more, and somehow, here I am, seething with the insatiable desire to wrap my hands around her throat until her eyes bulge from their sockets.

"Birdie, talk to me." Bo smooths the hair from my cheek and stares into my eyes. His touch is soft and gentle and unlike how he normally is.

Am I still dreaming?

Taking in the room, I recognize that I'm in Sydney's home—not in Prania.

My heart picks up its pace as I frantically put the pieces together.

"Wh-where's Dash and Wes? Did they make it out?"

"They're alive and well. They ran out of matches downstairs, so Wes went to light the fire. Dash is checking in on Jade."

Uncontrollable tears tumble down my cheeks. "Everest," I whisper, neither a question nor a statement.

"Don't worry about him. He's going to be fine."

My eyes widen and my mouth drops open. "Fine? He survived?"

Bo's cheeks turn up into the faintest smile. "They don't know what you did, or how you did it, but he was partially healed when he came back. You saved him, Birdie."

"We saved each other," I mutter the same words that he and Jade had shared once before.

"Are you okay?" Bo runs his rough palm over my shoulder and down my arm. "Are you in any pain?"

"I'm fine." I reposition myself, ignoring the aches in my body. They're nothing compared to the thought that I had lost any of my people.

My people. Is that what they are?

But how can I celebrate their lives when I never freed Prania of its tyrant, Parla?

Disappointment fills me anyway. How many more has she killed in the time I've spent unconscious?

"What's with the face, Birdie? What is it?"

"I...I have to go back," I tell him. "I have to finish what I started. Even if it's too late." I scoot out from under the covers and swing my legs off the side of the bed, noting that I'm no longer wearing my armor. Someone must have undressed and cleaned me prior to putting me here.

Bo doesn't stop me, but he says, "It's done, Wren. It's over."

I meet his dark stare. "What do you mean?"

Footsteps patter on the stairs outside our room, drawing our attention temporarily.

Dash rounds the corner first, his face breaking out into a contagious smile the second he's through the door. Wes is on his heels, the sheer sight of him calming my raging nerves. Bo might have said that they were fine, but seeing them in the flesh is something else entirely.

"You're awake," Dash says while rushing toward me. "Do you need anything? Water? Food? I could get you some cheese."

I wrap my arms around his torso and breathe him in. "This is all I need," I mutter into his chest.

He releases me and presses a soft kiss on my forehead. "You had us worried."

I shift my sights on Wes and hop off the edge of the

bed, doing my best to walk normally over to him. My body throbs but it isn't anything a couple days won't mend. My injuries were much more severe when I was in Prania, meaning only one thing—Wes healed me.

"You should get back in bed." Wes cups both sides of my face between his hands and runs his thumbs over my cheeks. He pulls me closer and kisses the tip of my nose before dragging me toward him. "I thank the Angels that you're okay."

I allow myself one full minute of his embrace, my body melting into his and reveling in the reality that all four of us made it out alive. But once that minute is up, I break away and stand on my own. "Bo said it was done. What did he mean?" I glance around at my men, waiting for one of them to answer me.

Bo reaches for my hand and tugs me back to the bed. I comply and sit along the edge, grateful for the ability to get off my feet again. I've been worn out after battle before, but this is something else entirely. It's almost like my insides were taken out, thrown in a blender, and put back in without any consideration of where they belong.

Wes looks to Dash, the two of them making eye contact for an unbearably long moment.

"Someone tell me what's going on or I'm going to go back there and find out for myself," I say to them.

"She's gone, Wren," Wes finally spits out.

"Gone like, she got away?" My stomach turns at the

idea of her possibly escaping and continuing to wreak havoc on demons wherever she is.

"No," Dash confirms. "Gone like her body was ripped apart into so many pieces that when it was all said and done there was nothing left of her."

My lips part but I find myself unable to speak words.

"It's true," Wes says. "Dash and I witnessed it."

I tilt my head toward Bo, but he just shrugs.

"I was here with you, Birdie." He rubs his hand over my back.

"You didn't stay?" I ask him. "And continue to fight?"

He shakes his head. "My fight is where you are."

Has hell frozen over and Bo been body swapped with someone else? How long until he runs out of the room to avoid his emotions?

I don't push him, not yet. I don't have the energy to chase after him if he decides to flee.

"So you're saying Parla is dead. We all made it out alive. And Everest survived, too?" That's when it hits me, we weren't the only ones there. "Willow?"

"She's fine," Wes is the first to say. "Silas was waiting here for her, pissed that she went without him. But other than that, she's okay. Everyone made it except..."

"Tremont," Bo finishes where Wes left off. "Whatever magical bullshit you guys did, it killed him. He went down first, then you did shortly after. You had so much blood covering you I could barely tell what was yours."

"Pippa? The wendigo?" I hold my breath because there's no way we got *this* lucky.

"They were alive when we left Prania. They were celebrating. The hunters and demons were celebrating together." Wes folds his arms over his broad chest. "I wish you could have seen it, Wren. The sky, it was bright blue, the air, it was nothing like here in Arthlia, but it was fresher than it ever had been."

"I don't understand," I admit.

"When Parla died, the barrier disappeared," Dash says from his spot leaning against the bedpost.

"You did it, you really did it," I choke on the words as more tears threaten to break free. I've never cried this much in my entire life. Well, except...

"No," Bo places his large hand on top of mine. "You did it, Birdie. None of this would have been possible without you."

"She killed my mom," I blurt out. "And then she altered my memory to make me think demons did it."

Bo removes his hand and wraps it around my shoulder, pulling me toward him. "It's over now. She can't hurt anyone else."

"I'm so sorry," I tell them. "I can't believe how easily she manipulated me. I..." This is the part where I tell them the truth, where I admit that I was the reason

Parla had as much power as she did. The part where they grow disgusted with what I had done and decide that they no longer want to be with me. I'd rather keep the truth concealed, never allowing anyone to know how terrible of a person I am, but how can I lie to the people I love and not give them the chance to make that decision for themselves?

"Don't be so hard on yourself." Dash lowers himself onto the bed next to me, sandwiching me between him and Bo.

Wes kneels at my feet and puts his hands on my thighs. "You did what anyone else would have. We don't blame you for that."

I sniffle and brace myself for the moment when I ruin everything. "That isn't it," I say. "There's more. And I understand if you change your mind about me. But I can't continue to keep this from you."

Wes grips my legs tighter and forces my gaze on him. "We know, Wren. We know and we understand."

I shake my head. "You can't possibly."

Dash puts his hand on my back and rubs gentle circles. "That's why she wanted you so badly, because you could take the power without dying."

Bo sighs. "We kind of put it together on our own, Birdie. But we don't fault you for following orders. Whether you knew what you were doing or not, that isn't who you are anymore. You've shown us, and anyone who meets you, what kind of person you are."

"You don't hate me?" I hate the way my voice cracks when I ask such a simple question.

Each of them holds onto me a bit firmer, telling me everything I need to know. That they aren't going anywhere. Not now, not ever.

I don't know what I did to deserve them, but damn do I feel like the luckiest girl alive.

23

WREN

"Are you sure you want to do this?" Willow asks me. "It's only been a week since you got back."

"I would have done it the night I woke up if you would have let me," I tell her. "I don't enjoy not sticking to my word."

"Who could have blamed you? You were off saving the world."

I laugh. "One realm is not the whole world."

She smirks at me. "It is to some people."

We step through the threshold to the Harper Shadow Academy, students passing us by without a second look in our direction.

It's strange being this near both humans and super-naturals, but I'm growing used to the weirdness of this realm—how very non-threatening it is.

When you've run to and from danger your entire

life, it takes some getting used to not assuming every single person that crosses your path is a threat.

"This way," Willow tells me as she leads me down a hallway off the right of the entryway. "I was able to buy some time on the other obligations, but I wanted to guide you through assisting in the barrier spell."

"Is it difficult?" I step into an empty classroom and immediately, I focus on the far corner where a sort of ripple in the seam crackles. "What is that?"

"That would be a shadow realm." She holds the door open long enough for Headmaster Walker to come in behind us, and then latches it shut. "Morning," she says to him.

He extends a cup in both of our directions. "Good morning, ladies. Coffee?"

Headmaster Walker has always been kind, especially to Willow. It's almost like he's a father figure in her life. If I didn't know better, I would assume he *was* her father. But Willow has told me of her biological father and the great lengths it took to locate him. Another one of the many mysterious and dangerous adventures she went on in her journey to free the Olivers of their curse. Still, that doesn't make the relationship she has with the Headmaster any less important. He was there for her through the darkest of times and that alone forged an intense bond between them.

"Thanks," Willow says to him while taking one of the cups.

"Thank you." I do the same.

"Sydney's been teaching me, so hopefully it doesn't taste horrible." He rubs his hands together and points to the ceiling. "We're overdue for reinforcing the barrier."

"I'm sure it's great." Willow takes a cautious sip and nods. "It's great."

Walker smiles triumphantly. "I can do advanced spells and somehow manage running a covert supernatural academy, but damn if making a good cup of coffee isn't the most challenging thing I've ever had to do."

"Sometimes the hardest things are those we cannot use magic for." Willow steps farther into the room and glances up at the ceiling. "I see the breakage here."

Walker follows her over. "I suspended all shadow classes the second I spotted it. Wouldn't want a repeat of your first semester here."

"No, we wouldn't." Willow sets her coffee on a nearby table and focuses on me. "That's a story for another day."

I take a quick drink from my cup, savoring the rich warmth of the coffee. "You're right, this is good."

"I went with mocha today," Walker adds.

Setting my cup next to hers, I join the two of them under the glistening magical forcefield. "What is that thing?"

"It's an opening to a realm very near to ours where students do a lot of their supernatural training. It's one of the ways we're able to conduct magical classes without the other students having any knowledge of it. It's only visible to the supernatural eye. But, if not maintained, it can grant direct access to anyone trying to enter our dimension. Good or bad," Walker explains.

"Wouldn't want that to happen." I study the hazy purple as it floats near the corner of the ceiling. "What do you need me to do?"

"Take my hand, like we did back in Prania." Willow steps toward me.

Without question, I slide my palm in line with hers. I haven't known her long, but I'm not sure there isn't anything I wouldn't do for her. She's not just family, she's a damn good person. She didn't have to come to Prania and fight a battle that wasn't hers, but she did it anyway, and for that, I will be forever grateful.

If it weren't for her, I may not have made it out of there alive. Willow might be the very reason *any* of us lived to see another day.

And surprisingly enough, Tremont sacrificed himself to make that happen, too. He gave his life to prove that he had changed. And I'll spend the rest of mine doing that same thing.

"Now take your other hand and hold it up like this." She points her palm to the ceiling, her magic already dancing along her flawless skin. Soft purple mixed with a faint pink flutter on her hand, and for a second, I'm completely mesmerized by how beautiful it is.

I do as she says, hoping that the movements are

similar enough to hers to do whatever it is that needs to be done.

"Good." Walker opens a small leather-bound book and traces his finger along the text. He mumbles a few of the words but I can't quite make out what they are.

I focus my attention on my arm and grow amazed when a reddish hue appears in the same way the pinkish purple did for Willow.

Expecting discomfort, I wait for whatever Walker is saying to do what it's supposed to do. But instead of pain or distress, he simply snaps the book shut and says, "All done."

I blink a few times and hesitantly lower my arm. "That's it?" I rub at where the magic was only moments prior.

"That was easier than I thought it was going to be," Willow chimes in.

"I'm not surprised." Walker leans his butt against the nearby desk. "Willow, you alone made this tedious task tremendously simple, but add the both of you, it's a cakewalk."

"Speaking of cake. I'm kind of hungry." I ate a banana before leaving the house, but I find myself suddenly famished.

"That's normal," Willow tells me with a kind smile. "Doing any kind of magic will typically leave you feeling a bit ravenous." She pats my shoulder. "You'll learn what to expect the more you practice. Some spells will take more out of you than others. That's why I have to be careful about where I spend my energy."

"Well, now that we know I can be of assistance, maybe I could pick up some of that slack." If I'm going to be living in her husband's house and eating their food, the least I could do is help. She's already done so much for me.

"Yeah." She nods and glances over to Walker. "That would be nice."

After saying our goodbyes to Walker, Willow and I exit the academy and make our way to her car. It's a bit nicer than Sydney's, with sleek edges and more comfortable seats.

I buckle in and wait for the death mobile to roar to life.

"Thank you," I say. "For trusting me with today."

Willow pushes a button that turns the car on, unlike Sydney's where you must insert a key. Does this one not require such things? I would ask but it seems too silly to bring up.

She pivots her body toward me. "It's what family does."

I breathe in her words, grateful for how welcoming she and her men have been. They could have easily dismissed us and thrown us aside. Instead, they've been more gracious than I probably deserve.

"I know you didn't want to get involved with the

Prania thing. But I hope you know how grateful I am for that. For the talk with Balial, for coming to my rescue. I...I couldn't have done it without you." It's strange to admit that for once in my life, I couldn't handle things just on my own.

Freeing Prania was a group effort. It took everyone coming together as one to defeat that evil bitch. Me. Dash. Bo. Wes. Everest. Willow. Sydney. Tremont. Pippa. The wendigo. Heck, even Gary. And finally, the remaining demons and hunters that had enough of her tyranny.

"I'm grateful it had a happy ending. Not all stories have one of those." Willow stares past me like she's recalling a memory of a time when things didn't go well.

"And I'm sorry if I uncovered any old trauma from being with Tremont." I can't imagine how Willow must have felt when she found out he was shacking up in Sydney's house.

Willow sighs. "Our relationship was complicated. But it's been long enough that I've healed, at least partially, from what he had done. And if I'm being honest, I forgave him a while ago. I just didn't want him to know that."

"Really?" I ask her.

She bobs her head up and down. "It doesn't serve me to hold onto all that anger. Hanging on to grudges is like poisoning yourself over and over. Eventually, you have to be the one to stop, move on, and recognize that you can't control anything other than how you react to situations. Did I hate him for what he did? Absolutely. But I had to stop giving him that power over me long after he was gone. I defeated him. I was strong enough to withstand any attack if he came back. There was no chance he would ever have the upper hand on me again. And with that, I finally gave myself permission to let go. I forgave him, but I would never forget. That was enough for me."

"You are a wise woman, Willow."

She chuckles. "When you've been through the shit I have, you learn a thing or two." Willow puts the car into gear and pulls us out of the parking lot in front of the school. "Maybe one day I'll tell you all about it."

I press the button to lower my window and shove my arm out. "That would be nice."

We step into the kitchen of Sydney's house to find everyone gathered around. Jade sits on the counter with Everest standing between her legs. Just the sight of him warms my heart, something I wasn't sure I would experience again when he was brutally injured in Prania. Somehow, I had shoved healing magic into him before forcing him to return home. I still don't understand how I did it, but Sydney and Willow have told me that magic doesn't always make sense, and you have to come to terms with not knowing the hows or whys.

If only I could figure it out though, because then I would have the ability to help those in need. Until then, I'll keep trying to uncover whatever lies hidden inside of me that allowed me to heal him.

Bo leans against the wall in the far corner with his arms folded over his chest. He's been more present lately, but still stays just on the edge like he's ready to leave at any moment. Either way, I'm grateful that he runs away a heck of a lot less lately.

Dash sits on a stool at the counter with Sydney standing opposite of him. Wes shuts the refrigerator door and pops the top on something called cherry cola. It's too fizzy for my liking, but Wes can't get enough of the bubbly drink.

Willow walks directly over to Sydney and wraps her arm around his waist. He slings his arm over her shoulder and pulls her close, pressing a kiss to her forehead.

"Missed you," he whispers.

She tugs him tighter. "Missed you more."

The love they share flows out in heaps.

"How did it go?" Dash asks us.

"Really well," I tell him as I approach and climb into the stool next to him.

"She's a natural," Willow adds.

"Sounds a little like you, Mrs. I-didn't-know-I-was-a-witch," Sydney teases Willow.

She giggles and pokes him in the ribs. "I can't help that I was a late bloomer."

Dash drags the hair from my face and tucks it behind my ear. "I'm glad it went well."

I look across the way at Everest. "You feeling okay?"

He rubs Jade's legs and nods. "Better each day."

"I was doing some thinking," Sydney says as he shifts from light-hearted to serious mode. "This house... prior to you all coming here. It was just sitting empty." He glances at each of us before continuing. "I don't know why I ever hung on to it, really, but maybe this is why. Maybe I knew someone would come along that needed it. So, here's me formally offering it to you. If you'd like to stay, it's yours for the taking."

"You're not serious," I say in disbelief.

Sydney chuckles. "I am."

"I don't know how we would ever afford it," I tell him. It's not like any of us have Earth money or Earth jobs. I can't imagine living in a place like this would be cheap, and I don't know the first thing about owning a home.

"We would work those details out if you say yes. The house is paid off, the only real cost would be utilities, taxes, and upkeep." He looks at Willow briefly. "You don't need to make a decision now. You can think about it. The house isn't going anywhere." Sydney slides his hand down Willow's arm and weaves his fingers through hers. "We'll get out of your hair and let you talk it over. No hard feelings either way."

Willow walks over and latches onto my hand with her free one. She gives it a gentle squeeze. "I hope you'll stay." She releases me and the two of them disappear in the direction she and I had come from only moments ago.

The door shuts behind them, sealing us in here with the gracious proposal they gave us and the silence of everyone being lost in their own thoughts.

"I wouldn't mind living here a bit longer until we figure out our next move," Jade is the first to speak. "It would be nice to catch our breath for once."

Everest tilts his head up toward her. "I'm in if you are."

"I do really enjoy how comfortable the mattresses are." Dash shrugs. "And we don't exactly have any better options on the table."

I look at Wes and wonder what's going through his head.

"Couldn't hurt to stick around." Wes takes another drink of his cherry cola.

So far, every vote has been to stay, which leaves things up to me and Bo.

Bo's intense gaze meets mine. "Can we talk? Privately."

My heart stutters and I worry that this is when he finally tells me the truth, that he's leaving for good. That he's going to take Balial up on his offer and spend the rest of eternity in hell being Balial's bitch. The idea of life without Bo weighs heavier than any scruni collapsing on top of me ever could. Still, I slide myself off the stool and follow him out of the room.

Once I'm at his side, he ascends the stairs and makes his way into the bedroom that we have claimed as our own.

He points to the bed. "Sit down."

I comply even though my chest aches with every second he waits to say whatever it is he needs to say.

Bo paces in front of me. "Birdie..."

When he doesn't continue, I say, "My mother used to call me that."

He pauses and looks at me. "Really?"

I draw in a breath and exhale. "I must have suppressed the memory, but yeah. When I dreamt of Parla having her killed, I remembered the moments prior. She told me that my father was as obsessed with cheese as I was...and that she preferred bread." I force a smile. "Like you."

Bo's shoulders relax and his resolve softens. He drops himself to his knees in front of me, taking my hands into his. "I'm sorry."

I pinch my brows together. "For what?"

"For everything. For how I've treated you. For that damned mark on your neck." His gaze flits to the scar he left behind. "For not being honest with you. For not being the man you needed me to be."

I cup his face in my hand and tilt his head up toward me. "I forgive you."

"You shouldn't."

"Good thing it's not up to you."

"I never wanted to be selfish with you, Wren. But I don't think I'm strong enough to withstand my feelings anymore."

"What do you feel, Bo?" I bite at the inside of my lip and hope he doesn't do the thing he always does—leave.

"I'm scared. Scared that you might not actually want to be with me if it weren't for that mark on your neck. Scared that if you do, I might keep letting you down. I've never been more conflicted in my entire life but all I do know is that I worship you. I am honored to be in your presence, and I am terrified that I have ruined things between us."

"Bo..."

"I never want to be apart from you. Not in this lifetime or the next. I can't explain it, Wren, but you need to know, you own me. Body and soul. My heart, my love, you can have it all. It's yours. Whether you choose to accept it or not, I will spend eternity worshipping at your feet and be forever grateful I'm privileged to breathe in the same air as you. I'm yours."

The heavy weight I was carrying dissipates with each word he mutters.

I run my fingers through his dark hair and hold onto the base of his neck. "I love you, too, Bo."

He blinks up at me, his dark gaze glistening. "You love me?"

I break out into a grin. "Yeah, you idiot."

Bo rises to his feet, swooping me into his arms and lifting me from the bed. He presses his forehead against mine and squeezes me so tight I could possibly break in half if he applied any more pressure.

With my hands wrapped around his neck, I graze my lips along his. "Are you going to kiss me, or what?"

Bo crashes his mouth onto mine, his touch cool and warm and soft and intense all at the same time. His tongue spreads my lips and cascades itself passionately. My heart skips a beat, and I die in the best way in his arms.

He breaks away, resting his head on mine again as he catches his breath.

"That's the first time you've ever kissed me," I tell him.

Bo presses a quick one on my lips and smiles. "It won't be the last."

Someone clears their throat at the door. "Are we interrupting?" Wes asks with a hint of *about damn time* lingering in his tone.

"She loves me," Bo tells him while lowering me onto the floor. "Can you believe it?"

Wes and Dash file into the room and Dash shuts the door behind him.

"You're only just now realizing this?" Wes strolls over, plants his hand on the bedpost, and shakes his head.

"Took you long enough," Dash adds.

I shove Bo playfully in the chest. "He can't help that he's a little slow."

Bo snatches my hand and kisses the top of it. "Better slow than never."

I stare up at the man who has finally given me a piece of him that I wasn't sure he ever would. "Can we finally get rid of this alpha mark or are you going to keep teasing me about it?"

Bo's nostrils flare. "I don't think you know what you're asking for, Birdie."

"You love to repeat yourself don't you." I wink at him.

He glances at Dash and Wes. "I'm going to need your help."

I tilt my head and cross my arms. "You think I can't get you hard?"

Bo chuckles and it's the most beautiful sound I've ever heard. "You're going to wish I wasn't hard when I fill you so full you can't take any more." He runs his tongue along his teeth and rakes his hand over his face.

"What do you need us to do?" Dash walks over and plops himself onto the edge of the bed. He scoots back and settles his head into his hand, laying sideways towards us.

"If this is what you really want, Birdie, I think you should let the guys warm you up first."

I narrow my gaze. "Why, so you can make another comment about passing me around to whoever wants a go?"

Bo growls and steps toward me quicker than I can react. He grips my chin and peers down at me. "No one, other than the men in this room, will get to be with you," he mutters. Do you hear me?"

I swallow and fight the urge to latch myself onto him right this instant. "I hear you, loud and clear."

It took him a couple months to finally come to his senses, and now that he has, his possessiveness drives me completely wild. Is this what he's been hiding this whole time?

"Good girl," he says while staring into my eyes.

Wes pushes off from the bedpost and stalks over to place himself between me and Bo. He causes Bo to take a step back and grazes his hand over my cheek. "You sure you want to do this?"

"Is it okay with you?" I ask him, unsure if he and his hound are willing to share me with yet another man. It was one thing when Bo was playing hard to get, but now the reality of me being intimate with one more guy is upon us. I don't know what I would say or do if Wes refused, but I find myself asking for his approval either way. We've had a couple intimate encounters with the four of us, and Wes has been aware of my feelings for Bo, but we've never gone all the way.

Wes leans down toward me, his lips just a breath from mine. "I want what you want, my love."

I stand taller and kiss him, our mouths hungrier than they ever have been before.

He wraps his arm around my torso and lifts me off

the floor with ease, backing me closer to the bed. Wes lowers me carefully onto the mattress, his tongue dancing with mine.

Dash repositions himself behind me, his hands finding the bottom of my shirt and dragging it over my head, forcing me and Wes to break apart for the split moment my top is removed.

I meet Bo's fierce gaze in that sheer second and continue kissing Wes.

Wes moans into my mouth and my arousal builds.

Someone, who I assume is Dash, glides his hand over my back, skimming it around the front, and slithers it into my pants. His gentle touch grazes my clit, and he dips his fingers along my wetness.

I arch toward him and all but beg for his fingers to penetrate me.

"Take her pants off," Bo commands whoever might be listening.

Wes breaks from my kiss long enough to drag my bottoms down and over my ass, discarding them onto the floor. He's usually the tidy one, but right now, that must be the last thing on his mind.

Completely nude in a room of fully clothed men, I spread my legs and wait for whatever it is they're about to do to me.

Starting at my ankle, Wes moves his way up slowly, his eyes glowing and locked onto mine. He skims his tongue over my flesh until he halts at my core.

"Please," I beg while leaning back onto my elbows.

Dash comes around my side and lowers himself closer, his mouth landing on mine for a heated kiss. Our tongues swirl together as Wes does his own exploration of my center.

I moan into Dash and whimper when Wes trails his finger over my clit before shoving it inside of me.

He turns his palm upward and slides another finger in, rocking them gently but firmly.

Dash weaves his hand under my neck, supporting the back of my head, and uses his other hand to skate over my bare breasts. He stops at my nipple, pinching it between his fingers, and I nearly come undone.

"That's it," Bo breathes, his presence closer than it was moments ago.

My core tightens and I find myself unable to withstand the pleasure any longer. I climax hard, biting down on Dash's lip and shuddering around Wes. My entire body shivers with bliss, and all too soon, Wes withdraws himself from me.

A second later, I hear the brief hissing of a zipper and feel the weight of Wes crawling onto the bed, on top of me. With no other warning and my mouth still melting with Dash's, Wes glides the tip of his cock over my entrance and pushes himself slowly in, stretching me with gentle ease. He fills me gradually and hooks his arm under my frame to lift me toward him.

Still trembling from my first orgasm, I tense around Wes's shaft, his hardness filling me so fucking full that I grow concerned about Bo's warning. There's no way he's bigger than Wes...but when I think back to having his cock in my mouth, he might actually be. Especially if he shifts into his demonic side. Those barbs that penetrated me were only just the beginning of what Bo has in store for me.

"You're doing good, Birdie." Bo exhales and from the sound of his footsteps, he must come closer.

Wes slides into me deeper, his girth and length spreading me open.

I reach my hand and search for Dash's groin, finally landing on his hardened cock concealed in his pants.

He moans against my touch but doesn't take his mouth off mine.

Wiggling my palm under his waistband, I secure myself around his shaft, gripping and tugging him. I stroke Dash as Wes fucks me and Bo watches from his close distance. Having the attention of all three of them is overwhelming to the senses and makes me crave them that much more.

If only Bo would stop biding his time and join in on the fun instead of being a voyeur.

Wes grips my waist and pulls me upward, the change in position sending a newfound spike of pleasure through me. A thumb finds my clit, and when I briefly peek through my lids, it's Bo that's touching me. With one of his hands bracing himself on the bedframe, he uses the other to apply steady pressure on my most sensitive area. His muscles bulge the plain dark T-shirt he's wearing, and just the sight of him heightens my arousal.

I keep my eyes on Bo, my mouth and hand on Dash, and rock my hips to allow Wes to fuck me. My center tightens and my breath catches as my climax builds. Wes's cock hardens inside of me and alerts me to his near orgasm, too.

Sweat glistens on Wes's brow and accentuates his already gorgeous features. His gaze darts between his cock pumping in and out of me and my eyes. He doesn't seem at all bothered that two other men are touching me.

Bo pinches my clit, and I cry out into Dash as Wes pumps inside of me, both of us falling over the edge into bliss together.

Wes groans, his face contorting, and somehow, it's the sexiest sight I've ever witnessed.

I grip Dash's shaft and ride out the orgasm with Wes, this one lasting much longer than the first. My pussy quivers around him, and he thrusts inside of me, each one slower than the last, until he's fucked me all the way through.

With even more caution, he gently pulls out, leans down to kiss my cheek, and steps away with a slight smirk on his face.

Bo dips his fingers into his mouth, making no attempt to fill the space that Wes just vacated.

And because I'm still hungry for more, I nudge Dash

into the empty spot, breaking my mouth away from his, and saying, "I want you to fuck me, Dash."

"Are you sure?" he mutters as he climbs into position anyway.

He hooks his hands under his waistband and shoves his pants down, allowing his cock to spring out.

I sit up and grip his shaft, spreading the precum over his tip before lining it up to my mouth and swirling my tongue around the edge. We both moan when I slide him inside, and his dick twitches.

Dash pulls the hair from my shoulders and holds it behind my head.

I glide his girth in and out and bounce the tip of his cock against the back of my throat.

"Angels," he moans.

Squeezing the base of his shaft, I stare up into his eyes and continue to suck him until I almost bring him to the brink. I slow down, smiling as I slide him out, and flip over onto my stomach, bringing myself up onto my knees, leaning down, and arching my ass toward him.

"I don't think I can last with you looking this damn good, Wren." Dash cups my ass with one hand and steers his dick to my entrance with the other. He skates it over onto my throbbing clit before entering me carefully.

Immediately, I tense around him, grateful for the penetration. I gather two fistfuls of the bedsheets and back my ass onto him; the motion fills me full of Dash's thick cock. He isn't nearly as long as Wes, but he is wider.

Bo strolls around the bed and stops in front of me, his intense gaze boring down onto me. He takes my chin between his fingers and tilts my head up toward him. "You almost ready for me, Birdie?"

"Mmhm." I nod and lick at my lips, wondering how it's possible to want more. Maybe it's the thrill of Bo's warning that drives my excitement, or maybe it's the immense love I have for each one of these men.

Dash picks up his pace, and I buck against him to match his intensity and give him silent approval to keep going. "Fuck," he sighs with both hands hooked at my thighs and dragging me back onto him.

I release one fist from the sheets and latch onto Bo's waistband, my eyes on his as I pull him closer and unbutton his pants. He doesn't stop me, so I continue unzipping. His cock bulges against his pants, dying to be set free, and because he isn't wearing any underwear, the second the zipper goes down all the way, he pops out.

"You want a taste?" Bo asks me.

I answer by latching onto and tugging him closer, not caring at all how rough I'm being. If his warning was any indication, things are going to get even more intense than they already are. My sights trail to the cock in my grasp, my mouth watering at the sheer size of him. He's bigger than I remember, and we're only just getting started. Still, the thought of him ruining me sends a jolt of heat straight between my legs where Dash is currently fucking me.

"Tell me," Bo says, his voice gruff.

"I want you," I whimper and open for him.

Bo skims his juicy cock over my lips, taunting me.

I graze my teeth gently along his sensitive flesh and widen my mouth to fit the tip of him.

"Fuck," Dash moans again. "I'm going to..."

Pushing the weight of my body back onto Dash, I manage to fit as much of Bo in me as I can, my eyes watering from the size of him. My arousal heightens and I stifle a moan on Bo's cock.

Dash explodes inside of me, my orgasm following his and pulsating my pussy around him. I fight through the tears and choke on Bo as Dash fucks us through completion. Dash is gentle but firm, both with his thrusts and his hands gripping my hips. He leans forward, his body pressing onto mine, and kisses my shoulder.

Dash whispers into my ear, "That was fucking divine." He pulls out, his absence allowing cool air to wash over my ravished pussy.

Keeping Bo still in my hand, I remove my mouth and sit up on my knees, daring a glance around to see where Dash and Wes have gone.

Wes sits at the front of the bed, one knee brought up and his elbow resting on it with his head in his hand, watching us intently. He winks at me, and it's enough of a confirmation that everything is still okay.

His irises glow and tell me his hound is good with this, too.

Dash repositions his cock inside his pants and pulls them back over his waist.

Still, I'm the only naked person in the room.

"Where do you want me?" I ask Bo, turning my attention back to the only man remaining who hasn't fucked me yet.

Bo steps away, freeing himself from my grasp, and shimmies out of his bottoms. He climbs onto the bed, claiming the spot next to Wes, and puts his back against the pillows at the headboard, with his legs straight out and his cock on full display. He takes the base of it into his hand, standing it upright.

I swallow down the lump in my throat and eye him.

"Crawl to me, Birdie."

And because I'm apparently a newfound obedient little thing, I drop down onto my hands and knees and crawl the short distance over to him, our eyes locked onto each other the whole time.

He reaches underneath of me, grazing his palm over my dangling breasts, giving both an equal amount of attention.

I kiss the tip of his shaft and span my lips over his hardness.

He uses this new closeness to drag his hand over my body until he reaches my center. Bo tangles one hand in my hair and uses the other to glide his fingers over my clit and onto my soaked vulva. Dipping a few of his fingers into my hole, he doesn't penetrate me any deeper; instead, he teases my entrance and spreads the wetness all over, coating me with the remains of Dash and Wes.

"It's too big," I tell him. Bigger than I thought it was going to be.

"You have to want this," he growls.

"I do."

"Climb on top, Birdie," Bo commands and drags me toward him. "If this doesn't kill you, you're going to be dying for more."

"Cocky much?"

"Not cocky. Confident."

I straddle his legs, his hands resting on my hips, his cock positioned between my pussy lips. I drag myself along his shaft and wonder how it's possible that he's going to fit inside of me.

"I need you to talk to me, Birdie. Tell me if it's too much." Bo glances at Wes and then Dash. "I need you two to keep her comfortable and relaxed. Can we do that?"

We collectively murmur, "Yes."

Wes rises from his seat and kneels beside me, stroking my hair out of my face. "If you want to stop, all you have to do is say so, okay?"

I nod and lean toward him, kissing his lips. "Okay."

Dash comes over to my other side. "Whatever you need, we're here for you." He plants a soft kiss on my cheek.

"I'm ready," I tell them, because if I'm being completely honest, the anticipation is fucking killing me, and if I don't do this soon, I might back out. It isn't that I don't want to be with Bo or remove the mark, it's the not knowing every little detail it entails that drives my control-freak mind insane.

What if I'm bad? What if he regrets marking me? What if the guys get upset and realize they're not okay with sharing me? What if Bo's giant monster cock rips me in half?

Whatever the outcome may be, I'm surely going to find out soon enough.

I've cross-realm traveled, won a war against an evil tyrant, and survived near-death experiences numerous times—I can handle sex with Bo, right?

"Fuck I can't do this."

"Do you want to stop?" Bo pauses.

"No. Give me all of you."

"Easy, Birdie." Bo guides my hips up and releases one hand to hold onto his shaft. He lines it up with my dripping entrance and looks into my eyes. "Is this okay?"

I lower myself onto him, his girth spreading me wider than I ever have been. "Yes." Carefully, I continue down his cock.

"You're so fucking tight," Bo whispers.

"Does it feel okay?" I ask him.

He narrows his bushy brows. "Are you serious?" Bo shakes his head. "It's like I've died and gone to heaven, Birdie. Don't worry about me. The focus is on you."

At this, Wes draws my attention, pulling my face toward him and distracting me with his fiery kiss. His tongue darts into my mouth and seductively grazes over mine.

My body relaxes and slides farther down onto Bo's cock as he spreads me so fucking wide.

Bo cups my tits in his hands and keeps his body still, allowing me to be in control of how far he penetrates me.

Dash moves from his spot at my side and comes around between Bo's legs, behind me. He trails his fingers over the back of my thighs and squeezes my ass gently. Having so many hands on me at once, it really does sort of distract me from the massive cock inside my pussy.

"You're doing so well, Birdie." Bo pinches my nipples harder. "Tell me if you want to stop."

I drag one hand up his chest and settle it along the crook of his neck, digging my fingers into his flesh, my other hand weaving along the base of Wes's skull, tugging his face closer to me to intensify our kiss.

Dash surprises me by gliding his tongue over my inner thigh and spreading my ass. He blows cool air on the back of me and glides his tongue over my stretched-out pussy.

Moaning into Wes, I arch slightly toward Dash but not enough that it causes me any pain.

"Grip the base of my cock, Dash," Bo says. "That way she won't go too deep."

Dash complies, his hand sliding under to settle his fist against the base of Bo's shaft and my pussy. The friction from his hand dances along my clit in the best way possible. He wiggles his thumb to tease my asshole and then inches himself closer to lick it. Dash swirls his tongue across, and up and down.

I push myself lower onto Bo, surprising myself at how much of him I can take. Maybe this won't be as bad as he warned after all. Dash's hand prevents me from going much farther but I'm grateful that he's there to act as a buffer against what might be too much. Each time I get closer, he uses his thumb and index finger to tease my clit and asshole.

Wes breaks away from my kiss to grip my face. "Are you still okay?"

"Yes," I breathe and rest my forehead against his.

"Are you ready for more?" Bo tweaks my nipple harder, the pain shooting straight to my pussy.

I focus on him. "I'm ready for more."

"This is going to hurt," Bo tells me. "Are you sure?"

"Have you ever done this before?" I stare into his dark eyes.

"Not like this, Birdie. And I've never meant it."

I swallow and bask in Dash's mouth still exploring my ass. "I'm ready."

Wes roams his hands over my body while Bo

breathes in deeply, like he's giving everything he has to concentrate on what comes next.

My gaze widens as Bo's cock grows inside of me, the sides of it morphing into ridged edges. He widens me even more, and I gasp at the fullness.

"Fuck," I blurt out.

Bo halts but I cut him off from saying anything. Dark, thick scales appear on his arms, and his teeth sharpen into pointy fangs.

"Keep going," I tell him. "Keep fucking going." I inch my legs apart and grant him more room to ruin me.

Dash keeps his hand locked around the base of Bo's cock, no doubt feeling the changes himself as Bo shifts into his demonic side. Dash laps at my ass and continues to lick at the back of my pussy, his tongue gliding over Bo's shaft on his exploration of my rear.

"Hold her hair back," Bo tells Wes, who immediately gathers all my hair into his fist, wrapping it around his hand. The tautness heightens my pleasure.

Bo looks into my eyes, his gaze darting back and forth between mine. "I'm going to bite you, Birdie. Is that okay? I have to reopen the mark."

I nod and tilt my neck toward him.

"I need you to say it."

"Bite me, Bo."

A sly grin forms on his rugged yet handsome face. "Good girl."

I lean closer to Bo, exposing the soft flesh of my neck to him.

His cock continues to contort inside of me, but I remain focused on seeing this through.

If we stand any chance of being together, we must complete this ceremony.

At the same moment his fangs graze over the scar, Bo rocks his hips up, giving into his desires for the first time since we started. He sinks his teeth in and digs his fingers into my sides, dragging me closer. He doesn't stop there, he pivots his hips harder, crashing his monster cock into me. If it weren't for Dash's hand gripping the base of Bo's shaft, Bo might actually tear me apart.

I lean into him, my face resting against Bo's shoulder as he drinks from my vein and his cock swirls and swells inside of me. I breathe in, the scent of him mixed with all this sex sending me into sensory overload. Without processing my next move, I latch my own mouth onto Bo, kissing his skin at first, but the second he moans, I drag my own teeth over his flesh and drive them down until I break through, his blood pooling in my mouth.

Warm decadence pours into me, and I suck harder, no longer recognizing my carnal desires but succumbing to them either way.

I grow lightheaded and hot all at once, but I don't care—not about anything other than Bo finally giving in to being with me. I thrust down onto Bo and moan against his neck as he plunges into me and drinks the blood gushing from my neck.

All at once, Bo breaks away and drags my face toward his, our mouths melding into one another, our essence mixing together as one.

I lean forward and brace myself on the headboard with one hand while Wes takes my other hand and drags it to his rock-hard shaft. I grip it tighter and stroke him with his hand on top of mine guiding me through my distracted state.

"Come for me, Birdie," Bo mutters. "Come *with* me."

With our breaths ragged, my pussy tightens around his enormous, bulbous cock, my orgasm hitting me like a brick wall.

I scream out but, luckily, the sound is muffled on Bo's lips as he thrusts deeper and finishes inside of me.

He releases me, his hand finding my cheek, his gaze meeting mine. "Are you okay?"

"I'm okay," I pant, my hand still stroking Wes's shaft even though Wes finished, too, his climax lost in the chaos of the entire situation.

Dash plants soft kisses over my thigh and lower back.

"It's not over yet," Bo warns.

"It's not?"

"Don't move, Birdie." The barbs on Bo's shaft pierce my pussy, the pain fierce and hot on my completely sensitive and still throbbing area.

I stay still for a moment but grow curious about the sensation and shift my weight slightly. The barbs penetrate deeper like they're trying to keep me in place, and I push against them, allowing the pain to consume me.

"Are you fucking crazy?" Bo pants, his hands on my sweat-soaked cheeks.

"Maybe," I grin.

He latches his palms onto my thighs to steady me from moving any more. "It'll be over soon."

But what if I don't want it to be?

I've never been much of a masochist, but damn am I enjoying this torment.

Bo's cock shifts again, the barbs piercing harder before withdrawing themselves. At first, I wince, but the second they're gone, I'm numb to the pain. Only, a moment later, his shaft swells and swirls, sending equal parts pleasure and anguish before cutting me deeper than it has yet.

My head spins and I fall forward, Bo catching me with his strong arms.

"Birdie," he says, his voice layered with concern. "Fucking heal her."

I lie there, still and pressed against his chest, my entire body radiating with sheer bliss despite being utterly ravished. I want to move, to reassure them that I'm fine, but I can't bring myself to move a single muscle. It's like I'm paralyzed by the pleasure and stunned by the pain.

Dash and Wes shuffle around, the two of them acting fast like they're worried I might actually die as a result of sex with Bo.

But I just sigh and melt into Bo and revel in the possibility that eventually I'll be able to have control over my body again.

The mark on my neck tingles, but different than when we started. It no longer radiates the same sensation, yet now it's altered into something else entirely.

Does that mean that it worked? That Bo was able to successfully change it from an alpha mark into a fated mate's mark?

Bo raises me off his shaft but keeps me tightly to his chest. A cooling sensation washes over my pussy as words are whispered by who I can only assume is Wes.

A split second later, my eyes flutter open and strength is replenished in my entire form, the fatigue being replaced by pure fucking ecstasy.

I push off Bo's broad shoulders and exhale. "Did we do it?"

Bo leans back onto the headboard and looks me over. "We did it."

Lowering myself down, I press my lips onto his for a quick kiss. "We did it," I repeat and collapse willingly at his side. "We did it," I tell the two other beautiful men who are mine.

Bo scoops me into his arms and manages to climb off the bed. He glances over his shoulder on his way to the bathroom, "You guys coming?"

I scoot higher in his embrace and smile as Wes and Dash hop off the bed and follow us in, a look of contentment on both of their faces.

"I love you, guys."

Dash rushes ahead and turns on the shower before Bo can get me there.

Wes comes to Bo's side as he lowers me onto the tiled floor, careful to give me an extra hand to ease me down as gently as possible. "We love you, more."

Dash takes my hand and leads me into the steamy oversized shower, pulling my hand up to his lips to kiss. "Yep, so much more."

I'm overcome by emotions, tears welling in my eyes at how far we've come.

I once thought I hated these men and everything they stood for—never would I have imagined I would feel the way I do today.

First, I was stolen by monsters.

Then I was fighting for them.

Now, I'm fated to monsters.

And I couldn't be any happier that I've fallen for the enemy.

EPILOGUE – WREN

"Wait, tell me again, which beats which, a straight or a flush?" I glance at the cards in Bo's hand and those laying out on the felt-lined table.

Bo narrows his gaze at me and presses his cards down to conceal them. "If I lose because of you I'm going to…"

But I cut him off. "If you lose it's because you're bad at poker."

Deghan laughs and reaches for his soda, tipping it back and taking a healthy swig. "A flush beats a straight. But a straight flush beats both."

I sigh. How could I retain enough information to successfully assassinate any target, minus Wes, but I can't remember which set of cards triumphs over the other? Maybe poker isn't for me.

"All in," Dash says from his spot across from Silas.

Silas looks at Dash, and if I wasn't certain of his

character by now, I'd grow concerned about the intensity of his stare. That's how Silas is. He's mean and broody and a bit too serious for his own good. But he's harmless, at least, unless you cross Willow or the rest of his family.

Silas pushes a stack of chips in, which I think means he calls Dash's bet.

Bo tosses his cards onto the table. "I'm out."

Sydney glances around at the remaining card holders.

Wes discards his, and Cameron follows behind.

"Turn 'em up, boys," Sydney tells Silas and Dash.

Silas flips his cards over, not saying a word.

Sydney scans them and slides three of the other cards from the five on the table up higher than the other two. "Flush, queen high." He turns his attention to Dash, who lays his cards carefully down in front of him.

A grin breaks across Sydney's face as he takes Dash's cards. "Flush, king high. Dash wins." He shoves the chips toward Dash, who had gone completely all-in on that hand, taking quite a chunk from Silas's pile.

Silas lets out the faintest sigh and folds his arms across his leather jacket-covered chest.

"Aw, don't be a sore loser." Willow plants her hands on his shoulders and kisses his cheek.

His resolve softens and he turns to plant one right on her lips. "He's just having beginner's luck."

Bo eyes me. "You keep looking that good and I'm going to put a baby in you."

"Ew, no you aren't." I giggle and shove him. "You're too much of a baby yourself to have one."

"Doesn't mean I won't do it." He pokes me in the side and latches onto my waist, pulling me into his lap. "One of these days, one of us is going to."

"Gross," Jade says from her spot near the door. She plugs her ears. "You're going to scar your sister for life."

I weasel my way out of Bo's grasp to rise from his lap and walk over to where she stands.

"No offense," she says.

I laugh. "None taken." I lean against the doorframe and take in the sight in front of us. So many various people and creatures coming together for something as simple as a game of poker in one of the many rooms in Sydney's childhood estate we now call home. "Think you can handle things around here while we're gone?"

"And get a little peace and quiet from Bo tormenting me all the time?" Jade side-eyes me. "I think I can handle that."

Willow strolls over and stands next to me. "How long will you be gone?"

"Not sure, but I can't imagine it'll be much in Arthlia time. A week or two? Long enough to help Pippa and Diego rebuild."

"Diego's the wendigo, right?" Jade asks me.

I nod. "Yep. I finally got tired of calling him *the*

wendigo so I asked his name. Kind of felt bad after all we'd been through."

"I'm sure he'd been called worse things," Willow adds.

"Bullshit," Bo calls out before slamming his hand against the table, chips splattering from various piles. The rest of the guys, minus Silas, burst into laughter. Bo shakes his head and leans back in his chair, the two legs barely supporting his large frame.

"I keep telling him he's going to fall if he continues doing that." I stare at the legs and wonder how much longer they'll last.

Willow sighs. "You'll have to let him learn the hard way." She turns toward me. "Speaking of, when you return, how about you enroll in some classes at the academy? I could really use your help around here and I'd love for you to learn proper magic."

"Yeah?" I say, my heart nearly bursting with the idea that I might finally come into my powers fully.

A gentle knock sounds on the front door, and a second later, it opens, and a dark-haired girl comes through.

Willow immediately rushes over, throwing her arms around the new person. "Lills," she squeals. "I've missed you." Willow releases her and grips her hand, dragging her over to us. "Lillian, this is Jade."

Jade and Lillian shake hands as I wait for my introduction.

"And this is Wren, Wren Oliver." Willow nearly dances with excitement.

I fit my palm into hers, noticing the spark of energy that pulses between us. "It's so nice to meet you," I tell her.

"Likewise," she replies. "I've heard a lot about you. All good things."

A smile creeps across my face and I tuck my hair behind my ear nervously as I wonder what Willow could have said.

Willow points into the room where the rest of the group is. "The guys are in there. The big one with long, dark hair is Bo. The red-headed one is Dash, and the other guy is Wes—all of which are Wren's mates."

Lillian raises a brow at me. "I see the Oliver likeness. Good for you, girlfriend."

I chuckle and my cheeks turn red, my attention turning to the men who have stolen my heart.

Lillian leaves Willow's side and walks into the room, hugging each of Willow's men briefly before shaking hands with each of mine.

"Who's that?" I whisper to Willow, who remains at my side.

"Family," she says. "You have family all over." Willow turns toward me, "You never have to be alone again, Wren."

Suddenly, it dawns on me that Willow was right.

As I look around at this space, so full of family and love, I realize something.

All the pain in the world was worth it to get here today.

Thank you for reading Fated to Monsters! If you want more from this magical universe, check out Willow's 5-book completed paranormal academy series: Harper Shadow Academy.

All caught up with both series? Make sure to join us to chat books in Luna Pierce's Gritty Romance Squad on Facebook!

Or sign up for the exclusive newsletter so you get details on upcoming releases and sales! www. lunapierce.com/subscribe

Acknowledgments

A massive shoutout to my readers for being so incredible and supporting me through so many books. This wouldn't be possible without you, and I am eternally grateful.

To all the amazing women in my life, I see you, I love you: Mini me. Mom. Vivi. Carolyn. Tiffany. Kate. Kelsey. Amanda. Michelle. Sam. Grace. Cassia. Joli.

S.J. Fowler. Tori Ellis.

The folks over at Patreon, I appreciate you so very much: Natasha. Payton. Kiana. Heather. Mandi. Laura. Grace. Ellie. Ashley. Michelle. Clayton. Tyler. Victoria.

To everyone who has tagged me in a video or post or shared your love for the worlds I create, I love you very much.

Thank you.

About the Author

Luna Pierce is a paranormal and contemporary romance author who loves getting lost in her stories. She brings you tough characters that love fiercely and fight for what's right, even if that means burning the city down for the ones they love. Luna adores all things gritty, and even supernatural.

When she's not writing, you'll find her consuming way too much coffee, making endless to-do lists, and spending time with her daughter and cats in small-town Ohio.

Join the exclusive reader group: Luna Pierce's Gritty Romance Squad

Join Luna's newsletter to receive updates at:
www.lunapierce.com/subscribe

Also by Luna Pierce

Falling for the Enemy

Stolen by Monsters (Book One)

Fighting for Monsters (Book Two)

Fated to Monsters (Book Three)

The Harper Shadow Academy Series

(set in the same story universe as Falling for the Enemy)

Hidden Magic (Book One)

Cursed Magic (Book Two)

Wicked Magic (Book Three)

Ancient Magic (Book Four)

Sacred Magic (Book Five)

Harper Shadow Academy: Complete Box Set

Sinners and Angels Universe

(Dark contemporary romance)

Broken Like You (Standalone)

Untamed Vixen (Part One)

Villain Era (Part Two)

Ruin My Life (Standalone)

www.ingramcontent.com/pod-product-compliance
Lightning Source LLC
Chambersburg PA
CBHW051001210726
48287CB00004B/1321